DARKEST BEFORE DAWN

A DARK BILLIONAIRE ROMANCE

LEE SAVINO

SILVERWOOD PRESS

FREEBIE - THE DARKNESS IN HIM

Get Roy Roy's point of view in The Darkness In Him, a freebie available here: https://geni.us/thedarknessinhim

CONTENT WARNINGS

Content warnings: assault, murder (past and on page), loss of family, stalking, violence, vigilantism, BDSM, non-con/reluctance, stabbing, surveillance, corruption, erotic scenes.

This a dark romance with intense and sensual themes. The erotic scenes depicted are dangerous and not an actual representation of BDSM, which should be conducted between knowledgeable and trusted partners with plenty of conversations about boundaries and consent.

PROLOGUE

I *nara*

FOR YEARS, I've dreamt of my own death. Not any details, just the feel of an explosion, of sparks and smoke blasting into my face. Pain and the sensation of falling.

LOVE FEELS LIKE THAT. Maybe not for everyone, but to me, it feels like dying.

AS I FACE MY DEATH, I hold on to that. My life may be bookended by pain and tragedy, but there was a moment when I was loved, and I loved in return.

IN THE END, nothing else matters.

1

R *ex*

THE NIGHT my parents died was the worst night of my life. Until now.

I stand with my little bird in my arms. Her eyes are wide with terror and sadness. We're surrounded by cop cars and crime scene tape, but Inara trembles like she's trapped in a nightmare.

And there's nothing I can do to help but hold her.

I swore on my parents' grave that I'd make my city safe for innocents. I honed my strength and power so I could make a difference. I protect the weak.

But I can't protect her from this pain. In the span of a few moments, she faced a gruesome crime scene and then found out she's the target of a stalker calling himself BK. The same initials the Bondage Killer used. She must feel like she'll never be safe again.

I can't stand it.

Her legs give out, and she crumples. I swing her up into my arms. I love to carry her and keep her close, but with every step, her breath hitches, and it's tearing me apart. I want to hide her away from the world forever.

I want to tear off my suit jacket and howl. I want to use every bit of tech and surveillance equipment and weapons I have at my disposal and hunt the killer down. Eradicate this monster from the face of the Earth.

It's what I was born to do. I was born to own her. Protect her. Fight for her.

She came to me. I'll never let her go.

I carry her from the crime scene to my waiting ride.

"Ivan," I call to alert him. He's already scrambled around the car to open the back door. I slide both Inara and me into the seat.

She looks dazed. She's still clutching the letters the stalker sent her. There's a stench rising from the paper, like smoke and filth. I want to rip them from her fingers and throw them out the window. And if they weren't important evidence, I would.

Damn the Bondage Killer for targeting my little bird. Damn him for rising from the dead to torment new victims. If it is him. It might be a copycat.

Whatever it is, it's a threat to my little bird. Hunting the killer down takes second place to making sure Inara is safe.

"Back to the helicopter," I order Ivan.

First, though, I need to get us both home. And then, once I know she's safe and secure, I'll figure out how to destroy the one who's threatened my little bird's life.

～

*I*NARA

I'M TRAPPED IN A DREAM, standing in the yard in front of a house. The front door hangs open, swinging in the wind. The family is inside, still alive, but they won't be for much longer. A long, crooked shadow creeps up the hall.

I'm not too late; I can stop it. Stop him.

My legs sink into the concrete walk. I struggle, but I'm trapped, buried up to the knee. I can fight all I want, but I can't move.

I open my mouth, but no sound comes out. I'm helpless, stuck, with no way to warn the family. No way to stop their murder.

I've failed. Again. It doesn't matter how much I try, the murderer always wins. I learned that lesson decades ago, and now I'm forced to face it again.

The dream changes, and now I'm in bed, huddling under the covers, hearing the floorboards creak. Hoping it's just the dog moving around beyond my door, but knowing it's not.

It's him. The killer has come for me.

I feel the same rush of terror my childhood self felt the night the Bondage Killer came for my family. This time, I'm a grown woman but just as frightened and helpless as I was then. My whole body is frozen in the bed.

And then the screams begin.

I come awake with a gasp, clawing the blanket off of me. I'm too hot and too cold at the same time. My skin is clammy with sweat. My stomach cramps, and I clench my teeth to keep from retching. I haven't eaten, so I'd be puking up nothing but stomach acid.

"Inara?" Rex sits up beside me, and I startle as I register his presence. He's here and huge and warm. A shadow moves, and I flinch before realizing he only lifted a hand to touch me.

"It's okay." He waits until I reach for him and slides his arms around me. "You're here with me."

I sink into his warmth. My teeth are chattering, not because I'm cold but because I'm afraid. I cling to him like he's my only hope, my only bastion against the encroaching terror.

"Shhh, little bird." He soothes me. His voice is a deep well I can fall into, but there's a tinge of sorrow like his heart is breaking.

"You're safe," he says.

But he's wrong.

It's not just a dream. The Bondage Killer is back. I'm trapped in a nightmare I can't escape because it's real.

"Another bad dream?"

Rex doesn't know about my visions. The secret is swelling, pressing on the inside of my skull, screaming to break free. But I can't give in.

"I dreamed I was back at the house." I don't clarify and I don't have to. He knows I mean the victim's house from earlier. Did it all happen less than twenty-four hours ago? It feels like it was long ago. I feel like I've aged a hundred years.

I touch the metal encircling my neck. So much has happened in the past few days. I came to Rex to entrap him and learned more than I dreamed I would. I fell into his arms, and it felt right.

Too right. I can't give in to him, and yet, right now, he's the only thing keeping me sane. I need him. His comfort and his darkness.

I can't allow him to own me fully, but I can allow him to hold me, if only for a moment.

"It's not your fault." He brushes my cheek, and I realize he's swiping at my tears.

I withdraw from his warmth, wrapping my arms around myself. I still feel like I'm encased in concrete. It was only a dream, but the sensations followed me, lingering like a vision. My psyche is tormenting me. "I was there, but I couldn't stop it." And that's true, isn't it? I had a vision of the latest victim's death right here in this bed. And I did nothing.

I don't deserve rest or comfort. I should be at the precinct, working through the night to stop the man who destroyed my family. But I'm so exhausted. My head is filled with cotton, fuzzy and full of funhouse mirrors reflecting fragments of my visions and nightmares back to me.

"You're not the one to blame."

I shake my head, and he catches my chin and says in his dom voice, "You're not."

I swallow. As soon as he lets go, I cover my face with my hands. "I feel like I'm going mad," I tell him. It hurts to get the words out. It's so hard, flaying myself open like this. Letting him see my insides.

"You're not. But even if you were, it'd be alright."

I peek through my fingers. He's cloaked in darkness, but I can still imagine his beautiful face. "You'd still want me?" It's meant to be a joke, but it comes out ragged, close to a sob. He doesn't know the full extent of my brokenness. He knows me better than anyone else, but I've managed to keep some secrets from him.

"I'll always want you." He sounds so confident, so assured. I want to squirm away. I don't want anyone to see me like this, but especially not him. He sees too much of me already.

"I just want to be okay," I whisper. I worked so hard to

hold myself together. But I was never whole. I've lost any hope of healing. I'm broken and always will be.

"You are okay." His hands cover mine. Not coaxing me open but holding me, reinforcing my own barriers so I feel safe.

"You're here with me. No one can touch us. No one can hurt you. Unless. . ." He wraps his hands around my wrists, and my pulse jumps. "Unless you need me to."

I let him draw my hands down. His touch is light but reminds me that he's strong enough to shackle me any time he likes.

"You're tired," he says. "You need rest."

He's right. I need to sleep, and not just so I can wake up refreshed enough to do my job and find the killer who's terrorized so many. I'd give anything to fall into oblivion. "I can't sleep."

"I can help you. I can take your mind off things if you'll let me."

I raise my head. I want that. It would be smart to keep my distance, but right now, I'm craving what only Rex can give. "How?"

2

I *nara*

THE BEST THING about being bound by rope is being forced to surrender. I had plenty of chances to escape when I presented my wrists to Rex. I allowed him to loop the rope over and over into a makeshift harness that would support me when he hoisted me into the air. The more the loops of rope touched my skin, the more I relaxed.

Now I hang suspended in my woven cocoon. I'm tied in a diving position with my arms secured behind me and my legs slightly splayed. Even my hair is wound with rope and suspended.

I can't move. And yet, I feel so free. All the worry bleeds from my brain. There's nothing but the rope snug around my limbs, the collar around my throat, and the shadowy presence of my dom. My Rex.

Warm air blows on my bare skin, but beyond the circle

of neon light, there's a chill. Rex could've brought me to his gorgeous dungeon to tie me up. Instead, he brought me to the dark cave he's converted into his secret head-quarters.

I peer into the darkness beyond the spotlight, trying to discover any clues as to the inner workings of his psyche. Rex has many secrets. I might be one of the only ones who knows the full details of his alter ego, his crimes.

It's what drove me to his mansion. A few days ago, I was on the warpath, searching for a way in, searching for evidence to expose him.

Now I'm tied up and suspended, at his mercy. And all I feel is relief.

It won't last. Rex and I can't be together. He's still a killer, and I'm still a detective sworn to uphold justice. But I can allow him to comfort me, just this once.

His touch ghosts down the back of my calf, and I shiver.

"I don't think you're focused." His voice is deeper, darker. I feel the vibrations of his rasp in my core. Wetness drips from my labia. I would squirm and press my legs together to relieve the ache, but I can't move.

"I promised I'd help you take your mind off things. Give you what you need so you can sleep. But you're still thinking too much."

He runs a hand up my thigh and brushes my sex. His touch is barely there, but I know he's collecting the moisture dripping from my pussy. "At least one part of you is paying attention." There's a smirking edge to his tone. "But I wonder. . . What will it take for you to let go?" He walks around to face me. He's dressed in black slacks and nothing else, and his hard torso is a feast for the eyes. All sexy muscle and sinew, power incarnate.

He rubs my own essence over my lower lip. "You're so

beautiful like this." He pushes a thumb into my mouth, and I run my tongue over it to thank him. "Good girl."

All too soon, he moves away, and a band of black fabric falls over my eyes. The darkness falls, and I sigh, relaxing further.

I spent so many years with a white-knuckle grip on my life, keeping myself isolated so I wouldn't dream of anyone's death. I craved connection so much that it hurt. And then, when it'd been so long I couldn't remember human touch, I craved the pain.

It's wonderful to give up control. I don't know what Rex and I are to each other, but I do know he's the only one who's been able to give me what I need so perfectly. I fell for him once, when he was my mystery dom, before I knew who he truly was.

It's tempting to fall for him again. But I can't give in forever.

Just this once, I tell myself. I've told myself this before, but this time, it has to be true.

After this, I'll distance myself from him. After tonight, we'll go our separate ways.

"Give in to me," he whispers, and for the next few moments, I do. My submission has an expiration date, but for now, I can forget myself and be completely his.

When I'm blindfolded, every touch is a revelation. He's wound rope around my torso to suspend me, but he left my breasts hanging free. Now he toys with my nipples, pinching them until pain sings through me. I gasp and flinch and moan, and I sense him watching me, taking in every reaction. Even though I can't see, I can feel his attention, and I soak it up like a parched plant soaking up the rain.

His hands are large and warm, cupping my breasts and tormenting my nipples. I can't lean into him, and I can't pull away. I can do nothing but hang from the ropes and take it. It's horrible and wonderful all at the same time, just the way I like it.

His fingers trace circles above and below my waist where the ropes cinch me. I shudder. My pussy weeps.

"My sweet submissive. You look like you're flying. Like a little bird." He pokes a finger against the rope binding my thigh and adjusts it a little. "I can keep you here for hours. You can't get away." He pushes my hip, and I swing in the air. He's toying with me, and it only makes me wetter. "Would you like that, little bird? Hanging here, at my mercy, for as long as I please?" He brushes my bottom, and goosebumps break out all over me. "I think you would. You might say no, but your body tells me the truth."

For a moment, I allow myself to imagine this level of possession. What if he never lets me go? He told me I would belong to him. He wants forever.

He's already proven he doesn't have limits when it comes to controlling me. He's stalked me, trapped me, killed for me. What will he do when I try to leave? There's no reasoning with a monster like him. He takes what he wants, and he wants me.

What if he locked me up for the rest of my life? I would fight, of course, but the submissive part of me would feel so free.

The submissive part of me doesn't get to make the rules. But just imagining it pulls me deeper into the scene.

He strokes the insides of my thighs. Does he know what he's doing to me? What I'm imagining? It's scary how much he sees. My darkest desire and my deepest fear warped and morphed into one.

"Just let go and be mine," he whispers and rubs a

knuckle between my lower lips, stroking beside my clit. It takes barely any time for my orgasm to rush closer.

"Rex," I gasp, and he withdraws his hand, only to let it fall in a hard, open-palmed smack against my sex.

I cry out in shock and wonder.

"No," he barks. "That's not who I am to you here." His rebuke rings through me, more painful than the slap.

What? I sort through my thoughts to figure out what he's talking about.

When I'm inside you here, you don't use my name. You call me Master. And you come when I tell you to come.

He told me this last time he took me in his lair.

He smacks me again, more lightly, and suddenly, I'm on the precipice, ready to tip into ecstasy.

"Oh gods," I gasp.

"No," he purrs. "I'm not a god. Who am I to you? Tell me, and you get to come."

"R—" I start to say his name, and he pats my sex, not hard enough to make me come, but hard enough to make me groan. "Oh fuck."

"I'll fuck you after you give me what I want. Can you do that? Can you be a good girl for me and tell me what I want to hear?"

If I call him *Master*, he'll allow me to come. He'll give me everything I want. I did it before, just last night. I don't know why it's so hard this time.

I should've known he wouldn't allow me to withhold any part of myself. He's always sought my submission.

And I've always given in. Like now.

"Please..."

"You beg so prettily, sweet submissive. But you still haven't given in to me. What do you call me when we're in here?"

"Master." It's the barest whisper, but he hears me.

"Good girl." He presses against my side, gripping my hair below where he's bound me with the rope, and shoves his fingers into my sopping sex. He uses the rough edge of his thumb and rubs the needy spot next to my clit, hooking two blunt fingers in to massage the inner wall above my entrance. My orgasm blows up so fast I scream. I explode, fragmenting around his fingers. The convulsions rock me, making me swell and strain against the ropes.

I'm tied up tight, and I'm flying. I'm free.

"Such a good girl for me," Rex murmurs, and gods, I need him. I need him to hurt me, to bring me down from this painful ecstasy. I need him to shove his cock into me, so I can focus on pleasing him. So I can earn his praise.

"That's it." He thrusts his fingers in and out, giving me a little taste of what it will be like when he's moving his cock inside me. It's not enough, but my inner muscles clench, milking him desperately. "You need this, don't you? You need me to tie you up and spank your pussy so you can get relief." He withdraws his fingers. With one last swipe over my sex, he moves around to my front. "Here. Taste yourself." He smears my juices over my face before shoving his fingers into my mouth, deep enough to make me gag.

"That's it. Open up for me. Show me you can take it."

It's almost too much, being bound and helpless and humiliated like this. But I don't care. I love it.

He withdraws his fingers and wipes them on my bare breasts. He's making a mess of me, and I want him to. *Yes, please. Wreck me.*

"Now it's my turn. You're going to suck me, and if you do a good job, I'll fuck your pussy until you come all over my cock."

I open my mouth wide, ready for him. I don't care if it's

humiliating to beg like this, with my face wet from where he used me like a rag. There's nothing I won't give him right now.

He steps close, and I smell his delicious scent, cedar and spice and a tang of sweat. He teases me, brushing the head of his cock over my mouth, painting my lips with his pre-cum. I lick my lips and extend my tongue, chasing another taste. His dark chuckle rings in my ears, making me blush. He's mastered me, and he knows it. But he gives me what I want, pushing past my lips and filling my mouth. There's a tug on my hair. He's holding the ropes back around my hair again and using them to control me. "Lick the underside," he orders, and when I do, he groans. "That's it, baby. Gods, you feel so good."

He presses forward, hitting the back of my throat. I gag a little, and he backs off, only to push forward again. He tugs my hair with one hand and strokes my neck with the other, coaxing me to take him deeper. "Relax, little bird. Let me in. Yes, like that. Fuck, how you please me."

His dick knocks at the back of my throat. I breathe through my nose and keep my muscles loose. *I love this,* I tell him by swirling my tongue around him. *Give me more.* I push my head forward and hum. He curses and tugs me back by my hair until tears leak out from under my blindfold. My pussy throbs, aching and empty, but I feel so satisfied, licking him, choking on him the way he likes.

"You're too good." He pulls out. I'm panting, my face painted with our combined essence, and all I feel is immense satisfaction at having pleased him.

He trails his fingers over my swollen lips. His scent wafts over me when he leans in to kiss me. I respond with eagerness, craning my neck to push into the kiss, straining towards him as much as I can while being restrained.

"Shall I give you your reward?" he whispers. His big hand cups my cheek, and I lean into it. My sex thrums with anticipation, but I'm content to soak in this moment of tenderness. This is why I love submitting to Rex. He thinks ahead to the next move. All the decisions rest on his shoulders, and I can just. . . be.

"Whatever you want." I turn my head to kiss his fingers. "Master." I still hesitate to call him that, but when I force it out, it fills me with peace. There's nothing left for me to do but surrender.

"My gods." His normally certain voice shakes. "You were made for me."

He walks down the length of my body, his fingers never leaving my skin. He's tied me up at the right height to pull my hips towards him and thrust into my entrance.

I'll never get used to how his thickness stretches me. We both moan from the pain that's on the edge of the pleasure, and the pleasure that's on the edge of pain. He trails his fingers across my skin, tracing the sensitive line of flesh at the edge of the bindings. The rope creaks as he begins to move. I can't push against him, can't escape; I can only hang here and take it. His movements make me swing, and as the cool air rushes over me, I focus on the place we're joined. The way I'm stretched around him, the way he probes me, driving deep, using the swinging momentum to slam into me, tipping my senses into blissful overload.

And when he's thoroughly used my body, he grips the tied length of my hair, bowing me back further. Making me feel his control. Obliterating me until there's nothing left but pleasure. No more Inara. No more Rex. Only us.

I spent my whole life running from this level of intimate connection. Only Rex, with his passion to consume me, could coax me to this level of surrender.

In another life, Rex would be perfect for me. We could be together. Joined completely, allowing our bodies to sing to each other in counterpoint. It's a tempting fantasy.

It'll have to remain a fantasy.

After this, no more. I can't allow myself to be with Rex.

But I'll always remember this moment, this feeling of being totally his.

3

R^{ex}

THE BEST THING about a long scene is the aftercare. I carry Inara's limp body to our bedroom. The first stop is the bathroom, where I wash us both clean. The ropes left red marks snaking over her golden skin, and I admire them before massaging the braid-like indentations. I offer her painkillers and arnica, but she mumbles and shakes her head, so I bundle her up and take her to bed. I wrap myself around her and sleep like the dead until morning.

Two things wake me—her leaving the bed and my rock-hard dick. I roll to my back and admire her shadowed silhouette. She sneaks to the bathroom, and then returns, but not to bed. She tiptoes to one of the closet doors, sneaking a glance inside.

I give the command for the curtains to open. Daylight pours in, startling her.

"Going somewhere?" I ask.

"I need clothes." There's a glow to her skin, a hint of a blush, and she's looking everywhere but at me.

"Do you?" I want to tease her, introduce the idea of walking around naked except for her collar, but she crosses her arms over her chest, and I relent. She's feeling vulnerable, which is making her pull away. If a few thin layers of fabric make her feel safe, then there's no harm.

"Here." I cross the room and open the door to the correct walk-in closet. "This is all yours."

"What?" She peeks in, and her eyes widen. "Of course," she murmurs mostly to herself. I've given her a wardrobe before, back when she stayed at Hotel Magnifique. She's starting to get used to how I anticipate her needs.

She wastes no time selecting a pair of jeans and a button-down shirt, grabbing a lingerie set almost as an afterthought. To my disappointment, she disappears in the bathroom to change.

I make use of the moment of privacy to receive my morning report from my AI assistant. Stock prices, corporate negotiations, and, more importantly, the results of the forensic testing Hamish ran on the letters sent to Inara. So far, there's no DNA or fingerprint evidence linking the Bondage Killer to the letters, but if there is, we'll find it.

By the time Inara emerges, I've dressed for the day. She's sleekly groomed and gorgeous in the casual clothes she favors for work. Her expression is closed off, a little wary. Her hand is at her throat, playing with the silver collar I placed around her neck.

She must have a lot on her mind, but she's acting strange around me. Almost. . . shy.

I want her to be comfortable, but I savor her uncertainty.

It says something about the monster I am that I enjoy having her off balance.

Even her trepidation is delicious.

"Are you sore?" I ask.

"Not really." She's still guarded. "Rex, we need to talk."

"Of course." I hold out my hand. "Let's go."

"Where?"

"Breakfast."

She glances at the window. "It's late."

"Brunch then." She's acting like she has somewhere to be. I need to have patience. Yesterday, she insisted on going to work. Now that a killer is stalking her, things have changed, and she's probably adjusting.

I can take her mind off of everything for a little while.

"Let me show you what Roy Manor has to offer." I've already ordered a full brunch spread, but I take the long way to the breakfast room, guiding her through two ballrooms and a gallery or two. She lets me lead, holding my hand and taking everything in with wide eyes and a solemn expression.

Only once does she tug my hand for me to stop. She stalls in front of a portrait of my family. Me, as a boy with my parents. Back when they were still alive.

She studies it but says nothing. I brace myself for the sight of my dead parents and force myself to look up at the painting as if it's a bland landscape that means nothing to me.

The faces look the same, and I wonder how many of my memories have shifted to match this painting versus the reality of how they actually looked. Have I forgotten them?

But no, when I remember them, I hear their soft voices, the sound of their laughter. There was so much love saturating each moment we spent together. It doesn't matter what they looked like. All that matters is the love.

That's what I lost.

And now I stand before them with the woman I've chosen. I know what they'd think of her. But what would they think of me? I've become someone they wouldn't recognize. Certainly not the sort of man they raised me to be. My father was a doctor, my mother a philanthropist, both focused on saving lives, not destroying them. They wouldn't approve of my intense focus on keeping the city safe at all costs. They wouldn't condone the lines I've crossed. The lives I've taken. They might mourn the man I've become.

But they would approve of Inara.

"I was seven when this was painted," I tell her because I need to break the silence between us. I need her to know me in a way I haven't allowed anyone else to know me since my parents died. "They hired the same master who did their wedding portrait. Family tradition."

She looks down the long hall full of oil portraits on the wood-paneled walls. Generations of Roys stretching back to before my ancestors came to New Rome. "Ah."

"After my parents died, I avoided this hall for years. Something about the way they're smiling. They look like they're looking forward to something." I swallow, and it feels like razors are lining my throat.

She steps closer to me, and that makes the pain of talking about my parents worth it. "Like what?"

"Nothing. Everything. Life, I guess." I stare at the gilt frame, unable to look even the decades-old visage of my father or mother in the eye. They had so much life to look forward to.

She leans in, pressing against my arm. She might be moving closer to see better, not to comfort me, but I feel comforted all the same. "You're not smiling." She points out the blank expression on young Rex Roy's face.

"No. I wasn't."

Looking at the portrait has lost its appeal, so I look at her instead. Her profile is lovely. Enchanting, even though she's withdrawn from me this morning. She's possibly more enticing because of that. I always did love the chase.

I want to know what she's thinking. I'm about to ask when her stomach gurgles.

"Let's get some food into you." I take her elbow, and she lets me steer her down the long hall, leaving the likeness of my parents and younger self.

We have breakfast in the south wing in a dining room that gives us a view of my mother's gardens.

"This is incredible," she says once she's finished her omelet.

"What?"

"All this." She waves a hand around the cavernous room. This was my mother's favorite dining space, full of light. It was designed with white columns and cream and gold wallpaper, and she added large pastoral paintings in ornate frames.

"Oh." I set down my napkin. I say thank you because it's polite and not because I had a damned thing to do with the architecture.

"I can't imagine growing up here." For the first time today, she meets my gaze. We share a long glance, and I sense that she's not complimenting me on the grandness of the house. She's thinking of how it would be to live here as the last remaining Roy. So much wealth and grandeur and nothing to make it a home. "You must have been lonely."

"Hamish took care of me," I say lightly. "And I went to school."

"Until you were kicked out."

"I see you read my journals." I know she found my boyhood bedroom. I watched her on the surveillance cameras. We haven't discussed it yet.

She looks abashed at invading my privacy. "Only a few. But I don't need to read them to know how alone you were."

She knows because she's felt that deep, aching loneliness herself. She didn't have the comfort of wealth to buffer it. She sees me, and she understands.

As exciting as it is to have her know my secrets, I don't know if I'm ready to be dissected like this. "When you're finished eating, I'll give you a tour of the rest of the house."

"Rex," she hesitates, and I know she's going to say what's been on her mind since she woke up. "I'm not staying."

I half expected it, but it still hits like a body blow.

"Thank you for breakfast," she continues, "but I should be going."

I control my impulse to shout *No*. "Where will you go?"

"To the city. To do my job." She's toying with her collar again.

I clear my throat and look pointedly at her collar until she realizes what she's doing and drops her hand.

Only to raise it again to indicate the metal at her throat. "When are you going to remove this?"

"Why would I remove it?" I'll make her say it outright. Tell me she doesn't want this.

We both know she'd be lying.

She huffs. "I can't wear it forever."

"Why not?"

She looks around as if waiting for help to come. "Because I need to work. I need to get back—"

"No, you don't." I let my gaze roll over her. She's wearing the clothes I gave her and eating the food I provided.

She flushes because she knows how much she loves it when I care for her. "You thought I would, what, quit my job and be your full-time submissive?"

"Sounds perfect." Being with her is the most pleasure I've had in this grand room. I lean in, coaxing her to confide in me. "You love this. You love my control."

She averts her gaze, and I want to grip her shoulders. Make her admit what she seems so reluctant to voice.

"I'm not interested in being a trophy." She goes to touch her collar again, and that subconscious gesture tells me she's preoccupied with the physical evidence of my possession. She realizes what she's doing and brushes her hair back instead. "I do love what we shared. But. . ."

"I told you when you came to me, I'd keep you." My voice is soft but firm. "I keep my promises, little bird."

Her pulse flutters in her neck. "That was just a game."

"Such a lovely game." I capture her hand and bring it to my lips. I kiss and caress her fingers, and some of the tension in her shoulders softens.

"I enjoyed it." Her voice is low and throaty. "You know I did. But it can't go on forever. There's too much at stake." She withdraws her hand, looking resigned. "It can't continue."

She's pulling away. Earlier in the bedroom, she wasn't feeling shy and nervous; she was putting up her walls. Does she need evidence of how good we are together? Because I have plenty of that. "Last night—"

"Last night, I needed comfort. A place to land. I'll always be grateful, Rex, but—"

"You belong to me." It comes out too harsh, and I know it's a blunder. I'm being a clumsy negotiator, but dammit, she surrendered herself to me, and I'm never letting her go.

She shakes her head, and the light catches her collar, negating her refusal. "I belong to myself."

"You gave yourself to me."

"You want the truth?" Her chest rises and falls as if she's bringing out the big guns but is reluctant to use them. Sometimes in our arguments, I sense that she's being careful, almost reluctant to hurt me, as if she intuits that she's one of the few people who could.

I get control of myself. There's a panicked part of me screaming that I need to beg her to stay, but I refuse to act so needy. So pathetic. "Tell me."

"I came here to trap you. To see if I could gather evidence of your crimes."

It's adorable, her thinking she can entrap me. "I know. You see yourself first as a detective. You'd like to only be a detective instead of what you are."

"And what am I?"

"Mine."

She shakes her head as if dizzy.

I enjoy seeing her overcome by me, but I know it's not a fair fight because her desires side with me. "Has it occurred to you that I used your single-minded focus on justice to trap *you*?"

"Yes." She closes her eyes briefly. "I thought I could resist you. I told myself I would get close to you, give you what you wanted, and see if you'd make a mistake. Give me something I could use to nail you to the wall."

"So that's why you were snooping around." She'd found my childhood bedroom, my journals, and evidence of my search for her. And then she found my underground headquarters. "You found more than you bargained for."

She gives me her hard-edge detective glare, but the effect is diminished because she's still wearing my collar.

"Whatever you told yourself, it's time to admit it was an excuse. You manufactured all sorts of reasons to put yourself in my clutches. But whatever reason you gave yourself was quickly eclipsed by your desire." I pause to give her a chance to protest, but she doesn't. "You were fooling yourself."

"You're right. I was fooling myself. And now I'm not."

She's trying so hard to pull away. "I get it." I let my voice soften. "You're afraid of this, of us. It's new—"

"It's not that. I need to focus. You're not the priority anymore."

She's talking about me like I am only a target, not her dom. "Why are you denying what we have together?"

"Because it's not right. It's twisted." She swirls her finger against the outside of her water glass, collecting condensation. I want to put her in a posture collar and force her to look at me. "Maybe it's just who we are."

"And what is that?"

"We're broken. Both of us. I don't know if what we can have together would be right."

I get a flash of the inadequate feeling I felt earlier when I faced my parent's portrait. "We are right," I insist. "We make sense together. Inara"—I push back my chair to face her fully, with nothing between us—"you're the only thing that makes sense."

"Rex." She's looking at me with sorrow and pity. "Two broken people don't make a whole. There are things you've done, that I've done–"

"What have you done?"

She presses her lips together, and my anger flares. She's holding back. Again.

I knew I should've shattered her when I had the chance. Broken her into so many pieces that only I could put her back together.

There's still time.

If she thinks I'm a monster, I can prove her right.

I want all of her. I need her mind and body under my possession, and if I don't get it, I'll go mad. And then the monster will truly be unleashed.

I grapple with my intense feelings and force myself to speak softly. "You're saying this because you're terrified. You've always been afraid—and with good reason." I think of the terror she went through as a child. "But you know me. You've trusted me with your body." If I stripped her naked, she'd be covered in my marks, proof of our compatibility written on her skin. "You can trust me to keep you safe."

I'm appealing to what drew her to me in the first place. It's ruthless, but I'll use any weapon I have to keep her at my side.

And she looks tempted, her face filled with yearning when I murmur, "Let me be your safe place to land."

She shakes her head slightly. "Safety is an illusion. And I don't think you want me. You just want to own me."

I shrug. "It's the same thing."

"No, it's not. You've fixated on me. You enjoy dangerous games, but everything in your life has come easy. I was something you couldn't have for far too long. Now I'm just a challenge to overcome, a prize to be won."

I smirk. "Such a lovely prize." It's the wrong thing to say.

She pushes to her feet. "I'm leaving, Rex. I have a job to do, and it needs me more than ever."

I rise also, kicking myself. I forgot myself and fell into the fun of fighting with her and went too far. "No," I blurt, rage and panic pumping through my heart until I'm made of emotion. I need to stop her, but I can't lose control. "Inara, think about this. It's not safe for you—"

She whirls to argue, but we're interrupted when Hamish glides through the door.

"Sir, there's something you should see."

"Not now, Hamish." He wouldn't interrupt unless it was important. I don't care if every stock I own is tanking or every business I own burns to the ground. Nothing is as important as keeping Inara here.

"You'll want to see this news briefing. There's been another murder."

Inara blanches, and I reach to comfort her. She's just been through her worst nightmare, and I want to give her what she needs.

But she pushes past me and barks a demand at Hamish. "Show me."

In the short walk from the breakfast room to the study, Inara fully transforms into the hardened version of herself she becomes as a detective. She's wan and withdrawn, the flickering light of the television emphasizing the bruised hollows under her eyes.

"I'm on location at the scene of a second murder," the TV reporter says, standing on a sidewalk corner with the wind tugging at her blonde hair. "An inside source says this new murder might be related to the horrific Green Street killings we reported on yesterday. NRPD has yet to comment."

Green Street is the crime scene where I met Inara yesterday. Where she almost collapsed after seeing a scene that matched her family's murder.

"In both cases, the killer entered the home at midnight while the victims slept. This time, his target was twenty-five-year-old Emily Rodriguez—"

A picture of the victim flashes on the screen. It shows the young woman at a happier time, when she was alive and well, instead of as a now mangled corpse. Horror hits me. The shape of the victim's face, her long dark hair—she looks like Inara.

The reporting continues, showing B-roll of the neighborhood, charming brownstones and old oak trees now marred by yellow crime scene tape. I don't hear a word over the high-pitched whine in my ear.

The killer wanted Inara. He targeted her first with the letters and then with a series of murders. First, a family was killed in the exact way her family died years ago. Now, a woman who looks like Inara. It can't be a coincidence.

I need to focus, to think. But all I can see is Inara lying dead on the ground. It could've been her.

Maybe it's because I just studied their portraits, but for a moment, I'm transported to that horrible night in the alleyway outside the theater, the smoke of gunfire hanging over my mother and father's prone bodies. One minute we were laughing and talking, the next, they were dead. Leaving me with nothing but the echo of gunshots and the loss I would carry for the rest of my life.

Inara is in danger. She could die, just like my parents. She would've died last night if the killer had found her.

Only I can keep her safe. And I will do anything. There's no law I won't break, no boundary I won't obliterate.

Nothing matters but protecting her.

Inara

THE BONDAGE KILLER has struck again. This time, instead of a family, it's a single woman. She was alone in her apartment when he broke in. I feel a flash of terror and anguish, and I don't know if it's mine or a psychic response to the victim.

They show a picture of her when she was alive, smiling, with her arms around her dog. The mention of a dog tugs at my memory. The detail matches my dream last night, where I was a grown woman lying in bed, hoping the sounds outside my room were made by the dog and not an intruder.

Dear gods. It wasn't a dream.

"Pardon, ma'am?" Hamish mutes the TV and cranes his head as if to hear me better.

"Nothing." I didn't mean to say that aloud. No one knows the truth about the visions I see of victims before they die, and no one ever will. It's a secret I'll take to the grave.

I shake off the sick feeling of psychic horror and try to focus on the facts of the case. There's no time for me to collapse, not now.

"Are there any more details?" I ask. On the muted TV, the news broadcast has switched to images of Chief Jordan waving away microphones. The chyron announces an upcoming police press conference.

"I did make a few inquiries and learned a detail left out of the press reports," Hamish says. "There was a note left on the latest scene. Much like the ones sent to you, Detective Ramos."

I jolt. Of course. The letters. "What happened to the letters?" All I remember is gripping them while getting into the backseat of Ivan's town car. "I need to get them to the precinct. They're evidence."

"We have them," Rex says. "They're in my lab. We took the opportunity to run some forensic testing."

"You did what?" It's bad enough that Hamish so easily uncovered sensitive details of the case, but tampering with evidence? He's gone too far. I channel my shock into anger and round on him. "There are rules about the chain of custody for a reason. The letters are our best hope of finding the killer, and now they're tainted—"

"Because evidence is never tainted in police custody." Rex doesn't bother to hide his sarcasm.

"I guess you would know." I remember how easily Rex made evidence disappear in the Martin case, and my face and chest grow hot. "You have no right—"

"Do you want to know what we found?" Rex interrupts.

I pause with my mouth open. If he compromised the evidence, I might shoot him. Not anywhere fatal, but maybe in the leg or something. He's lucky I'm not armed now.

But I do want to know what he found.

I nod, and he beckons. "Come see for yourself."

We end up back in his HQ or, as Hamish calls it, his "lair." Beyond the illuminated workspaces, the place is as dark and forbidding as ever. Rex leads me across a metal bridge to a large glass cube, a makeshift room filled with lab equipment. There are stainless steel counters and a hanging array of computer screens.

"This can't be sterile," I mutter.

"Alfie?" Rex asks, and the computer answers in a cheerful, artificial voice. "We maintain the strictest sanitation levels and disinfect all surfaces regularly. Would you like a decontamination report?"

"That won't be necessary." I roll my eyes.

"Here." Rex guides me to a long plastic case that holds each letter. "We hoped for fingerprints, but there are only yours. The writer must have worn gloves. The paper is aged, but it's common card stock, a brand that's been sold in craft stores across the nation for over twenty years. We're analyzing for mold spores, bacteria, anything that can give us a hint of the writer's location."

I lean over the case, studying each letter. I didn't have to read the ravings of the madman to know it was the Bondage Killer. I feel it like a dark cloud hovering over my senses. A poison spreading through my psyche, making me want to rip at my skin to shed the suffocating feeling.

"Most interesting was the handwriting analysis," Hamish says. He's pecking on a computer, pulling up toxicology reports that would rival the best forensic lab. "The signature matches that of the Bondage Killer." A picture of a similar letter, written on cream card stock, appears on the screen nearest to me. "This is a letter sent to the Elyria police station sixteen years ago, around the time the Bondage Killer was active in that area." By 'active,' Hamish means murdering people. Families like mine.

"I remember," I say. I've seen photocopies of the Bondage Killer's letters in my mentor's files. "He was confident. Baiting the police. It helped them catch him."

"Indeed, Detective."

"We'll catch him again," Rex says. There's a bleak finality to his tone that makes me turn to him. Earlier, he tried to comfort me. Now he looks solemn, like a man who's just learned he's been conscripted to go to war.

The letters all have the same handwriting, a spidery scrawl that gets wilder and harder to read in the latest letters. The latest one reads *I'm coming for you* in barely legible script. I fight the urge to take a step back. My stomach twists like I'm going to vomit, but I force myself to swallow. "He's unraveling."

"He's fixated on you," Rex says. "Has he ever had any contact with you outside of. . ."

"The night he came for my family? No." I step away from

the letters and suck in air. Maybe I will be sick. "It's a delusion." I suddenly get a whiff of something foul and turn my head, coughing. "What's that smell?"

"Smoke and rot," Hamish says. "The paper is saturated in those scents."

"You said the paper stock was old," I say. "Could it be from BK's original hideout in the warehouse?"

"The one that burned down, supposedly with him in it? Perhaps. Hamish?"

"I'll see if I can run that particulate analysis, sir." Hamish presses a button, and a lab machine on wheels rolls forward to insert robotic arms into the protective case. "I'll have to take another sample."

This goes against all my training on chain of custody for evidence, but I have to admit that Rex has an advanced lab. I don't like it, but if he can uncover more clues faster, it'll be worth it. All that matters is stopping the Bondage Killer before he strikes again.

The scent of smoke coats my lungs. It's more than a smell; it's a taint soaking into my pores. The sensation is mostly psychosomatic, but I pace to the end of the glass cubicle to suck in some fresh air. The lair has great air circulation for being underground.

Rex follows me. "Are you all right?" He hovers at my side.

I rub a hand over my face as if I can wipe the psychic stink away. "A madman has come back from the dead to kill more people to get to me. I won't be all right until he's stopped."

"He will be stopped," he vows. "One way or another."

"Everyone thought he died in the fire." I never realized how much that comforted me. My family was gone forever, but the murderer met his karmic end. I could breathe easier, knowing that the case was closed.

Now, I feel like all hope has vanished.

I want to lean into Rex and accept his comfort, but I don't. No more. I can't allow myself to indulge in him.

"Inara," Rex hesitates, as if choosing his words carefully. "Have you sensed anything since moving to New Rome? Anything strange, like the feeling of being watched?"

"Yes." I give a bitter, broken laugh. "But I thought it was you." Some of it was him. The body of my attacker on my doorstep, the gift box left on my desk—they were Rex's doing. I didn't realize another killer was also stalking me. "Where did you find the letters?"

"They were in your mailbox. A whole stack, all together. No envelope, so they had to be hand-delivered."

I shudder. The Bondage Killer was at my apartment. On my front stoop. "He must have been writing them and waiting until he found where I lived to deliver them."

"You're sure it's him? The original Bondage Killer and not a copycat?"

"It's him," I don't think before I reply. "I don't have proof, but I know it." My psychic senses tell me it's the same man who entered my bedroom all those years ago.

"All right." Rex doesn't ask how I know, he just takes me at my word. And it would be heartwarming, having him believe me without having to expose my secrets, if the reality wasn't so horrific. "We'll look for a connection, see what we find that can help us catch him now. How he could have escaped the burning warehouse and lived and what he's been up to all this time."

"Thank you." I glance back at the cubicle where Hamish is bent over a microscope.

Rex puts his hand on my back. The heat from his large

hand should comfort me, but it only makes me realize how chilly I am. "One more round of tests, and we'll send them to the precinct."

"When will the testing be done?"

"In another few hours. The crime labs are backlogged. This is the most expedient solution."

"All right." I want to get to work as soon as possible, but Rex is right. I'm uncomfortable with breaking the rules, but if unconventional methods are the best chance of stopping the Bondage Killer, I'm all for it. We don't have much time.

He's going to kill again, and soon. I know it.

"When you disclose that BK sent you the letters, you'll be at the center of this thing," Rex says quietly.

"I'm already at the center of this thing." I blow out a breath and say what needs to be said, even though it makes me want to weep. "I'm the reason he came back. He wants to finish what he started. It's my fault."

"Inara, no." His shadow falls over me. "It's not your fault."

If only Rex knew. For the past two nights, visions of the victims have haunted my sleep. If only I had heeded the visions earlier and figured out how to act, the family on Green Street and poor Emily Rodriguez would still be alive.

"You can't blame yourself," he says, but he's wrong. I can, and I do.

Stopping the Bondage Killer is the only way to atone for my failure.

"Little bird," Rex calls softly. He's right in front of me, but with all the thoughts crowding my head, he sounds far away. "Look at me."

A few hours ago, I would have let that deep voice soothe me. But now, comfort is a luxury I can't afford. I need to leave all intimacy behind. It's the price I pay in service of justice.

I shake my head. "I'm wasting time. I need to focus." My involvement in the case and my psychic instincts might be the only way to catch the Bondage Killer. "I need to get to work."

"I'll set up a meeting with the NRPD. They can interview you here."

"What? Why?" I glance up and take in his impassive expression. "I need to go in."

"You can't be thinking of going into the city. There's a killer looking for you."

"All the more reason for me to go in. I might be the only one who can stop him." I turn to find my way out of this cave, and suddenly, Rex is looming over me, standing in my way.

"If you think I'm going to let you leave here to hunt down the Bondage Killer alone, you're delusional." His voice is as hard as I've ever heard it.

"Excuse me?"

"You heard me." His gaze is so cold and hard it's like looking down the barrel of a gun. He's never looked at me like this, glaring at me like I'm the enemy.

I'm the one willing to cross him, so I guess I am his enemy. "Rex, you can't keep me here."

"Can't I?"

"You wouldn't."

He leans in. "Watch me."

4

I *nara*

MY BREATH COMES FASTER, staring him down. He's a formidable opponent and there's no way I can overcome him physically. And I haven't had much luck fighting him any other way.

I have to get him to see reason. "Let's just slow down." I raise a hand. "We want the same thing—to stop the murders."

"I'm not willing to sacrifice your safety for that."

I open my mouth to tell him I'll be perfectly safe, but I can't make that promise. Ever since he came for me, I've dreamed of dying. Ever since arriving in New Rome, I felt that my time would come soon.

If it's at the hands of the Bondage Killer, so be it. I'll just have to make sure I take him with me.

Knowing the end is close tears me up like knives in my

insides. But my visions always come true, so I might as well resign myself to it. No one can save me from my fate.

Not even a man as wealthy and powerful as Rex.

"It's not your decision," I say. "It's mine." I whirl and look to the left and right. "Get me out of here."

"Inara, wait." His voice has softened, so I pause.

"I can't let you. . . I don't want to lose you." For a moment, I hear the little boy he was, begging for his parents not to leave him. Begging the gods to let his mother and father live. "It's not safe out there. Please, let me keep you safe."

"I'm going to be safe. I'll be smart. But Rex. . . I have to stop him."

"You're leaving me," he says.

No, I want to insist, but I clench my teeth and nod instead. It's for the best.

For a second he turns to stone, as if bracing himself for a blow that already came. Then, his torso deflates with a sigh. "The elevator's this way."

I want to open my mouth and tell him I'm sorry it has to be this way, but what good will that do? Any bit of hope I give him that we can be together will be cruel.

He leads me over a metal bridge suspended with cables. The elevator doors open when we approach. I'm surprised and grateful when he steps in with me and hits the button for the correct floor. It's awkward standing with him, staring at the stainless-steel wall, but I would never find my way out of this place without him.

"There's nothing I can say to keep you here?" he says without looking at me.

Oh, Rex. My heart is breaking for us. Maybe if we were different people. Maybe if I had more time. But the circumstances that brought us together are the same ones that will rip us apart. "No."

The elevator doors open, and I exit, only to halt in confusion. I'm in an unfamiliar hallway.

"This way," Rex says, leading me to the right.

"This place is a maze," I mutter. I don't like this hallway. It has a low ceiling and not enough lighting. Rex opens a door and holds it for me, waving me through. I go through without looking first, which turns out to be a mistake.

I'm in a small, windowless room. The walls are black panels, there's a thick carpet on the floor, a low gray chaise lounge, and a bed made up with black satin sheets and a velvety coverlet, but no other furniture.

The door slams behind me, along with the unmistakable click of a lock. I grab the handle, but it doesn't budge. "Rex?" I pound on the door, but it's solid. "What the hell?" I ride the wave of anger, ignoring the tinge of panic. "Let me out!"

His voice comes muffled through the door. "Your life is in danger. I can't let you leave."

"Are you serious right now?" I shout, even as my organs turn to concrete. He's lost it. He's finally gone too far. "You can't do this."

I wait for an answer, and there's only silence.

The realization that he can do whatever he likes hits me. "You won't get away with it," I yell. But he will. He's rich and powerful enough to make anyone disappear. That he's doing it out of some misguided attempt to preserve my life doesn't reassure me.

I forgot that Rex isn't an ordinary, rational man who plays by the rules. He'll do anything to get what he wants, the law be damned.

"Please don't do this to me." I'm begging, and I don't care. The weight of what's happening hits me, and I slump against the door. If Rex wants to keep me here, he can. He can lock me up for a long, long time.

Who knows how many lives the Bondage Killer will destroy if I don't stop him?

"I have to." His voice is firm, even muffled by the door. "I just got you. I'm not letting you go."

He thinks he owns me. I thought we had something, but he only saw me as a possession. Something he can lock away whenever it suits him. He never considered me his equal. I was nothing but a trophy to him, a toy.

And that hurts more than anything.

Rex

I watch Inara lean against the door like it's the only thing keeping her upright. The room is secure and outfitted with cameras that will allow me to keep an eye on her.

Her hand is planted on the door, and I press my own palm opposite hers, imagining I can feel her warmth through the thick surface.

I'm not sorry to lock her up. She'll hate me for it, but it's for the best. One day she'll forgive me, but even if she never does, I stand by my decision. I'll do anything to keep her safe.

When I return to the cave, Hamish lifts his head from the microscope.

"Have you found anything?" I ask.

"The paper is old and dates to the time the Bondage Killer was last active."

"Really?"

"Yes, and I have a theory about the smoky quality of the paper. It might have been from the killer's personal supplies in the warehouse."

"How is that possible?"

"He could've slipped back in to salvage his possessions after he was presumed dead."

I curse. Damn this serial killer for returning to haunt Inara decades later. "Or it's a copycat. Someone who was obsessed with the original Bondage Killer and decided to hunt down the one person who escaped him."

Hamish inclines his head. "Another excellent theory. There's no way to conclusively confirm it without more evidence."

I have a thought. "You said the NRPD found a letter at the scene of the latest murder. Can we test that letter against these?"

"I'll see what I can do." He'll have to use his contacts to obtain a sample from the evidence locker. Not legal, but necessary. And right now, time is of the essence. Even now, the killer could be choosing his next victims.

"Has Detective Ramos left?" Hamish asks.

"No, there's been a change of plans." There's a little stone in the pit of my stomach, the tiniest regret. I wish I didn't have to lock Inara up. But it only takes a second of imagining what will happen to her if the Bondage Killer gets her in his clutches to harden my resolve.

Hamish has paused his work, waiting for me to explain further. He's not going to like this, but I tell him anyway. "She'll remain here as our guest while the killer is at large."

Hamish's eyes narrow. He knows when I'm glossing over the truth. "As a guest? Or a prisoner?"

"I prefer to think of her as a reluctant guest. Her unwillingness is temporary. She'll come around."

Hamish sighs. "I see." Over the years, I've grown used to his unspoken disapproval. He supports a certain amount of lawbreaking in the name of justice, but there are moral lines he won't cross, especially when it comes to torture and murder. I keep those activities off-site.

He doesn't approve of locking up a woman for any reason. But he understands how important she is to me and how I'd do anything to keep her alive.

"Sir, if I may give you some advice—"

"I don't want a lecture, Hamish."

He gives me his silence instead, which is worse than a lecture. Finally, I groan, "Say your piece."

"I know you've searched for her for a long time. But now that your search has borne fruit, you would do well to put some thought into how you will keep her by your side."

"Right now, under lock and key."

"I can't imagine she's happy with that."

"You don't have to imagine." I instruct Alfie to cast the surveillance footage on a nearby screen, and Hamish and I both watch Inara tear apart the room, running her hands over the walls and investigating the in-suite bathroom in her search for a way out. "I'll handle all contact with her. Meals, et cetera. She's off limits."

He presses his lips into a disapproving line but acquiesces. "Understood."

I should stop broadcasting the footage and get to work, but I can't take my eyes off Inara. Her expression is closed off and focused, but she's still breathtakingly lovely, marching around the room looking for ways to escape. I admire her determination, even while I want to soothe away the haunted look on her face.

I move close to the screen to block Hamish's view. I don't want anyone looking at my little bird. There's something satisfying about having her at my mercy. It's wrong to keep her this way, but it soothes my deep need to possess her.

Hamish speaks quietly to my back. "When I was a boy, I found a butterfly that had hurt its wing. I thought I'd care for it by placing it in a glass jar."

Oh gods, here it comes. A homily inserted in a fable. My childhood was rife with them.

"I thought the glass would protect it," he continues. "But when I woke the next morning, I found the butterfly had died. Suffocated."

"Let me guess. I'm the boy."

"I know you want to keep the ones you love alive and safe. But lack of freedom is a death in and of itself."

He leaves me staring at Inara's desperate face, feeling more unsettled than I did a moment ago.

INARA

I'VE GONE over every inch of the bedroom and its contents, looking for weakness. The door is solid. The furniture is sturdy enough to use as a battering ram, but I'm not strong enough to brute force the door open. The air ducts are up by the ceiling and too small to fit through.

There are no obvious knick-knacks lying around to use to pick the lock, but I learned a thing or two from my fellow inmates at the group home. One of the girls there who liked to sneak out to buy cigarettes taught me how to break out of locked rooms.

I don't have a hairpin, but I'm angry enough to take the bed apart, which is when I find some cuffs and chains attached to the frame. Most mansions don't have kinky implements in their guest rooms, but it fits with what I expect from Rex.

I can't believe he would do this to me. I can't believe I let him lull me into a false sense of security, thinking I was special. My psychic sense didn't warn me. It told me he was safe, and I wanted to believe that, so I let myself indulge in him.

Now I know the truth: there's nothing he won't do to get his way. He acted like he cared about me, but the moment I made a decision he didn't like, he treated me like a pet who tried to run away. He's made it clear that he doesn't think I'm his equal.

My heart is a cauldron of hurt and longing, so I ignore it and focus on my anger. I'm going to make him regret locking me in here.

I pry one of the chain links apart, breaking a nail in the process, and use the sturdy surface of the bed frame to hammer the metal flat. I need to act fast. I have no idea how long Rex will leave me alone.

I use my makeshift pick to tinker with the lock. The metal filament is too short to maneuver easily, but I somehow get the pins into place, and at last, the door clicks open.

I hold my breath and slip into the hall. I take a left and continue as quietly as I can.

I have no idea how I'll get out of this place or, once I'm out, how I'll get back to the city.

But I have to try.

Rex can't win.

The hallway ends at another locked door. I pick this one, too, gritting my teeth so hard my jaw aches.

The room is dark, but I can sense how large it is.

When the lights come on all at once, I stifle a scream. I'm in the long, red-walled room Rex uses as a dungeon. I'll have to cross it to escape.

I creep past the spanking benches, St. Andrew's crosses, and other heavy wooden contraptions fitted with iron chains that belong in a medieval torture chamber.

I'm halfway through the room when I hear his voice right behind me, "Hello, little bird."

I startle and break into a run, dashing toward the door ahead of me and freedom.

I've almost reached it when Rex's arms close around me. "No!" I shout, but he lifts me easily off my feet.

I fight, but it's no use. He's bigger and stronger, faster and way more used to grappling with enemies than I am. He drags me to the floor and pins me face down. Even with me thrashing and flailing, he overpowers me.

My screams ring loud in my ears. I'm a wild creature full of panic, unable to think or reason. If I had a weapon, I'd stab him.

He isn't the man who comforted me last night.

He isn't the dom who gave me the pain and pleasure I needed.

He's the monster dragging me into darkness.

I can't give in.

There's a hiss like a valve releasing, and I realize Rex has triggered a mechanism in his gauntlets that releases a plume of chemical-scented air. I breathe in a thick gas of some sort, and it clings to my face, filling my nostrils.

My limbs grow heavy like I'm moving through water. I sag in Rex's arms, turning into dead weight. He rolls me to my back and lays me out on the floor. My head lolls on my neck, and I stare up at the opaque glass of the helmet Rex is wearing.

He lifts it off, revealing his starkly handsome face. His eyes are black, merciless.

He tackled and gassed me like he would a fleeing criminal.

"Why?" I croak.

He says something but it's lost to my fading consciousness.

I *nara*

I WAKE up to a faint creaking sound and the sensation of being rocked like a boat on a gentle ocean. My throat is raw and sore, but the rest of me is warm and comfortable, cradled by a blanket.

My face feels clammy, and it's hard to fight my way back to consciousness. That must be from the gas.

As I lie here, fighting the slumberous feeling, I get a sense of deja vu. The morning I woke up after eating at Paisanos and then dreaming of my mystery dom, I felt the same way. There's a similar heaviness to my limbs.

He drugged me then like he drugged me now. Why did I ever think I could trust him?

I open my eyes, and the first thing I see are the bars. Round and shiny, painted gold, they stretch overhead to create a circular ceiling.

I push myself up. I'm lying on a thick pad, a makeshift bed piled high with blankets and pretty pillows. Light falls over me, bisected by the bars. I look around, and my insides tighten.

I'm in a cage.

I rise, and the structure sways slightly with my movements. The cage is tall enough for someone twice as tall as me to stand and wide enough that it takes several paces to reach the side. A short glance off the side tells me I'm still in the dungeon. The cage hangs in the middle of the room, suspended about ten feet in the air.

He's done it. He's caged me like a bird, locked me in here so I can't fly away.

A wave of weakness makes my legs wobble. I grab the bars, leaning against them until I can stand on my own. My shaky limbs and dry mouth catapult me past frustration and into fury. I can't believe the bastard drugged me. But now I know there's nothing Rex won't do. No line he won't cross. I never realized how much I assumed he had a basic level of decency when it came to me. I relied on it like a tightrope walker relies on a safety net underneath.

But there's no safety net anymore. Rex ripped it away.

And now I'm a bird in a gilded cage.

I rest my forehead against the bars. They're solid and shiny, too tightly spaced for much more than my hand and arm to fit through. I peer at the ground below, feeling dizzy.

My gods, I never thought it would come to this.

But what did I expect from a man who murders people without hesitation?

My strength returns slowly. I can't stop myself from giving the bars a desperate yank, even though I know there'll be no give to them. They won't budge. I go hand over hand around the circular cage, not so much trying to force my way out but to prove to myself that I really am trapped.

At the end of the room, a door opens, and Rex strides through. "You're awake." He's changed into a suit, the sort you wear to a boardroom meeting. His hair is freshly combed back from his face and shiny as a raven's wing.

I close my eyes so I don't have to look at him. My animal attraction to him is a weapon he wields against me. He's proven to me over and over that he doesn't see me as an equal, and that's the thought I need to cling to, not the memories of moments we shared together or all the ways he cared for me.

A mechanism whirs, and the cage lowers, but I still don't open my eyes, not even when it gently touches down.

His scent wafts over my face as he moves closer. "How are you feeling? There's water for you if you need it."

I step back into the middle of the cage as if that will protect me from him. My foot hits a water bottle I didn't notice before. I stoop to pick it up and sip it slowly, washing the dry feeling out of my mouth.

"Do you need anything else?"

I shake my head and recap the bottle and set it down, still half filled. "Is this how it starts?"

He cocks his head to the side.

"The torture before the murdering. Do you like to put your victims in a cage?"

"No, just you." He doesn't smirk, but his smug reply still rankles. "Like this dungeon that I had built for you."

I had liked that Rex did things for me and me alone. A part of me had thought his obsession was romantic.

But I had also believed there was some goodness in him, something that could redeem him. Not anymore.

"Escalation," I say to the cage ceiling. "Many killers start out as Peeping Toms. But voyeurism provides less of a thrill, and they need more. They start to stalk their victims. Collect trophies. And finally. . ." I stop quoting my criminal behavior textbook and give Rex a hollow look. "Well, you know."

"I'm not going to kill you, Inara." His tone is patient, almost condescending.

"That's good to know, I guess." The sarcasm is satisfying, so I lean in. "Although if you're lying, I'll take Paisanos as my last meal. At least I know it goes well with whatever you're drugging me with."

"I'm not lying. I've done a lot of things, but I haven't lied to you. I've told you everything. No one knows me better than you."

Oh, how I had reveled in knowing that knowledge. I was proud of the way I peeled his layers apart until I realized he's a psychopath all the way down. "Lucky me. Is this my reward? A complimentary stay in a cage at Chez Crazy?"

A muscle jerks in his sculpted cheek. "Little bird—"

"No." I hold up a hand. "You don't get to call me that. Especially not when I'm locked in here." I yank on the bars for emphasis.

"I know you're upset."

"Upset doesn't begin to cover it," I cry. I snatch up the water bottle and pitch it at his head, but it only hits the bars and rolls back to my feet. "You shouldn't have done this. Are you insane?"

"You can hate me." He stands strong, his face inscrutable. He looks like a statue of a man, a general facing down the enemy on the battlefield.

I still feel everything for him, even the things I don't want to feel. Conflicting emotions I never thought I was capable of. I want to cup his cheeks and kiss him. I want to muss his hair. I want to thump his chest and strangle him. "I trusted you. And you did this."

"But your safety is my priority. Everything I've done, I've done for you."

"Yeah, keep telling yourself that." First, I let him flog me, and then I let him hold me. I thought I could be careful, but I let him in. I let myself sink into his darkness. I hoped he could be my refuge from the world and the psychic forces that buffeted me. When we were in the cave with the letters, I tasted BK's evil, and it coated me like a poisonous film. I wanted to turn to Rex for comfort, but he's given into his darkness, and I'll never have that again.

It hurts so much that I want to howl.

"You know what? A part of me is glad you did this. I thought it would hurt to leave you. Now I can't wait to see the last of you. So thanks for making it easy." I mean for my words to hurt, cruel as a knife between the ribs. I watch his face closely and don't miss his flinch. But with it, I feel an echoing pain in my own chest.

I pick up the water bottle and thrust it through the bars, throwing it at his head. He catches it easily.

I press my face against the bars and remind myself that he's here to gloat. To prove his mastery over me. The thought strangles and kills any empathy I feel for him. "Now I know the truth. I'm just a possession to you. A trophy you can put on a shelf. I was fooling myself that you could ever see me as more."

He shakes his head, but I don't let him interject.

"You're like all the other billionaires who inherited Mommy and Daddy's money. But guess what, Rex? You want a trophy wife? You can have any socialite you want. They'd be happy to spend your money and look good on your arm."

"I don't want anyone else." His eyes blaze as he comes

closer to the cage. His controlled expression turns feral, making me glad there are bars between us. "You are it for me."

"No, I was just an easy target." All my sarcastic bravado slips away, and suddenly, I'm close to tears, remembering last night. The tender moments when he held and comforted me, the times he seemed to read my mind and anticipate my needs. "I thought I could resist you. I had spent so many years being careful. Following my rules. I thought I was strong, but I was actually so needy. And that was my downfall." I was so alone, hidden behind my thick walls, and when he got past my defenses, I was relieved. My armor became my weakness. I'd deprived myself for so long I couldn't be strong. I too quickly craved his touch.

It was easy to forget he was a murderer. That he snuffed out people's lives as deftly as he tied me up and made me come.

"I don't hate you, Rex. I hate how fucking weak I am."

His facade cracks, and I see the pain on his face. "Inara. . . no." He wants to save me from everything, including my own self-recrimination.

"The saddest thing is, you were it for me, too." Deep down, I know he's the only one for me. "And it hurts knowing the one person in the world perfectly suited for me is someone I can never be with."

"We belong together," he insists, with the cold command of a man who's never been denied.

"No. You have to let me go." I'm not going to submit to him.

"I'll let you out when you swear to me you won't run. That you'll let me keep you safe."

I shake my head. I can't bring myself to tell him what he wants to hear. I don't want to lie to him. Even now, I want to preserve the honesty we had more than I want to be let out of this cage.

"As soon as I get free, I'm going to leave. Go back to the life I was supposed to live."

Shadows burn in his eyes. "It doesn't end like this."

"It's already over!" I grab the collar around my throat. The smooth metal is not comforting anymore. It's constricting, and I can't stand it. I search for a lock or a latch, anything I can manipulate to take it off.

It's a sign of his ownership, and I can't bear it.

"I'm not yours," I say, spitting venom. My stomach is a pool of acid, and my skin is overheating. "I'll never be yours."

I give up trying to find a way to unlatch the collar and claw at it instead. "Get this off me!" I shriek. My nails scour my skin, but I don't care. I'm losing it.

"Calm down." He reaches for me, and I scramble away. "Shh," he murmurs like he's soothing a frantic pet. "It's okay. Let me." He pulls something from his pocket and holds it up to the collar. I don't know how it works, but there's a click and the metal falls away.

I back up from the bars, rubbing my bare neck. My breathing calms.

I'm surprised he took it off, but I suppose he enjoys acting like a caring dom.

He holds the collar, gripping it until his knuckles go white. It's the only sign he's feeling anything. He's cold and calm and in control. "Tell me what you need, Inara."

"I need you to let me out." I sink into the shadows in the center of the cage, curling up in a ball. "If you're not going to do that, I need you to go away."

"All right. If you're sure."

I don't answer. If the cage is my home now, at least it's

quiet and comfortable. As someone who's longed for safety and shelter, I can see the appeal.

There's a crinkle and a sound that tells me he's set the water bottle back inside the bars.

"The second you call me, I'll return," he says. "There are cameras everywhere. You won't be alone."

I huddle in the blankets and listen to his footsteps recede, leaving me to grieve the memory of what we were.

REX

I SIT IN MY OFFICE, swirling bourbon in a glass and watching the screen that shows the cage in the dungeon. Inara hasn't moved for some time, but she's not sleeping.

I sent Alfie the robot down with a tray full of food. She hasn't touched that either.

I hate it when she misses meals. It's only been a few hours, but I'm tempted to be the first to crack and let her out.

I need to be stronger than this. But I hate that I might have harmed her.

A rap on the door wakes me from my thoughts. It's Hamish, waiting in the doorway until I invite him in.

"I've finished testing the samples. The new letter left at the most recent murder matches the ones sent to Inara. Handwriting, paper quality, mold spores—all identical. I'm waiting on a sample from the original letters the killer sent to the Elyria police station, but from the photocopied versions, I can surmise the handwriting will be a match as well."

"Has the NRPD made a connection between these murders and the Bondage Killer?"

"It's one of their lines of inquiry, but they have no evidence linking the crimes. I suggest we send a package of our discoveries to the lead detective immediately." He pauses and clears his throat. "Unless you wish to free Detective Ramos and send them with her."

I glare at Hamish. He's unfazed.

"No. It's not safe for her out there. Not while this killer is fixated on her." I thump down my glass. "I have to find him." The faster I stop the Bondage Killer, the less chance he'll kill again. Maybe then Inara will forgive me.

"I have the utmost faith in your abilities, sir. But if I can make a suggestion?"

"Is it about Inara?" I fold my arms. I don't want to hear any more parables telling me if I love someone, set them free.

"It is not." He moves closer to the desk and speaks in a quieter tone. "In the past, you've gone through certain channels to solve problems. Channels some might find unorthodox but effective."

He's referring to the alliances I've made with St. James and his criminal connections. In the rare instance I've had trouble finding and destroying an enemy, I've hired an assassin to do it for me.

I used to think Hamish disapproved of these methods, so I'm surprised when he continues, "I was wondering if they might be a resource now?" He must be more shaken than he's letting on if, instead of nagging me to free Inara, he's encouraging me to hire an army of criminals to help hunt the Bondage Killer down.

"You want me to work with criminals?" I bristle.

"As much as you'd like to be, you cannot be everywhere at once."

I rub my face, hating him for pointing out my weakness. Hating that there are so many ways I've failed to make this city safe.

"If this is the Bondage Killer risen from the dead, we're up against an experienced killer. We don't have time to wait for him to make mistakes."

He's right. We don't have time for my pride. I'll sacrifice anything to keep Inara safe, even my last gasp at moral ground. "Make the calls. Set up a meeting."

"Consider it done." Hamish nods and leaves.

Building an alliance with St. James and his gang of murderers will be another sin Inara can judge me for. She sees the world in black and white, but I'm more practical.

There are those who would hurt Inara and those who would help me stand against them. I'm not picky when it comes to my allies. And if the choice is between keeping my hands clean and keeping Inara alive? There's no question what I'll do.

On camera, it looks like Inara has finally fallen asleep. But a frown mottles her face. Her limbs twitch, and she jerks like she's trying to wake herself up.

She's having a bad dream. I watch, on edge, until her mouth opens in a silent scream. And then I'm out of my chair and running for the dungeon, unable to be apart from her for another second.

INARA

. . .

I'M TRAPPED IN A SMALL, claustrophobic space. It stinks like smoke and rot, and ash fills my lungs. Every time I move, there's a dry, crackling sound, like I'm stepping on tinder. When I finally open my eyes, I realize I'm surrounded by the bodies of dead birds. The fragile bones snap under my flailing feet. Black feathers fill my vision, and when I scream, they fill my mouth—

"Inara." A large hand cups the side of my face, and I jerk away until I realize it's Rex. He picks me up and cradles me in his arms. I press my face into his solid shoulder, reveling in his immense strength.

Slowly the psychic horror of the dream recedes until there's only Rex, his scent, his warmth, his strength. I cling to him. Because even though I can't forgive him for locking me up, he's all I have.

He seems to know what I need and rubs my back, soothing me like I'm a child. "It's okay, baby. You're safe with me."

He carries me easily away from the cage and through the dimly lit dungeon. He takes me back to the bedroom I escaped from earlier.

I struggle to be let down, and his arms tighten around me like iron bands.

I stop fighting him and whisper, "I have to go to the bathroom."

He carries me there and gives me privacy, but I find him waiting right outside the door. Which is a good thing because I stumble in the dark, my body still heavy from sleep.

He sweeps me off my feet, and I let him, my arms and legs dangling while my head slumps against his chest. He settles us on black satin bed sheets. I find myself pressing my face into the side of his neck, sucking in his cedar scent. I missed this. I missed him.

He lets me burrow deep in his arms. Once I relax, he strokes the hair back from my face. "Was it a bad dream?"

"I don't know." It might have been a vision of the future or an echo of the Bondage Killer's past crimes. Either way, I can't share this with Rex.

But Rex notices everything, and he's not about to let me hide a piece of myself. "You said something earlier when we were watching the news. Something about a dream." He shifts me in his arms so he can study my face. "Did you dream about the killer? About the crime scene?"

I press my lips together and shake my head. *No, you don't get to know this part of me.*

"Inara, please. Let me help you."

It's tempting. Of all the people in the world, he could actually help me. Ease my burdens. But I can't trust him anymore.

"The only help I need is getting away from you." I sit up, finally putting some space between us. He only lets me move so far before his hands come to my back, pulling me into the circle of his arms.

I huff and look around the room. "Are you going to lock me in here again? Chain me to the bed?"

His cock twitches under my ass. "If that's what it takes. But right now, I thought I'd just hold you."

I do want him to hold me, more than he knows. His arms feel right around me.

This is when Rex is the most dangerous. When he's using a soft voice and gentle touch. This is when I want to give up, give in.

"I don't want to fight you," I say. "Not like this. The stakes are too high. We should be focused on the same thing— stopping the Bondage Killer."

"Agreed." Of course he agrees with this. We both want the same result. It's the steps we'll take to get there that are in conflict.

"I've spent my life dedicated to bringing murderers like him to justice. If you take that away from me, I'm not sure who I am."

"I know you want to do your job. But it's not worth your life."

I want to argue that the cost won't be my life, but the reality is I'm willing to sacrifice anything to put the Bondage Killer behind bars. Rex knows it, and it terrifies him. No wonder he overreacted. He's not used to feeling so afraid.

But I have to make him understand why I have to leave. "Imagine something with me." I brace myself before I continue. "A little girl wakes up to a nightmare. There's someone in the house. A stranger. He's already killed her parents. No one is alive to come help, when suddenly her bedroom door slowly swings open, and she knows her life will never be the same."

He rubs my back with a massive hand. "That little girl was you."

"No. That little girl is out there now. Her family's alive, but only if we put the Bondage Killer behind bars. And I'm the best chance at catching him. I'm the only one who's survived."

"That makes you a target. The danger, the risk. . . it's unacceptable."

"That's my choice."

He says nothing. He's done his damnedest to take away my choices.

"Don't you understand? This is why I survived. To become a detective, to stop people like the Bondage Killer from preying on innocent families." I dig down deep through the shards of myself to put my feelings into words. "After my family died, I didn't understand why—why they were murdered, why I had to keep living. And this is what I realized: every murderer I stopped meant another person lived. Instead of being a victim, they could survive and thrive. They could have a life with a home and a family..." I'm breathing hard, like I've run up a flight of stairs. Because it hurts to say this. It's hard to think about the responsibility I bear. And it hurts more to think of what little my life has become. "If I can save one little girl from going through what I went through, it'll be worth it. My life will make sense. Because she'll get to live the life that was taken from me."

"The life you won't allow yourself to have," Rex says, leaning in close enough that his hair brushes my forehead. "Because you'll never allow yourself to have a home. A family."

"I—" I can't refute that because it's true. I've dedicated myself fully to the cause of justice and sacrificed everything else.

"You've made yourself a martyr. Giving up everything for people who may not deserve it."

"She deserves it," I insist, even though I'm talking about a hypothetical child.

"She is gone," he snaps. "She became you."

I gasp like I've been slapped. My chest stings.

"As much as I know what it's like to focus your life on a single purpose, I can't let you sacrifice yourself." He grips my arms as if reassuring himself that I'm here. As if he's afraid I'll disappear.

"If you had any kindness in you. . . if you ever cared for

me as more than just a plaything you can train to orgasm on command. . . you would let me go. You'd let me be who I need to be and do what I need to do. You can call it my purpose or destiny, but it's more than that, Rex. Hunting down monsters and bringing them to justice is all I have. It's all I will ever have."

As I speak, his head bows like it's under a great weight. His fingers flex on my arms in an involuntary movement, and when he finally speaks, his voice is almost a whisper. "What about me?"

"What?"

"You're all I have, Inara. And I can't lose you." He raises his face, and the terrible sorrow written on his features is too much for me to bear. "You won't let me in. You won't make space in your life for us because you're afraid if you love someone, you'll lose them like you did your family. You think it'll be easier if you just don't allow yourself to have things. So you condemn yourself to being alone."

I stare at him, breathing hard. It would hurt less if he reached through my ribs and squeezed my heart.

"But I finally found you," he says, "and I'm not giving you up. You might be willing to throw your life away, but I can't allow it. You might be fine with sacrificing yourself for justice, but I'm not."

My lower lip trembles. "Rex," I whisper. I cup his cheek, and he leans into my hand, his eyes closed. I don't see Rex Roy, billionaire. I see a little boy standing at his parents' graves with a devastated look on his face. He's lost so much.

I want to hold him and comfort him like he's comforted me.

But I don't dare get closer to him. It's too dangerous to let him in.

"This is all I have," I whisper. "My mission, my fight for justice. It's all I have."

He presses his forehead against mine. "And you're all I have." The air gusts out of him like he's been punched. I feel his pain reverberating through my own body.

He turns his head so his lips brush my face. "I guess. . . I had hoped you'd say the same about me."

I turn from Rex, unwilling to face him any longer.

His arms tighten around my torso as if he won't allow me to retreat even a millimeter. He's already trapped my body, but he wants more.

He wants everything.

And even though we're fighting, I relax, soaking in his warmth.

"If you ever felt anything for me, if any of it was real, you would set me free," I tell him sadly.

My body doesn't know he's my enemy, and I'm too over-wrought to keep up my walls. It's a relief to relax. My subconscious doesn't see Rex as a threat. Quite the opposite. It's only in Rex's arms that I feel safe.

I don't know what to do with that, so I let it go and let my mind drift.

In a drowsy half-sleep, I fall into a scene from the past. It's not a dream, not a vision, but a memory.

I'm gripping twin ropes, staring up at the canopy of leaves. The sunlight streams between the green.

There's a golden quality to the air. I don't know if it's real or a halcyon haze coating my memory.

My father is behind me. He calls my name, and birds explode from the trees above my head, flying away in a dark group that blots out the sun.

This was my childhood. A simple time filled with whole-some moments. I'm sure it wasn't all sunshine and rainbows, but I only remember the good. My memory is like a faded photograph, showing only the happy smiles and none of the dark corners of the day.

My brothers and I went to school and then to the park, where Dad made us do our homework on a picnic table. When we were finished, he allowed us to play before going back to the house, where Mom would have her account books spread over the dining room table and something bubbling in the slow cooker.

I was happy then, and like anyone truly happy, I was completely unaware of it.

You think it'll be easier if you just don't allow yourself to have things, Rex said. And he's right. I have nothing of my old life —just empty cupboards and solitary meals, a life revolving around my work. A life my younger self wouldn't understand. A life that isn't a life at all.

That girl is gone. She became you.

I died in my bedroom that night. But the Bondage Killer didn't snuff out my life. I did.

More memories rise to the surface. *Christmas, making tamales while my mom, aunt, and grandmother weave a constant conversation over my head. My father's gloved hand squeezing mine, ready to lift me up if I slip on the icy path. My brothers and I lying on the floor surrounded by our toy cars and plastic dinosaurs, a tiny city of our own making.*

I haven't allowed myself to think of these happy times. The walls I erected kept everything out. The good, the bad, the pain.

But remembering the good is worth the pain. And Rex gives me a safe place to feel it.

You're afraid if you love someone, you'll lose them like you did your family.

He doesn't know how close to the truth he is. Everyone

I've gotten close to has died. I have no choice but to push them away.

You condemn yourself to being alone.

It's only now, imprisoned and secure in Rex's arms, that I start to wonder if I could live another way.

R *ex*

EVIL NEVER SLEEPS. Which is why I stay awake long after Inara falls asleep in my arms. This time, she rests peacefully, with no tremors or bad dreams.

I can't be the man she wants me to be, but at least I can keep her safe and watch over her while she sleeps.

If you ever felt anything for me, if any of it was real, you would set me free, she told me before she fell asleep.

I can see our future, where I hold her tight in my arms, keeping her safe even while she grows sadder and sadder. She's right; without her work, she'll be a shell of herself.

But her work also might kill her. I had to make a choice, and I'll always, always choose to save her. Even if it means the rest of the world burns.

But she won't let me own all of her. She's too stubborn for that. She's been holding back pieces of herself. I thought

I could coax her secrets from her in time, but BK escalated things, and now I don't know how to earn her trust again.

I'm about to do another thing she won't approve of, and the chasm between us will only grow deeper. But it's already too vast to contemplate, so what's another six feet?

After midnight, I rise, careful not to wake her, and kiss her perfect face. I could chain her to the bed—I have the chains ready and attached to the bed frame, including a replacement for the one she ripped apart—but I don't.

I hate leaving her, but after all the trouble Hamish went through setting up this meeting with the most dangerous men in the city, it's imperative I attend in person.

I fly to New Rome and walk into a nightclub called Club Inferno in the dark hours before dawn.

Two identical blond thugs escort me through the restaurant, bar, and strip club area, straight to a private meeting place. There's a long conference table in the center of the room, but only one chair at the head of the table. My guards lead me to the opposite end of the table, so I guess the chair isn't for me.

I thank them, but they don't say a word. They remain flanking me while the rest of the meeting attendees file in.

Seven gang members take their places around the table. They're mostly men, although there's a slim woman in a wheelchair with tattoos winding up her arms. Some are dressed in jeans and leather jackets like they're part of a biker gang, while others look more like businessmen in their tailored three-piece suits. Most of them also wear skull masks to hide their faces.

The one thing they all have in common is the huge silver rings decorated with a skull. Different colored jewels glitter in the skull ring's eye sockets. These are The Seven, the leaders of a gang called Fraternitas.

Hamish and I have cataloged as many of them as we can, putting names to faces in a private database we keep on all important figures in New Rome. Even with our thorough research, a few figures remain mysterious.

Fraternitas means "brotherhood," and the gang was founded by a group of street children who pledged their loyalty to each other above all. Now, their wealth and power are formidable. In a few decades, it might rival mine.

St. James is one of the last to enter in his signature gray suit. I know he's been up all night, but he doesn't look tired. He takes his place behind the single chair.

The man who enters last is shorter than St. James, but his presence sends ripples through the room. Surrounded by other powerful gang members, he's the obvious leader. I've never met him, but I know of him. He's Damien to his friends, but everyone else refers to him as The Devil.

There's no record of a man named Damien. No history, no childhood. Hamish and I have tried to gather information but found nothing more than hearsay and legend. In the early days of Fraternitas, he made a name for himself by murdering the heads of every gang and crime family in a bold and genius move. The coup created chaos and paved the way for Fraternitas to cement their control of all criminal activity in the city, from gambling and smuggling to the illegal fights under the city.

Like the rest of the gang, Damien wears the signature Fraternitas ring, but his ring is the only one that has a skull wearing a crown. If businessmen like me rule above ground, he's king of the underworld. At least in New Rome.

I nod to both St. James and Damien, but only St. James nods back.

Damien goes to the head of the table and stands in front of the chair but doesn't sit down.

"All right, Roy," he says to me. "We're here. What do you want?"

I don't waste any time. I paid a million dollars for the privilege of meeting with the heads of Fraternitas because money is the language St. James speaks fluently. If money talks, mine shouts the loudest.

"There's a new serial killer in New Rome. I'm hoping we can form an alliance for the purpose of bringing him down."

I look at the blond thug to the right of me, the one who took my briefcase while his identical twin frisked me at the door. He brings it to Damien, who opens it on the table and removes the files Hamish and I compiled on the case.

Damien studies the picture of the Bondage Killer. "This him?"

"Yes, that's the target, as he was decades ago. He's responsible for a series of murders in a small Midwestern town. He sent letters to the local police station to take credit for the crimes. Called himself the Bondage Killer. His real name was Dennis Bundy, and his killing spree ended when he was trapped in a warehouse fire and presumed dead."

Damien sets the picture down on the table for everyone to see. "And why should we care?"

"Because he's back in this city now. And he's killing again."

St. James shifts closer to the table to get his own look at the photograph. After a pause, he shares a long glance with Damien before saying, "This is a job for the cops."

"The cops haven't been able to stop him. Plus, he might be working with someone in the department." Hamish found Detective Lacy Collins's notes where she speculated that BK might have had an in with someone in the department, and that's why he always seemed one step ahead.

"Corrupt fucks," a masked man mutters, and a few others agree with him.

"I've come to you because I'd like him found sooner rather than later, and Fraternitas rules the underworld of New Rome." They're also responsible for their share of murders, but I don't mention that. Hamish and I have discovered that they take great pains to follow a strict code of honor. For example, they never hurt children.

Their history is gruesome and bloody, but the violence is mostly against the grown members of other gangs or corrupt city leaders. Which suits my own purposes just fine. If I were to punish Fraternitas for their crimes, a worse gang would take their place in the underworld. In this case, the devil I know is better than the devil I don't.

"I'm willing to pay handsomely to see this man brought to justice," I say. "I'm putting a bounty on his head." I make a point of meeting several of the masked men's eyes. "Double if you happen to find him dead."

"We're not killers for hire," Damien says.

"No, that would be me." A murmur comes from the door where a tall man with white-blond hair stands idly flipping a knife in the air. "Am I late? Has the party already started?"

There's a burst of movement from the masked men around the table. Several draw weapons and begin to charge at the stranger before St. James raises his hands for them to stand down.

"He's a guest," he says.

"Victor," I greet the newcomer. We're not really on a first-name basis because I don't know his full name. I suspect "Victor" isn't even his real name anyway, only a moniker.

"Roy." He dips his chin. "St. James. Everyone. Sorry to startle you." His smirk tells me he's not sorry at all.

"Next time, accept our escort," St. James warns him. "Trespassers end up in the Abyss."

"Understood," Victor says. "And I promise to never do it again. But tonight I needed to make an entrance to prove myself. I'm still auditioning for this job." He sidles up to the table and sifts through the pictures with long, pale fingers.

I've hired Victor before. He's an assassin of the finest caliber but semi-retired. I had to lure him here with a seven-figure advance, so he's joking about auditioning.

"You might be the only one in the running. We haven't accepted the job," Damien tells him.

The room turns expectant eyes on me. I need to sell this. "He's murdering families. I'm hunting him on my own, but I can't leave this to chance."

St. James stirs but doesn't say anything. He knows why I'm so invested in finding the Bondage Killer, but he wants me to explain why. I knew this meeting would require my complete honesty. It's a risk to reveal my weakness, but from what I've gleaned, Fraternitas understands loyalty. They have rituals revolving around their members claiming a chosen one, so I'm hoping they'll respect my commitment to Inara.

"He's targeting someone important to me," I admit to the room. "A detective named Inara Ramos. She happens to be the only victim of his who escaped."

Damien finds the copy of the front page of the newspaper that reported the Bondage Killer's crimes with a picture of Inara as a child in black and white. Hamish paper-clipped a second, more recent photo of her from the NRPD's employee files.

"She was a child," he states, frowning at the photos.

"Yes. The Bondage Killer murdered her entire family

and saved her for last. It's not clear why he spared her. She then became a detective to lock up monsters like him."

Damien rubs the lower half of his face. The back of his hand bears a tattoo of a skull, and the effect of his hand over his face makes him look like he is wearing a mask over his mouth. "What else do we know about this fuck?"

"You have everything we know." I dip my head toward the files. "Letters tie him to the current scene, but this is the first activity from him in decades. He was presumed dead in a fire."

I explain how the case in Elyria grew until the whole nation was watching. The feds got involved, but the break in the case came from Lacy Collins, who found the Bondage Killer's hideout in an abandoned warehouse.

Victor speaks up. "You say he's targeting your girl. What are your plans to keep her safe?"

"She's currently in lockdown at my estate."

Damien nods, and I remember he has his own bride. Rumor has it she was reluctant to wed him. Even though she was in danger from multiple factions, she tried to escape him, so he kept her under lock and key for the first few months of their marriage.

I should be disturbed that our methods are so similar, but I understand his reasoning perfectly.

"Is she?" Victor asks. "Maybe we just follow her around and catch the killer when he comes for her."

"Unacceptable. I won't allow it." I fix the assassin with a glare.

"It looks like the good detective has other plans." Victor flicks his fingers and carefully reaches into his jacket pocket to remove his phone. After a few taps on its screen, he holds it up to show me a picture of Inara in the passenger side of a black armored car.

I stiffen. "When was this taken?"

"A few minutes ago, when she entered the city limits. You'll need to keep better tabs on her if you're going to ensure her safety."

She escaped. Hamish must have helped her. I recognize that car. It's one I've made my own modifications to, so it's fully autonomous and has anti-surveillance equipment.

I curse, and Victor smiles. "Would you like to know where she is?"

~

INARA

MY DAY BEGINS in the strangest way possible: with a little robot chirping at me from the foot of the bed.

I rise quickly and realize the bedroom door is unlocked. Rex is gone.

"Alfie?" I greet the robot and it warbles an acknowledgment. "Good morning, Detective. Please dress and follow me."

I rise from the bed, feeling disoriented. Rex has been a constant presence claiming my days and my nights, and even though I've fought it, it feels weird with him not here. Is he somewhere in the mansion, and he just sent Alfie to summon me? Is this a test?

Last night I bared myself to him, and I felt his pain when he said, *You're all I have.*

I don't know where we go from here.

The robot chirps as if urging me to hurry. There are clothes and brown boots for me at the foot of the bed.

I dress quickly and follow it, still half-expecting a trap. Instead, it leads me through low corridors until we're walking out of a heavy exit door, straight into a long hangar with concrete floors. The lights snap on, and I shiver in the chill. We're in a garage filled with rows and rows of expensive cars.

Alfie rolls up to a black sports car, and sleek doors open upward, like wings. On the driver's seat are my purse and jacket.

"I don't know if I can drive this," I say.

"Initiate self-driving mode," Alfie announces, and the driver-side door closes. The car rolls out of its space and automatically comes to a stop beside us.

Oh gods. Do I trust this?

"Welcome, Detective." The car's speaker system greets me in a voice that sounds suspiciously like Hamish's. Is he helping me escape? I have a feeling he's behind this but is using the robot to cover his tracks.

Still, I hesitate. This car is Rex's. "Will Rex be able to track this?"

"Initiating stealth mode," the car responds in a cool voice.

I smile. It's nice when Rex doesn't get his way. It happens so rarely that I want to savor it.

Reality descends. There's a killer hunting in the city. I need to get back there and do my best to stop him.

I guess I'm not in a position to refuse the gift of a self-driving escape vehicle, so I slide into the passenger side, the door closing automatically. My purse contains all my things, including my badge and gun. In addition, there's a clear plastic case marked "For NRPD's eyes only." I'd bet it contains the letters and the lab findings. Crucial evidence gift wrapped for the department.

I have everything I need to do my job. So why do I feel bereft at the thought of leaving?

"Good luck, Detective," the little robot warbles and rolls out of the way. The car glides past it and increases speed.

It's official. I've put my trust in a self-driving car to escape a billionaire who's obsessed with me. What is my life?

At my feet is an insulated container that turns out to hold food—breakfast burritos with salsa verde. There's a second container with fresh cinnamon buns and a thermos of hot coffee. At least I'll be able to eat my feelings.

I did enjoy the concept of being taken care of before Rex went too far.

I can't lose you, he told me. *You won't let me in. You condemn yourself to being alone.*

He's right. But I am who I need to be.

"I'm sorry, Rex," I whisper and settle in for the long drive.

7

I *nara*

THE CLOSER I get to New Rome, the more I sense the darkness waiting for me. The pressure is like an oppressive blanket coating my senses.

The killer is waiting for me.

For the longest time, the car races at record speeds along a narrow tunnel. When it emerges, I'm in the warehouse district north of the city center. Dawn is breaking.

I made record time. Rex must have had a secret tunnel built connecting his mansion and the city for his own personal use. Because, of course, he did.

I reprogram the car to swing by my townhouse first. The Bondage Killer delivered the letters there. I want to see what my senses pick up.

When the car self-parks in front of my place, I half

expect to see a dead body on the stoop. There's a sense that something horrible is waiting for me inside.

I approach carefully, my psychic senses screaming at me. There's a fist around my chest, making it hard to breathe.

I open my door and choke on an awful scent.

At first I think I'm imagining it, but no, it's real. My floor has disappeared, blotted out with the glossy black of broken wings. Covering my floor, as far as I can see, are hundreds of dead birds.

I stagger, and bones crunch underfoot. The wind races in and raises a flurry of feathers, shiny as a deadly oil slick.

The Bondage Killer was here. Again. He knows where I live. I can sense his presence—the perverse glee, the longing, the hate. My throat has closed, and my head throbs. My legs wobble, so I hunch over and crouch, curling into a ball. I raise shaking hands to cover my eyes and my ears, overwhelmed by the evil battering at my psychic senses.

I don't know how long I sit there, reeling. I only know I wish Rex was here. He'd lift me in his arms, clear of the bodies, and carry me away. His presence would shelter me from the psychic barrage. He has his own darkness, but it's safe and warm, a shelter instead of an assault.

But then he'd lock me away in a cage. My only source of comfort is gone.

My phone rings, cutting through the buzzing sound in my ears. I answer it automatically before I notice that it's an unknown caller.

"Detective Ramos," the silken voice with a slight rasp on the line is familiar. I try to place it but can't before the caller says, "This is St. James. Are you hurt?"

"What? No. What do you want?"

"I've been informed that you're back in the city, but your life is in danger."

"Informed? By who?" Everything's happening so quickly that I can't keep up.

"Hamish wants me to keep an eye on you. He cannot assure your safety anymore. But I can."

Hamish spoke to St. James? Why? "What's going on?"

"Listen carefully because we don't have much time. Rex is already on his way to you."

"No," I gasp. I rise and back out of my townhouse, slamming the door.

"He's watching you even now."

I run back to the car. My best chance is to head right to the police station, but Rex is best friends with the Chief. What's to stop him from pulling strings and getting me ordered into protective custody? *His.*

I tried so hard to escape him. There's nowhere I can run that he won't hunt me down, but I won't go back without a fight.

"I understand you no longer want to be under Rex's power."

"I won't go back." He'll put me back in the cage.

"But no one can stop Rex from getting what he wants."

He's right. The sports car's lights flash, and I stop before getting in. I should abandon the car. I bet Rex has an override to the stealth mode, and if I get in now, the car might take me straight to him.

What should I do?

"If I may offer a solution," St. James continues. I almost forgot I was talking to him. "Come to the club. I can offer you a safe haven."

"Rex will find me."

"Eventually. But Club Empire has served as neutral territory before. I can convince him you'll be safer if you're working with him rather than against him."

The solution sounds so elegant, but I still hesitate.

There's a whirring sound overhead, and a black drone zooms through the air to hover at my eye level six feet away from me.

"Inara," the drone says in Rex's voice. "It's okay. I'm coming for you."

I drop my phone and pull my gun. "I'm not going back," I snarl, aiming for the drone. "I'll shoot you first."

To my left, a motorcycle rips down the street at break-neck speed, only to skid to a stop beside me.

I switch my aim to lock in on the motorcycle rider. *It's him*, I think at first, but the rider's build is slimmer than Rex's. He pulls off his black helmet, and I jerk back when I see a skull bandana covering the lower half of his face.

"Don't shoot," St. James is calling from my fallen cell phone. "That's your ride."

"We gotta go now." The rider holds out the helmet to me.

I have to make a decision. My townhouse is full of dead birds. Rex is coming for me. I don't really trust St. James, but where else can I turn?

"Inara, get in the car," Rex shouts from the drone.

Crack! I fire my gun and blow the drone away. Black pieces fly off it, and the hunk of dead metal plummets to the ground.

I flip the safety on my gun and holster it, scoop up my phone, and face the motorcyclist.

He's got long black hair and flecks of gold in his green eyes. I can tell he's young, in his early twenties, even with the skull bandana hiding the rest of his face. "Hurry," he barks.

I grab the helmet, slam it onto my head, and swing onto the bike. I'm barely on the seat when the rider jerks my arms around his waist and kicks the bike off the curb. His ab muscles flex under my hold. Before I can brace myself, we're hurtling down the street.

~

REX

SHE ESCAPED ME. Again.

And now St. James has her. Instead of helping me as he agreed to minutes ago, St. James has decided to become my enemy. For what? He loves his power plays, but what is his end game here?

I slam the steering wheel of my car. "Deploy more drones," I direct Alfie, who's installed in this car's computer system. "Find them."

"Deploying ten units now."

I'm racing down empty streets—I had Alfie hack the city's traffic lights and shut down all east and westbound traffic to clear my route to Inara—but there's a matte black Lykan on my tail. One of the identical blond twins from Inferno is behind the wheel, the skull mask covering the lower half of his face mocking me.

I let the Lykan pull level with me and then drop back. I'm in an armored car not unlike the one Inara used to get away from me, and I've paid good money for it to be as strong as a tank and fast as a sports car.

The Lykan tries to slow with me as I ram its back wheel at the precise angle required to make it spin out. The hit makes the sports car swerve out of control, smashing into a truck parked alongside the road. I accelerate around the crash and then wrench my car to the right, ducking down an alleyway to try to lose my tail completely.

"Alfie, I need you to clear an alternate route."

"Rerouting traffic patterns."

A black Jeep is waiting for me at the other end, blocking the exit. The second blond twin is behind the wheel. I order the computer into tank mode and smash into it, pushing it out of my way.

I shoot past the ruined Jeep and race up the road, only for a set of motorcycles to surround me. These riders also have grinning skull masks under their black helmets. I don't need to see their hands to know they all wear a Fraternitas ring.

Fucking St. James—always interfering. As soon as I have Inara safe and the Bondage Killer in the ground, I'm going to turn my focus to ruining him. He loves money, so I'll bankrupt him first.

"Hamish calling," Alfie informs me. I order it to answer and as soon as the call's connected, I snap, "What have you done?" I know he's behind Inara's escape from the Manor.

"I did my duty," Hamish says so stiffly. "To you and to the detective."

"You betrayed me."

"I've been more than supportive of your illegal nocturnal activities. I'll even allow that some lives should be snuffed out for the cause of justice, but I will not be party to imprisoning a young woman in our home."

"My home. You will pack your bags—"

"Undoubtedly, I will. But may I remind you that we have the same aim: to keep Detective Ramos alive and stop the Bondage Killer." The chill in his voice could freeze over hell. "You do not have time to throw a tantrum."

My brain shorts out. I'm so angry, I don't know what to say.

"Really, Rex, what would your parents think?"

And now my chest is seizing with pangs of guilt despite myself. I was just in the hall, looking at their smiling faces and realizing they'd disapprove of me.

When Hamish decides to pull out the big guns, he does not hold back.

"You dare—"

"I'm sending a team to the duplex." He changes the subject. "The killer has been there."

The air leaves my lungs. "What? How did this happen? The place was under surveillance." I'm angry at Hamish and St. James, so it feels good to direct my anger somewhere fruitful.

"There's something wrong with the security equipment. Some sort of glitch. I'm working to override it."

"I tried to pull up the feed from the cameras earlier, and they seemed to be offline. That's why I deployed drones. Are you telling me the Bondage Killer was on my property and all my tech failed to detect him?"

"It seems so," Hamish sounds preoccupied, and I can hear the computers chiming in the background.

A cop car slides in behind me, sirens wailing. I accelerate to lose him. I do not want the cops involved in this. A news helicopter is circling overhead, which means my stunt will be all over the stations.

Sure enough, Hamish says, "I'm getting traffic reports from New Rome. Are you currently involved in a high-speed chase on Central Avenue?"

"Yes," I grind out.

"Far be it from me to criticize, but is this the best time to pull resources away from the BK manhunt?"

"That sounds a lot like criticism, Hamish." More cops are on my ass, but there's a tow truck ahead with its ramp down and nothing loaded on the metal bed.

"Initiate turbo mode," I tell Alfie, and the computer takes over the wheel. The car hits the ramp at high speeds and sails over the truck. Parachutes deploy, allowing the car to float over the median into the opposite lane of traffic.

"Call incoming. Unknown number," Alfie tells me.

"Trace it," I bark and start evasive maneuvers, dodging cars to drive the wrong way down the highway.

"Trace complete. Location, Club Empire."

"Hamish, I've got to go. St. James is calling me. He has Inara."

"May I ask what you're about to do next?"

"I'm getting Inara back. Then I'll deal with everything else."

"You can't fight everyone and keep her safe. You need us. You need me. And you need her consent."

I want to shout him down, but he's right. I curse.

"Language, sir," Hamish clips, sounding just like he did when I was a surly sixteen-year-old. I automatically cringe.

A truck veers into my path, and I swerve around it. I've lost the cops, but it's only a matter of time before one of them spots me again. I jerk the wheel, crossing five lanes of traffic to dart into a tunnel.

"I've recovered the most recent feed from the townhouse," Hamish says. "Sending it over now."

I end the call with him and switch to the line with St. James.

"Where is she?" I ask.

"Hello, Rex. It's been a while." He's joking; it's been only a few minutes. I can hear his smirk over the line.

"Cut the small talk, Sebastian. You have something of mine. Give her back."

"Is the lovely detective a toy we're fighting over?"

"She's mine," I snarl in response, but Inara's accusations echo in my head.

I'm just a possession to you. A trophy you can put on a shelf.

Maybe it's the after-effects of adrenaline, but her words resonate with me now as they didn't before.

St. James continues, "The news is all abuzz about a high-speed car chase in the city. And it seems all the traffic lights on roads running east to west turned red. The police are out in force, trying to sort out the gridlock."

"And?"

"You came to Fraternitas to help you find the Bondage Killer." He changes the subject. "Is that still a priority?"

"My priority is Inara."

"So is mine."

"You have no right to her—"

"She doesn't want to see you. She told me so herself. She says you tried to lock her up. I'm just as much of a fan of keeping my partners in a cage—"

I grimace. I don't want to be anything like St. James.

"The good detective is shaken."

"Is she hurt?" That should have been my first question.

"She is unharmed and safe." Censure rings in his voice. First Hamish condemning me, now St. James. They all think I've gone too far.

Maybe I have. But the only opinion that matters to me is Inara's.

I remember how she pleaded with me. *If you ever cared for me as more than just a plaything, you would let me go.*

"You can't keep her from me," I say to St. James to drown out the memory of Inara's desperate begging.

"Do you want an alliance with Fraternitas or not?"

"I want Inara back."

"You can't fight me and protect her."

"Can't I?" I'll fight all of Fraternitas if I have to.

Except, that would be a waste of resources. Theirs and mine.

What am I doing?

"It would be wiser to turn our entire focus on catching our mutual enemy," St. James says. Since when did he become the voice of reason?

I'm almost out of the tunnel. In a few minutes, I'll be at Club Empire.

St. James continues, "I'm proposing Club Empire as neutral territory. I have Inara here, but I promised her sanctuary. You will not harm her."

I want to snarl that, obviously, I won't harm her, I only want to protect her, and how dare he even think otherwise—but my screen flashes, distracting me.

The video Hamish promised me appears on my dash. It plays in a loop: Inara walks into her townhouse, visibly recoiling at what she sees. Her body stiffens, her eyes wide. She raises her hands as if to fend off a blow, then sinks down, covering her face and rocking a little.

She had a full breakdown, and I wasn't there to help her.

I wanted to keep her safe, but she won't let me.

She'd rather face a serial killer alone than allow me to care for her.

What have I done?

"Rex?" St. James calls me back to our conversation.

"Agreed," I spit. "Club Empire. Neutral territory. I just want to see her."

"I'm sure that can be arranged." His noncommittal tone

has me grinding my teeth. "In the meantime, I'll do my part." He reminds me of the importance of his role in the situation. "I'll keep her here. I had to promise you wouldn't put her in a cage."

If you ever felt anything for me, if any of it was real, you would set me free.

She ran from me, right into danger. I can lock her up all I want, but if she escapes, she'll be lost to me.

Even if she doesn't escape, she'll still be lost to me.

"Destination, Club Empire. Time of arrival, five minutes," Alfie announces loud enough for St. James to hear.

"You can park in the underground deck," St. James says. "And you owe Kaiser a new Jeep," he adds before hanging up.

INARA

I JOLT in my seat when St. James enters the room but relax when I see it's him.

"He'll be here in five minutes," St. James tells me, pocketing his phone. His face is expressionless, but I can tell he's bracing himself for a fight.

I blow out a breath. I'm huddled on a couch, holding a cup of tea I don't really want. "All right."

St. James sinks into a chair across from me. "He wants to see you. To make sure you're unhurt."

"So he can drag me back to his mansion and lock me up?" I mutter.

"I won't allow that."

"You can't stop him."

"Not without risking full war."

I set my mug down. I'm all jittery, needing to run, to fight. If St. James wasn't here, I'd run right out of this room.

He must know that because he sits preternaturally still. His gray eyes track my twitchy little movements, but he projects an aura of calm.

His real aura is a thick fog, with something sinister lurking in the gray banks. It occurs to me I don't really know him, and that if I did, I would probably trust him less than I do Rex right now.

"Why are you helping me?" I ask.

The only sign that the question bothers him is a slight flex in his long fingers. The movement draws my attention to the ring on his finger. It's silver and in the shape of a skull with onyx eyes. It looks familiar, but I can't place it.

"Years ago, I tried to help someone I cared about. You remind me of her." A muscle jumps in his jaw. I hold still, getting the sense that he's lost in memory. After a moment, he blinks and bows his head. "Back then, I wasn't strong enough to protect anyone. Now I am."

I give a little nod, both grateful that he shared and wary of what it might mean. I get the sense that St. James doesn't open up to anyone. Ever.

He checks his watch and rises. "I should go. Our guest will be here soon, bellowing and ready to break things."

"Like a bull in a china shop." Although that isn't really fair to Rex. He can be subtle and gentle when he wants.

But not lately.

I start to rise, and St. James stops me with a single raised finger. "Wait here. I'll make sure he's contrite or at least ready for polite conversation."

I don't know if anyone can make Rex back down, but St. James is my best bet.

"St. James," I call. He stops halfway to the door but doesn't turn around. "Thank you."

"Anytime," he murmurs, leaving me with a sense of disquiet.

8

R^{ex}

I storm into Club Empire just as St. James strolls into the foyer. "I want to see her."

"Rex. Lovely to see you again." Now St. James looks weary, like he's been up all night and would like to go to bed instead of dealing with a lover's spat. It will be easier to overpower him in this state.

I remind myself that I can't kill him until he tells me where Inara is.

"Give her back."

"Right this way." St. James pivots and leads me to the elevator.

I'm surprised he didn't fight me. I almost wish he would.

But it seems he'll do me the honor of escorting me. A risk on his part. I might kill him before we reach Inara.

He leans in to press a button and close the doors, but the elevator doesn't move. He hasn't pressed a button for a floor.

I round on him. I'd knock him out right now, but I need to find Inara first.

He holds up a hand. "Before you speak to her, I need to know you'll behave. I've made certain promises to her, and I need to know you'll uphold them."

The thought of him speaking to Inara long enough to promise her anything makes me want to put my hands around his neck and squeeze.

No, I need a good, gruesome fate for St. James. A torture session followed by removing his tongue.

He isn't special. He'll bleed like all the rest.

But then St. James adds, "She's not hurt, but she is frightened."

I remember how she looked on the footage Hamish sent over, and the all-consuming rage leaks from my veins. I let my shoulders relax.

"What promises?" I growl.

"First, that you'll honor this as neutral territory. No dragging her out of here by her hair or anything else."

"I wouldn't do that." He makes it sound so distasteful, but I can't sugarcoat what I've done. "I'd drug her first." I'd cradle her unconscious body against me and hold her the whole way home.

"Ah. Then no drugging her, either."

I grumble my assent.

"One more thing," St. James says, then adds in a softer tone, "This isn't her request, but I'd advise you to take caution before touching her."

"What?"

"Before she met you, she didn't allow anyone to touch

her," St. James quietly reminds me. He must have read her scene requests when she first applied to be a member of the club. For a moment, we're simply two doms discussing how to best care for a treasured submissive. "Touch means something to her."

This is why St. James is so dangerous. He can sum up a person's deepest needs and darkest desires in a single glance. And he has no soul to stop him from using this insight against you.

But he's right about this. Godsdamn him.

Inara strapped to the cross, sassing me even as she quivered in anticipation for the flogger.

Inara shaking when I ran a gloved finger down her spine.

Inara, resting in my arms, sated.

I trusted you, she shrieked from the cage. *And you would do this to me?*

I'm the only one she allowed to touch her. And then I betrayed her trust.

I don't ask how St. James knows the intimate details of our relationship. I want this conversation over. "I won't touch her without her consent."

Without another word, he presses the elevator button to take us to the floor with the private rooms.

I thought he might be keeping her in an office or in the bar upstairs. But no, the elevator descends, and I'm reminded of previous visits on happier nights. Every night I met Inara here, I was full of hunger and a certain satisfaction in having trapped her. But also the wary anticipation a hunter reserves for vicious prey. I'd always known she'd be dangerous to me.

She's the only one who can destroy me.

Now, as the elevator descends, I wonder if I'm descending to my doom. She can scoop out my insides, leaving me a shell of a man, driven by lust and my need for control, with no softness to temper my monstrous desires.

Did St. James take this route on purpose? To remind me of my responsibilities as a dom?

Or did Inara choose our usual private room, knowing it would remind me of the times we had?

The elevator has almost reached its destination when St. James speaks again. "By the way, you're welcome." We're both facing the door, and I refuse to glance at his face or ask what he thinks I should thank him for. "For keeping her safe when you couldn't."

The only thing keeping me from stabbing him right here, right now, is the thought of having to face Inara with blood all over my hands. "You snatched her before I could get to her," I say to my blurred reflection in the metal door.

"She was ready to run away. She would've done anything to get away from you." He means to bait me—does he *want* me to kill him?—but his words batter me like bullets hitting a bullseye. All I can see is Inara crouched and screaming in that room of dead birds. Overwhelmed by fear.

In what I'm aware is a heroic act of self-discipline, I do not break his neck and leave him in a crumpled pile on the elevator floor.

The doors open, and I stride out, willing to give St. James the last word if it means I'm rid of him faster. I know where my private rooms are; I don't need him to show me the way.

"Do we have an alliance?" St. James calls after me.

"Yes," I say, without turning around.

"Excellent. I'll inform Damien and the rest. Oh, one more thing. In addition to owing Kaiser a new Jeep, you owe Jaeger bodywork on his Lykan."

"Send me the bill," I say and stride down the hall toward my room.

I burst through the door, but Inara isn't there. There's a mug of tea on a side table, still steaming. If that's hers, she was just here.

I move deeper into the room to see if she's standing in a corner when the door slams behind me.

I leap to grab the door handle, but it's locked. As I knew it would be. But that means—

"St. James?" I call out to see if he locked me in.

There's a pause, and my heart leaps at the first clue of who's beyond the door.

"It's me," Inara says. Her voice is quieter than usual. Not the firm, stubborn tone I'm used to.

"Inara." Her name leaves my lips in a rush. She must have been hiding in another room when I exited the elevator and took her opportunity to trap me. Now I imagine her standing only a few feet away. I rest a hand on the door between us, wanting to feel close to her. "Unlock the door."

"No." Her voice is stronger. "I'm not going to do that, Rex."

I huff. I could force the door, but if she's standing close to it, I don't want to hurt her.

And I don't want her to leave.

For the moment, she's trapped me. It's just a small taste of how I trapped her, but I hate it.

"I know what you're doing."

"This is the part where I tell you it's for your own good," she says. "But we both know that's a lie. It's really for mine."

I clench my fist, allowing her to have her revenge.

"Now you know how it feels."

Only a few inches of wood separate me from Inara, but it feels like a chasm. *She's safe,* I remind myself. *And she's near.*

I swallow my temper. "Are you hurt?"

There are many ways I could break out of this room, but I need to make sure she's okay more than I need to see her. And a part of me knows that if she feels safer talking to me from behind a locked door, then I want to give her that.

"I'm okay. It was just a shock."

She's talking about the collapse at her apartment. I'm all amped up about St. James, and she's still reliving the horror of that moment I saw on the footage Hamish sent me. "What happened?"

"He was there, Rex." She sounds like she's closer to the door, leaning against it. "He was in my house. It was awful, I can't—" She sounds close to hyperventilating.

"Shhhh," I rest my forehead on the wood, feeling helpless. The only thing stopping me from busting through this door is the fact that it might scare her, and she's already scared. "It'll be okay." I don't want to send her back to the state she was in, crumpled by her townhouse door. I keep my voice calm and soothing, even as my arms ache to hold her. "You're here, and you're safe."

"No thanks to you." Her voice hardens.

I keep silent because it's true.

"I thought you would keep me safe, Rex. Instead, you locked me up." Her voice rises in anger. Anger is good. Anything is better than the devastated sorrow I saw on screen.

"I know."

"Why are we fighting? There's evil out there; I can feel it. And I need to stop it. I need you to be on my side."

"I am on your side."

"Are you?" Her breath hitches.

I have to lay the truth of myself bare, or I'll lose her forever. "If anything happens to you, Inara, it would destroy me."

I can't apologize for locking her up. It seemed the best way and I'll do it again if I have to. But I am sorry that I broke the fragile bond between us. "I lost control." I search for a way to make her understand.

A good dom needs to have a handle on himself at all times. So does a serial killer, or things get sloppy; you make mistakes that leave your victims alive and leave clues for you to get caught. I know this. I've been careful and never had a problem until now.

Inara destroys all my control. It would be easier if I didn't care about her. But the monster in me wants to possess her completely and won't accept anything less than full access to all of her—body, her mind, and trust.

She's my greatest weakness.

"I haven't allowed myself to. . . feel things. For anyone. It wasn't safe. But I can't stop myself from feeling things for you."

Silence. She doesn't ask me what I feel for her, and I'm grateful. I don't have the words for it now.

"I felt something, too. But now I don't know if I can ever trust you."

"Please," I murmur, knowing I don't deserve another chance. I'll need to prove myself, prove that I can give her what she needs.

"I should go now."

"No," I say, my panic rising. The monster wants to break down the door, but if I give into violence, it'll prove to her that I'm out of control again. I'll lose her forever.

I'm trapped. The words burst out of me, full of fear. "Don't leave me. Inara, please, I'll do anything. I'll make any vow. Just, please. . . don't leave me now."

. . .

INARA

I CAN HEAR Rex's desperation through the door.

"Don't leave me." He sounds like a little boy lost to a nightmare.

And isn't that all we are, two orphans struggling through life, keeping everyone at arm's length? Why would I expect him to be healed of his trauma when I'm still carrying around mine?

We are the same. And I would do anything to keep him from feeling this pain.

I wrench open the door, and he's standing there, a few inches away, in an elegant suit that does nothing to hide the coiled tension in his muscles. His hair is mussed like he's been running a hand through it.

He faces me, and even though his lingering gaze tells me he longs to touch me, he doesn't move.

I stand in the doorway, clenching the doorknob. I should be running away from him. He's made himself my enemy.

But then his cologne reaches me, and I sway on my feet. I'm tired of fighting. So very tired.

"Inara," he says, and I can't hold back any longer.

I go to him, close enough to feel his warmth wash over me.

Still, he doesn't move.

"Can I touch you?" he asks, and I suck in a breath. I didn't expect the respectful question, and it is everything. In this moment, in this familiar room, we've rewound to the time when we were just two scene partners on the brink of something exciting, something necessary. Carefully negotiating so we didn't harm the fragile connection growing between us.

"Yes," I whisper and let him envelop me in a hug. I tuck my head against his chest.

"Are you okay? You didn't get hurt, did you?" His hands roam over me. He puts some distance between us only to check for wounds, for blood.

"I'm okay. No one touched me. I opened the door and just couldn't. . . I got overwhelmed."

His lips press together. I can sense his latent anger, like an atomic bomb ready to be unleashed. But I know it's directed at the killer, not me.

"I'm okay," I repeat and lean in to hug him again. This time, his arms come around me slowly, almost reluctantly. He cradles the back of my head.

"You scared me."

I can hear the fear of a lost little boy in his voice, and it melts me. But we both scared each other. "You locked me up. I had to escape."

"What possessed you to go to the townhouse?"

"I wanted to check on it. If the killer dropped the letters there. . . " I thought I'd get a psychic impression, and I did. I just didn't expect it to be so overwhelming. "He's fixated on me. There was a bird feeder, and I used to like watching the birds. He must have poisoned them all and put them in the house—" I'm shaking, babbling, letting all the poisonous fear leach from me.

Rex murmurs soothing things and guides me to the couch. He's still holding me, but he's not threatening to lock me up, so that's a win. Maybe I look too fragile right now.

I feel fragile. I've made a habit of falling apart in Rex's arms. A day ago, he pleaded with me to let him be my safe place to land. I denied him at the time, but the truth is, he was already my safe place.

"Do you want this?" He shifts so he can pick up my mug.

I close my hands around it, cradling it like he cradles me. "I didn't know you drank tea."

"I don't." I wrinkle my nose. "But I couldn't get warm."

He strokes my face. "St. James said you were shaking."

I let my thoughts turn to the moments after I opened my townhouse door—the overwhelming darkness, like an oil slick coating my senses. "I could feel him. . . his energy. His sick interest turning into hatred." My stomach turns, but talking this out is helping. And Rex is the only one I feel safe enough to share this with. "He wants to be with me, but more than that, he wants to control me."

I stare at Rex, realizing I could say the same about him. The difference is that I've always felt safe with Rex. Even after he locked me in a cage, I slept in his arms.

I'm more afraid of the intense swell of emotions I feel when I'm around him than I am of him. I've tried to avoid feeling anything for anyone. Then Rex burst into my world and made me feel everything. Of course it's frightening. It's new.

"I'm sorry," he says.

"It's not your fault." But I can tell he's taking the blame.

"I failed to keep you safe."

I hand him my tea so he can set it down, then cup his face between my mug-warmed palms. "You can't shield me from everything."

The sculpted planes of his face harden underneath my hands. "I've sent a team to lock down the townhouse. They'll analyze the scene, dust for prints, and clean it up."

I drop my hands and sag into him, feeling even more relief. On the long car ride from Roy Manor to the city, I allowed myself to wonder what it would be like to work with him to solve the case. To use his lab, his tech, his unlimited resources. I bet he's already surveilling half the city.

"They'll need to send anything they find to the department," I say.

He hesitates, probably thinking about how that will put me in the middle of a murder case. Again. But he says, "Of course. It's your choice."

I lift my head. "Really?" I never thought I'd hear him say that, not after everything he did to stop me from leaving his house.

He doesn't look happy, but he bows his head in a reluctant nod. "If it's what you want, I'll comply."

It's what I want to hear, but I don't know if I believe him. "What's changed?"

"I realized you'll keep running from me if I continue to push too hard. You're stubborn and will probably run right into danger."

I huff. I could say the same about him.

"And if I lock you down, a part of you will die. I'm not willing to live without any part of you."

He's going to try to control me no matter what I do. I have nothing to lose if I simply surrender.

I take his hands. They're large and capable, and was it only a few weeks ago that I didn't allow him to touch me? Now I can't imagine going any length of time without his hands on me.

"Rex, I need to tell you something."

He holds his breath as if waiting for a blow.

"I can't fight you anymore." I pick up his hand and hold it to my cheek, needing his comfort as I admit, "I can't win, and even if I could, I don't want to anymore."

"What do you want?"

"I want. . . I need you to help me. I can't do this without you." The darkness I felt at my townhouse is gone, obliterated by Rex's presence. I need him.

Without him I won't survive long enough to do what I need to do.

Without the pressure banding around my head, my tears are leaking out. I haven't cried for so long—not since my aunt died.

I fight my tears back, letting my words rush out of me. "I don't want anyone else to live through this nightmare, Rex. Please, please, just help me." I give up and press my face to his strong shoulder. He's so solid, his free hand tracing comforting circles on my back. Our bodies are always so in sync; why can't the rest of us fall in line?

"Of course, I will," he murmurs. "Inara, I'll do anything for you."

My breath shudders out of me. I let my tears disappear in the dark fabric of his expensive suit and raise my head. Time to negotiate terms. "I need to go into work."

His hand on my back stills, but he says, "All right."

"And you can't come. You can't interfere with the investigation."

"You can't stay at your townhouse. Your room at the Hotel Magnifique is always available for your use."

I take it as a good sign that he's not ordering me to stay there.

"All right. Then that's where I'll sleep. It beats a giant golden birdcage." The joke slips out before I can stop it.

The side of his lips quirk.

"Where did you even get a cage that big? Never mind. I don't want to know. Just don't lock me up again."

"I'll try."

I shake my head at him, almost smiling as we fall into our familiar pattern of banter. "You'll try? You, the great Rex Roy, who succeeds at everything?"

"Not everything." He sobers and kisses my hand.

I bite my lip, remembering the accusations we threw at each other in the heat of the moment. I need his help, but I don't trust him anymore. Not like I did.

But maybe we can start over.

"Truce?" I turn my hand over so he can shake it, and he does.

"Truce."

9

I *nara*

I'M STILL a little shaken when I arrive at work, but I fought hard to get to this moment. I can't fall apart now.

But I still feel Rex's warmth from where he cradled me. "You are everything to me," he murmured.

"Then don't destroy me," I whispered back.

He agreed, with a few conditions, to let me do my job. He respected my boundaries, like when he asked to touch me. He didn't call me 'little bird.' He's trying to respect my wishes, but a part of me wishes we could rewind time to when I allowed him full mastery of my body.

Will I ever hear him croon *little bird* to me again? I'm wondering if we can repair the damage between us.

Time will tell.

I'm lost in my thoughts the whole way to work. Good thing that Ivan's driving.

Just before we reach the final block, Rex texts me.

Sir: The team is analyzing the evidence left at your townhouse. I'll update you as soon as I know more.

It's the perfect text to get my mind back on the case. But at the same time, he's reminding me that he's still "Sir" in my phone. Maybe he's trying to tell my brain to remember what we once were. I told him to take care of me and give me what I needed. Maybe he knows that seeing "Sir" pop up on my phone will both soothe and infuriate me. Being annoyed with him is a safe outlet, one that won't send me spiraling but will distract me from the horrors of the case.

Or maybe he's just being his same old arrogant self. He plays this game on many levels. Every move can have five meanings, and I'll go bonkers trying to figure them all out.

But I'm grateful that he texted. It makes me feel like I'm not so alone.

"Here we are," Ivan announces when the precinct comes into view. "Good thing they fixed that thing with the grid earlier, or we'd still be in traffic."

"There was a thing with the grid?" I ask, and he waves it off. "It happened earlier. Don't worry about it."

When he gets out and comes around to open my door, identical blond twin giants are waiting for me. They're tall and built but move light on their feet, like professional fighters. These are the bodyguards I agreed to. I let them trail me to the station doors, clocking all the double takes and funny looks we get.

"Have a nice day, Mrs. Roy," one of them says.

Mrs. Roy? I jerk out of my thoughts and frown, but my bodyguards are already drifting away, so I don't call them back to correct them. I pull out my keycard and swipe it to open the door.

Instead of the light flashing green to signal the door unlocking, it flashes red. I try swiping my keycard again, but get the same red error light.

"Ramos," Diego Silva, the crime scene investigator, sidles up to me, a takeaway cup in his hand. "Did I just see two members of Fraternitas walk you to work?"

"What?" I glance back, but the twins have disappeared. "Do you know them?"

"Do I know them?" He looks at me like I'm nuts. "No, I just recognized their rings. I'm not on speaking terms with the most powerful gang in New Rome's history. Which begs the question—why are you?"

"I don't know them. They just—" How do I explain that Rex Roy himself made me agree to a security team before he'd let me leave the sex club we both attend? "Long story." I give up trying to swipe my key card. "It's been a few crazy days."

"Your card not working?"

"Guess not." Just add that to the pile of stuff I have to deal with.

"Here." Silva swipes his card, and the door locks clunk loudly before the light flashes green to signal they're open. "The desk sergeant will sort you out."

"Thanks. I actually need to talk to you about the most recent murders."

"Which ones?" Silva asks.

"The ones on Green Street. And the murder of Emily Rodriguez."

"Of course, you mean those. We have murders every day in this city, but the news cycle is only focused on them."

"They are linked. And I know who killed them. It's the Bondage Killer. He's back."

To his credit, Silva doesn't immediately roll his eyes. "How do you know?"

I hand over a packet of letters Hamish practically gift-wrapped for me. "These were sent to my home. They match the letter left at the site of the last murder."

He swears when he turns the packet over and sees the BK script. "The killer sent these to you?"

"Yes. I can explain everything, but right now, I need you to get these to the lab. Front of the line. The works."

"Bonds needs to know about this. There's a whole task force set up, and he's the lead," Silva graciously explains. He hasn't asked why I disappeared for several days— maybe he's been too busy to notice. I'll have to think of a way to explain my absence to my bosses, though.

"I'll tell him. I'm going right now to give my statement." It'll suck being at the center of a murder investigation, but I have to tell the truth. My privacy is a small price to pay for stopping a madman.

It's your choice, Rex told me. Before I left, he told me he'd support me in any way he could and protect me from the fallout. The thought warms me before I push it away.

Silva tells me good luck and heads off. I go to the room reserved for the task force. It's the same one we used for Gregory Martin's murder. I track down Bonds and pull him into an interview room, where I tell him as much as I can— about the letters sent to my home and how they tie the Bondage Killer to the current murders.

"These are photocopies of the original letters." I spread them out. "The originals are already in the lab. But I have initial findings." I lay out the lab reports Hamish worked up. "Handwriting is a match to the original Bondage Killer."

Bonds grabs a few pages and reads quickly. His face goes blank in a way that tells me he's processing all of this. It's not every day a serial killer comes back from the dead.

"Where did you find these?"

"A friend was collecting my mail and brought them to me." I explain that they were in my townhouse mailbox. "The killer probably wrote them over a period of days and delivered them all at once." Talking about these letters gives me a creepy crawling feeling and the sensation of disgusting film coating my skin. I try not to twitch.

MY Swallow is the greeting of one letter. Bonds spots it right away.

"Are you Swallow?" he asks.

"I think so." This is miserable, being a witness on a case I'm supposed to be working. I swallow down the sick feeling and keep my responses as cool and professional as I can.

"I believe it refers to my name. I was named for my great grandmother Enara." I spell it for him, and he writes it down. "It means 'swallow' in the Basque language."

"Huh." He keeps reading. "He mentions seeing you in a park. Was that recent? Did you know you were being followed?"

"It's possible. Maybe he didn't follow me for long." I shudder, remembering the cold feeling on the back of my neck. The sensation of being watched.

I have another terrible thought. "It could also be a reference to me as a child. There's evidence he cased families before. . . " I let my voice trail off. Bonds gives me a nod, and I rally. "He might have stalked me in a park, then and now."

My memories are back. *My father, holding my hand. My brothers running ahead, eager to get to the ball field. Me, insisting my father push me on the swings. The golden light sifting through green leaves.*

"Why now?" Bonds is asking, and I pull myself back to the present. "What triggered him to put these in your mailbox all at once?"

"It's possible he found out where I lived when a murdered man was dumped on my doorstep." Rex inadvertently led a killer to me. The irony.

"When he was last active in Elyria, he always seemed one step ahead of the police, even though he was sending letters to them. A detective on the case speculated he might have ties to a member of the police force. I can put you in touch with her." Lacy Collins was a detective on the Bondage Killer's case and, in many ways, my surrogate parent. But I haven't spoken to her in years. I'll have to break the silence now.

"It's not uncommon for a killer to embed themselves into their own investigation," Bonds tells me what I already know. "Or return to the crime scene."

I point to the lab report. "There's evidence that the card stock for the most recent letters matches the paper he used before. He might have returned to the warehouse and raided his own supplies."

"And kept them all these years, just in case he needed to start another letter-writing campaign?"

I have to brace myself before I ruthlessly explain. "The Green family was murdered in the same way my family was. And Emily Rodriguez looked a lot like me." It's taking everything in me to sound detached, like I'm talking about a case and not my own life. "It's possible BK is angry that I got away from him and now he's come back to finish the job."

"Fuck me." Bonds throws down the papers and scrubs his face with his hands. The details are finally dawning on him. "If this is true, we've got a serial killer resurfacing after, what, sixteen years? And targeting his former child victim, who happens to be an actual detective working on the case?"

"It's true." I'm impatient for him to catch up so we can start tracking the Bondage Killer down. *Rex believed you right away,* my mind points out. I have to admit, it's nice when Rex is on my side. The thought that right now, he's doing all he can and scouring the city for clues makes me feel better.

"All right. I'll set this as a line of inquiry."

I start to interrupt, but he holds up a hand. "No, Detective. You're too close to this. I'll need a profile from you, but you're too involved in this. You're off the case until further notice."

White hot rage slices through me. "Are you seriously sidelining me? I'm your best bet to understand how he acts, how he thinks—"

"Like I said, I'll take a profile. I shouldn't even allow you to do that, but you're right. I need you. But other than that, I don't want you anywhere near this case."

I'm speechless. I'm ready to give my all for this case, and now I'm being ordered to stay away? Does he think I'll be too emotional to keep a clear head and do the work? Because that's fucking sexist.

Bonds doesn't meet my gaze as he stacks up the papers I delivered and heads out. I was also supposed to tell him about the dead birds in my townhouse. Rex has a team there analyzing everything, so now I think I'll find out what they have to say before letting the department know. With my luck, Bonds will insist I go into protective custody because the killer is targeting me. Rex will be thrilled.

Maybe Rex was behind this.

I pull out my phone before I can second-guess myself.

Me: You promised to stop meddling

Sir: I did.

Me: They took me off the case

My phone rings. I usually don't have any cell reception in an interview room, but somehow, Rex is able to get through.

"I thought we had a truce." I want to sound angry, but I can't keep the hurt out of my voice. *I need you on my side.*

"They took you off the case?"

"Yes. Conflict of interest. I thought you were done interfering."

"I had nothing to do with this."

And why should I trust you? I want to shout. "You're sure? Swear it to me, Rex. Swear it on your parents' grave."

"I swear."

I sag back in my seat. He didn't hesitate. Maybe it wasn't him.

"You don't need access," Rex says. "Anything they have, we can get, so it doesn't matter. The PD is several steps behind anyway, and even if they aren't, we can get any information you need."

He's right, of course, but it was only a few hours ago he was dead set against me being a part of the investigation, and I'm still raw. I'm still getting used to the idea that he's serious about helping me.

"If I find out you're behind this, I will never forgive you."

"I understand. Give me a chance to prove myself."

"All right." My voice betrays how much hope I have in him.

Damn this man.

But if Rex makes good on his promise to help, I will have

full access to any evidence NRPD turns up, plus the resources of his lab and anything else we might turn up.

It's too easy to step outside the bounds of the law, so I'll have to make sure any evidence we find sticks when it's time to go to trial. But Rex is right; this will go much faster if I'm not hemmed in by procedure. I'm willing to break the rules if it'll save lives.

I wonder if that's how Rex feels.

I snort. If Bonds thinks he can stop me, he has no idea what I've already overcome just to come into the station today. I'm working this case, and that's final.

First, I'll get him his damn profile. I have my own notes, but the files from the original case will be a big help, so I head to the bullpen to put in a request for them through official channels. I wish Rex hadn't chased Mina off; she can get her hands on almost anything in a matter of hours versus days or weeks.

I shoot an email to an old FBI pal of mine, Dirk Larsen. He brought me in on a few of his cases as an unofficial consultant and owes me a few favors. I'm also pretty sure he doesn't know I have personal ties to the BK murders. He emails back immediately to say he'll see what he can do, but the person who has the most information on the case is Lacy Collins, a former detective who worked on the Elyria force back in the day. She discovered BK's true identity as an alarm system salesman named Dennis Bundy and tracked him to the warehouse where he was hiding out.

Dirk offers to put me back in touch with her. I tell him there's no need and I still have her number.

Then I pull out my phone and pull up her contact info.

Lacy Collins was more than just my mentor. She found me as a runaway. She was my hero and adoptive family rolled into one.

And then I cut ties with her. I moved to California and started a new life. I had no friends and no family, but there was also no one I could hurt.

She, of all people, could guess my worst secret, the one that keeps me running from city to city without putting down roots or making friends.

Do I dare call her now? Will it put her in danger? Is it worth the risk?

I'm squeezing my phone so tight my knuckles are a sickly white.

Finally, I decide she needs to know. I hit the *Call* button, my heart pounding painfully with every ring. Her voicemail picks up, and I catch my breath at her voice. Firm, kind, no-nonsense. "This is Lacy Collins. Leave a message at the beep."

My own voice sounds shaky and unsure. "Hey. It's me. I'm sorry I've been MIA." An apology can't begin to make up for what I've done, so I continue in a rush. "But I need your help with some cases in New Rome." I hesitate but then decide blunt honesty is best. "It's BK. He's back."

I end the call and clutch the phone tight, my throat clogged with emotion. All my old demons are rising up to strangle me.

You should've died with your family, my uncle told me all those years ago. *If you had, none of this would've happened.* My aunt had just died, and he was grieving, but I knew he was right. I'm cursed.

I've never told anyone what happened in the years after BK destroyed my life.

It started with my parents and brothers. First, I dreamed of their death, and then I lived it. You'd think their murders would be the worst thing that happened to me, but then I went to my grandmother's, and within a year, she was gone.

I had a vision of her slumped over the kitchen table and walked in after school to find her exactly as my vision had predicted. Slumped over the table, dead from a heart attack.

My aunt took me in, and the cycle continued. I had a vision of her collapsing on the deck. This time, I shared what I'd seen, but it was no use. She died a few days later, and her husband could no longer bear the sight of me.

You're an angel of death, my uncle said. My aunt wasn't cold in the ground before he kicked me out of his house. *You killed her. I want you gone.*

Everyone close to me dies. My parents and brothers, my grandmother, my aunt. Lacy Collins helped me, and I rewarded her by cutting off all contact as soon as I was old enough to do so.

I haven't allowed anyone to get close to me since.

Not until Rex.

But I can't think about that right now. I'm already too close to falling apart.

I stop by the task force room and survey the wall full of evidence, including the pictures of the crime scene.

Luckily, Bonds isn't around to shoo me away. I've also avoided seeing Burgess or Cucinelli, which is always a win.

A photo of the scene around the body of Emily Rodriguez catches my eye. There's a dead bird in the frame.

The door creaks open, casting a light over the black feathers to make them shimmer green—

I suck in a breath, blinking back the memory of the dead birds at my townhouse.

"There was a dead bird left at the scene?" I say to myself.

An old-timer—a retired detective who volunteers a few days a week—hears me and limps over. "Yes. That detail wasn't released to the public."

Which is why I didn't see it on the news.

"Terrible business." The old timer peers at the photo of Emily Rodriquez with her dog, leaning in so close his nose almost touches the corkboard. "Reminds me of the Blackbird murders."

"The Blackbird murders?"

"Yeah, from a decade ago. Two murders where the killer left a dead bird at the scene. Just like this."

"A blackbird?"

"Different types of birds, actually. The press never gets it right. The victims were both young women with dark hair and eyes. Looked a bit like her." He nods to the victim's photo, then glances up and does a double-take when he sees my face. "And a bit like you."

"This all happened in New Rome?"

He nods, still staring at me. His back may be stooped and his eyes bleary, but I can tell there's a sharp mind working behind them.

"Did they catch the killer?"

"Nope." He shakes his grizzled head. "A friend of mine was on the case. Could never let it go. Worked it on and off for years before he retired. He passed a year ago; otherwise, he'd still be working on it."

I have the sense of a key clicking in a lock, the same feeling I get when I uncover a clue. "I need to see that case file." I straighten and start to head out.

"Won't be here," the detective calls. "It'll be down in storage at City Hall. That's where they keep the cold cases."

"Thank you," I say. I have an urgent feeling that I need to see the Blackbird case file immediately.

Beady black eyes open in death. The feathered body placed at the foot of the victim, wings spread—

This isn't a memory. It's a vision. The birds are a clue. The Blackbird murders are another piece of the puzzle.

I head down the hall, striding with purpose. This is part of the case that I crave the most—when a picture is forming, and I have a line of pursuit.

Before I leave, I remember I need to get my keycard replaced so I don't have trouble getting back into the precinct. Bonds might want to cut off my access, but I'm still a member of the force. Plus, I should check in with the desk sergeant. Explain why I fled the Green Street scene and haven't returned to work until now.

But when I go to greet him, he says, "Detective. I didn't expect you back in so soon. You sent that email saying you were taking a couple personal days."

"Oh, yeah," I say slowly. Rex must have logged into my work account to send that email, covering for me while I was distraught. It would be considerate if it wasn't so on the nose and overbearing. So perfectly Rex.

I would be lying if I said I wouldn't miss the way he took care of me. Even when he invaded my privacy to do it.

The sergeant continues. "And then I saw your name change and it all made sense. Here." He slides an envelope towards me. I pick it up, unsure of what it is. "By the way, congratulations."

Congratulations? "What?"

"On your nuptials? At least, I assume that's why your name changed."

"My. . . what?"

"I assumed you got married, and that's why you changed your last name." The sergeant looks as confused as I feel. "I didn't mean to overstep."

"No, no. . . it's fine." Slowly I make sense of what he's telling me. "You said my last name has changed?"

"In our system. That's your new badge there." He nods to the envelope he handed over.

I open it and shake out the new white badge. I can guess what the last name will be before I see it.

It reads, "Detective Inara Roy." I have a surreal sense of deja vu and shake my head to clear it. It's not a vision, just a feeling that I've entered some sort of alternate reality.

Roy. So that's the reason the sergeant thinks I got hitched. Somehow, someone changed my name in the system.

"There're a couple of forms for you to fill out, too," the sergeant prattles on, oblivious to the fact that my brain is glitching. "Do you have your new ID?"

My shock is fading, drowned out by disbelief. I can't believe this is happening. "There's been a mistake. I haven't changed my last name."

The sergeant frowns at the computer. "Our system says otherwise."

I stare at the badge. *Inara Roy.*

I don't need a detective badge to solve this mystery. There's only one man who has the power and influence to do something like this: Rex fucking Roy.

You belong to me.

Are all billionaires like dogs needing to pee on their territory and advertise their ownership in any way they can? Or just the one billionaire who's obsessed with me?

Either way, I'm going to kill him.

"Your system is wrong," I grind out.

The sergeant doesn't seem to know what to say.

I sigh. "How do I fix it?"

"Name changes are processed at City Hall. You might go talk to them."

"Great. I'll get right on that." I don't have time for this, but I need to push back.

And I have to go down to City Hall anyway to look up old records anyway.

New badge in my pocket, I head outside, texting as I go.

> Me: Wtf

> Me: You changed my name.

> Sir: Good morning, Mrs. Roy.

UNBELIEVABLE. I ignore the way my heart feels a little thrill, knowing he's publicly claimed me.

> Me: Marking your territory?

> Sir: Now everyone will know you belong to me

GAH! I knew it. I add a few angry emojis to my next message.

> Me: everyone will think we're married

> Sir: Exactly.

IS HE SERIOUS?

. . .

> Me: I'm changing it back. enjoy it while it lasts

> Sir: I will

I CAN FEEL his smugness radiating from my phone.

I TEXT HIM:

> I thought you were going to back off

> Sir: Never

A MINUTE AGO, I felt like I had lost everyone I'd ever gotten close to. But here's Rex reminding me he won't leave. It warms me through more than I can say.

Biting my lip, I shoot back a reply.

> Me: Maybe I wanted you to take my last name

> Sir: that can be arranged

> Sir: Shall we hyphenate?

DESPITE MYSELF, my lips curve into a smile. It's just so ridiculous.

> Sir: Roy-Ramos has a nice ring to it.

> Me: NO

> Me: we're not changing our names. We're not married

> Sir: I have paperwork that says otherwise

DID he really file for a marriage license? No. He has to be bluffing.

> Me: get ready for the fastest divorce in history

I POCKET my phone before walking out the front doors of the precinct.

And all hell breaks loose.

10

I *nara*

THE SECOND I step out of the police precinct, I'm hit with the flashes from a hundred cameras.

"Mrs. Roy! Mrs. Roy!" There's a mob in front of me, reporters waving to catch my attention, and a row of TV cameras behind the line of photographers. "Inara, over here!"

Shit fuck! I hold up a hand to shield my eyes as another round of bright flashes explode in my face.

"Is it true you're now married to Rex Roy?" someone shouts.

"When was the wedding?"

"How did you meet?"

Reporters push forward, microphones in hand.

"No comment," I yell, but my shout is lost in the fray. I

am seriously overwhelmed. The crowd surges, driving me back towards the doors.

A man with a camera around his neck presses close. He grabs my arm, and his disgusting breath hits my face. "How does he like to fuck you?" He looks manic and eager, and an oily sensation slides over my senses. I'm gagging, too overcome by his nauseating aura to call on my defensive moves to break his hold on me.

Before I can do anything, someone grabs him by the collar and tosses him aside. The blond twins push through the crowd to flank my sides. "This way," one barks at me. We move forward as one, and if people don't scramble out of our path fast enough, they get shoved to the side by one of the twins. One guy refuses to budge, and the twin on my right grabs the guy and tosses him into a bank of reporters without breaking stride.

They get me into the back of Ivan's waiting car and guard the door until he pulls away from the curb.

"You okay?" Ivan asks.

"Fine," I clip, too breathless to say much else. I can't even wrap my head around what's happening—my name was changed without my knowledge, and the press thinks we're married. "I need to get to City Hall. The sooner, the better."

Fortunately, Ivan doesn't need an explanation. "Understood," he says cheerfully while accelerating toward a group of cameramen who stand in the street, right in our way. A few of them scream and dive for the sidewalk. At the last second, Ivan jerks the car and swerves to keep from hitting them.

Ivan laughs and lets out a string of words that can only be curses, then apologizes. "Pardon my Russian."

There aren't enough cuss words in any language for me

to express how I feel about Rex right now. What was he thinking, pulling a stunt like this?

The fact that he did it so thoroughly and quickly is kind of impressive. Only Rex would think of something like this and have the means to pull it off.

Inara Roy-Ramos. Why does it have a nice ring to it? I fight a small smile.

Not that I'm letting him get away with this. If the good people at City Hall can't undo what Rex has done, I'll have to explore more drastic options.

"Hamish wanted me to give you this," Ivan says, passing me a lunch cooler. "I'm supposed to report back if you prefer something else to eat."

I typically munch on a meal bar or sip a protein shake for lunch, but I'm pleased to find a lightly dressed salad with grilled chicken and an iced, honey-sweetened green tea.

"This looks great, thanks." At least I'll have a full belly while I deal with the mess Rex has made. "Ivan, do you know any assassins?"

"I can probably hook you up." He winks at me in the mirror, then lays on the horn all the way to City Hall.

Rex

I'm WALKING into my office when my assistant approaches. I can tell by the fast clip-clop of her stilettos that she's in a hurry.

"Sir, you have messages from *The Post*, *The Press*, and *The Times*. They want a statement about your recent nuptials?" She can't keep the questioning tone out of her voice.

"Tell them I'll be holding a press conference by EOD.

Location TBD. And clear my schedule for the rest of the day."

She nods, looking harried, and rushes off.

So far, I've had a productive day. Inara is safe in the precinct and now has the protection of the Roy last name. If she leaves, Fraternitas is on guard duty. I have a team of more conventional bodyguards assigned to her detail, but nothing sends a message like having a member of Fraternitas personally escorting her to and from work. The New Rome underworld will understand she's off limits.

The rest of Fraternitas is on the street, shaking down their own contacts to sniff out the Bondage Killer. Not to mention Victor, the assassin I hired.

I don't usually outsource hunting down a target like this, but I want BK taken out before he has another chance to torment Inara. She's suffered enough.

His days are numbered, and when I get my hands on him, I will paint the town red with his blood.

I'm in the middle of reviewing my messages when an incoming call from Hamish interrupts me.

"I've spoken with the team at the duplex," he says. "They've confirmed a man entered yesterday evening around ten and spent some time carrying full garbage bags from an unmarked delivery van into the townhouse. A neighbor thought he was moving in."

Unbelievable. I brace my hands on the desk, willing my heart rate to slow down. "How did he get past our surveillance?" Inara's townhouse wasn't being as closely monitored now that I was no longer spying on her while she stayed there, but one system should've at least been operational.

"He was wearing a police uniform. Our outdoor system didn't flag him because of that. Inara's residence was recently a crime scene and, therefore, the site of increased police activity."

I close my eyes. I'm the one who made her doorstep a crime scene. It's my fault a police presence wouldn't trigger the system or alarm the neighbors.

Hamish continues. "We can't be certain, but it seems the intruder used a device that scrambled the camera's signal but didn't activate any emergency response."

"I want to know how." All this tech and surveillance was at my disposal, and I failed to protect her.

"I'm still gathering the details, but it's clear the intruder had an inside knowledge of security systems. If you'll recall, Dennis Bundy, the self-named Bondage Killer, worked as a security expert."

"It was him. He was right there." I thump my fist into the top of the desk. "We could've had him!"

"We also have to consider that this is the work of a copy-cat. Or he's working with someone in the police department."

"I want all the original records on Dennis Bundy ASAP." I already know Inara left a voicemail on retired detective Lacy Collins's phone, probably wanting Collins's own notes on the BK case.

"Understood. I've hacked the Elyria police department records and sent an agent to retrieve the hard copies. They should be here by tonight."

"Good." My jaw aches from how hard I'm clenching my teeth. In my mind's eye, I see Inara opening her townhouse door and collapsing over and over again. "It's my fault."

Hamish says nothing.

"If only I—" Could have what? Rewind time? There are some mistakes no amount of money can undo. "We have to catch him. He'll make a mistake, and we'll get him."

"Indeed, sir. In the meantime, you should know the news is reporting that New Rome's most eligible bachelor is now a married man." His brief pause speaks volumes of censure. "Is there something I should know?"

I suppose now is as good a time as any to tell him. "As of ten a.m. this morning, Inara and I are married. The paperwork went through this morning." Technically, there's a thirty-day waiting period between getting a marriage license and tying the knot. The bride is also supposed to be present to sign the forms and actually have knowledge of the impending nuptials. But no problem is insurmountable with a big enough bribe.

"Ah. Does she know?"

"She does now."

"I shall instruct our lawyers to draw up a postnuptial agreement."

"No need. What's mine is hers." She might accept me if she realizes how much fun it is having billions to your name. The thought fills me with satisfaction. Gives a new meaning to golden handcuffs.

"Then I shall order her a signature seal, as well as some stationery."

"Hold that thought. She might not be too keen on taking my last name." I smile as I scroll through her annoyed texts.

"Trouble in paradise all ready?" Hamish does not sound surprised.

"I'm working on it." I've spent much of my courtship with Inara pissing her off. Why stop now?

My phone lights up with an incoming text from one of the Fraternitas twins guarding Inara.

Kaiser: Wifey is on the move.

She's going to hate that codename. I look forward to her blowing up at me when she finds out.

"If you'll excuse me now, Hamish. I'm off to hold a press conference." It's time to make it clear to this city that anyone who messes with my wife messes with me.

INARA

A SWARM of reporters beat us to City Hall. My blond bodyguards hustle me past them and into the quiet depths of the grand old building. I go to wait in line, but once I show my ID, an official rushes over and escorts me to a private room. Someone flagged my maiden name, and I'm recognized as the newest Roy. It seems my association with the wealthy family is enough to award me special treatment, whether I like it or not.

I sigh and figure it will be faster if I take advantage of the quick service than if I insist on waiting in line. Maybe I can reverse all this today.

"There's been some mistake," I explain to the official. "I haven't actually gotten married or changed my name."

The man fumbles with his computer, his brow creasing as he clicks and mutters to himself. "It says the forms were filed this morning."

"But not by me."

"Is this your signature?" He shows me the screen, and I grit my teeth.

"It's a forgery." But a perfect match to my own. Maybe there's a journal of Rex's somewhere full of practice lines. I take a moment to imagine a page filled with schoolboy script and "Inara + Rex" decorated with little hearts. The absurd image makes me bite back a laugh.

This whole thing is absurd, so I might as well let it

amuse me. I was annoyed at this distraction, but it's nice to have something to smile about, even in the middle of a case.

"But that's fraud," the official gasps. "Do you have any idea who would do such a thing? Or why?"

Apparently, to mark me in a way society will accept. I won't wear Rex's collar, so he went with something more conventional.

Now everyone will know you belong to me.

"It doesn't matter." I don't want all this getting out. Rex makes headlines by walking down the street. This sort of scandal will be gossip fodder for years. "I think it was supposed to be. . . a joke." I wince when the official gasps again. "I just want the record corrected."

"The thing is, ma'am, as of this morning, you're legally married. Do you want to file for divorce?"

"There's no way to. . . I don't know. . . just change the record back?"

The door creaks open, and a young woman sticks her head in. "Hey, George, there's a bunch of reporters out here tryin' to get a word with a Mrs. Roy."

George gulps and stares at me. There's a sheen of sweat on his bald head.

The young woman zeroes in on me. "Is that you? You married Rex Roy?"

"Uh, no—"

"Actually, Denise, Mrs. Roy would like to file divorce papers."

"Are you serious?" Denise props a hand on her hip, showcasing her acid-green nails. She looks me up and down, chomping her gum. "You just hooked him, and now you're throwing him back?"

"Uh—" I glance back at George, who gives me a weak smile.

"Can I have him?" Denise waves a finger. "'Cause honey, the whole package works for me, you know what I'm sayin'?"

No! I'm surprised by a sudden surge of possessiveness. *He's mine.*

Denise doesn't give me a chance to answer. "I'll get your divorce forms, stat. Fault or no-fault?"

I blink at her, trying to understand what she's asking me. Before I can recall what fault or no-fault divorce means, she snaps her fingers to get my attention. "Will Mr. Roy be contesting?"

"Absolutely," comes a deep voice. Rex appears behind Denise. Her mouth opens so wide her gum tumbles out. George also gapes.

But Rex has eyes only for me.

"Hello, wife."

11

I *nara*

REX SMILES AT ME, cool possession in his gaze. My whole body flushes at the sight of him. I'm already amped up, but now I'm suddenly giddy, like I'm riding an adrenaline high. He's claiming me publicly, and I'm not annoyed; I'm excited. I'm used to my body interpreting pain as pleasure, but this is a new type of masochism.

Or else I'm craving complete ownership more than I thought.

"Excuse me," he says. "Can I have a moment to speak to Mrs. Roy?"

"Of course, sir." George scrambles out of his own seat to offer it to Rex. It's a revelation, watching Rex move through the world like the rich celebrity he is.

"Thank you." Rex's smooth tones remind me of a politician's. "We'll just be a moment."

"Take all the time you need!" George hustles out, taking a starry-eyed Denise with him, but not before she wrangles an autograph out of Rex.

And then I'm shut in a clerk's tiny office. Alone with Rex. My new husband.

The room feels smaller with him in it. Like there's not enough air. I stand to face him, crossing my arms over my chest to keep myself from touching him. I need to make clear that he's in trouble, and swooning into his arms will give the wrong idea. "Does Roy Manor have a doghouse? Because that's where you'll be sleeping tonight."

"No, darling. But you can have one installed on the grounds. You're the mistress of the manor now."

I narrow my eyes on him. If he thinks that's tempting. . . he'd be right. The mansion is beautiful. I could spend years exploring all the rooms. I drop my arms and close the distance between us. The pull to go to him is too strong; I can't resist it. I don't want to. "I can't believe you changed my name. Rex, what the hell?" I playfully smack his chest.

He grabs my hand and kisses it. The touch of his lips makes my pulse flutter. He is so sinfully handsome when he's being bad. "Inara and Rex Roy-Ramos. Sounds perfect."

He joked about hyphenating before, but hearing it out loud sounds more serious. "You'd change your name too?"

"It's only fair. Everyone will know I belong to you, too."

My knees weaken. Rex's charm offensive is hard to resist. Denise had it right. *The whole package works for me, too.*

"That's not. . . you don't. . ." I sputter, trying to figure out what to say. "We're not actually married."

"According to the world, we are."

"You didn't even ask me."

He opens his mouth, probably to declare himself, and I hold up a hand. "It's too late." If he gets down on one knee, it'll be all over. I already feel myself wanting to give in. He'll win. "It's already done. We're not even in a relationship."

"Aren't we?"

I don't know what we are to each other. But this is a dangerous topic. I can't think about it right now.

I don't know what it says about me that I'd rather focus on the gruesome details of serial murders than discuss the state of our relationship.

"You said you'd stop meddling. You promised."

"I'm not meddling. I'm giving you my name. For your protection."

My mouth falls open. "What protection? The paparazzi was all over me!"

"I know. I've made it clear that's not to happen again. You'll be assigned your own security detail. We'll also give select media some access, and after a few interviews, the press will settle down."

I frown. Interviews? Access? What the hell?

"Speaking of interviews, we'll be holding a press conference today. Don't worry. You don't have to say anything if you don't want to."

If meeting the press is anything like the mob earlier, I don't want anything to do with it.

"I'm used to these," Rex reassures me. "I can do all the talking. You can just stand there and look pretty."

I grit my teeth, and then I clock the gleam in his eye. "Are you riling me up so I'm mad instead of nervous?" I ask.

"Is it working?"

Yes. "Keep it up, and I really will kill you."

He shifts forward into my space. "Is that what you want?" Only Rex would think my threat is an opportunity for us to flirt. "You'll be a very wealthy widow."

My brain glitches out. "Really?"

"What's mine is yours, Inara."

Rex is a billionaire. Does this mean I'm one now, too?

That can't be right.

I can't think about this right now, either. "This isn't a real marriage. I need you to understand that."

"Understood." He sounds serious. "The Roy name means something to New Rome. It'll attract attention, but there are many people who respect it."

Like George the clerk. Although Denise didn't seem too impressed with me.

"Please, Inara. Keep it until this is all over. I only want to help."

I blow out a breath. "All right. As long as you understand it's fake."

"Of course." He dips his head, agreeing so quickly I don't think it's a real concession. "We can work out the details over dinner tonight."

Give this man an inch, and he thinks he's a ruler.

I raise a finger between us. "Don't get too comfortable, Mr. Roy. I'm already interviewing assassins."

The door opens just in time for George to hear my last statement. "Um, is this a bad time?"

"We're almost done," Rex says. Without taking his eyes off me, he breaks into a superstar smile. My insides quake under the full force of his charm.

A tall woman with a black headset fixed over her long box braids leans in past George. "Mr. Roy, Mrs. Roy. We're ready for you."

"Thank you, Nadia. We're ready." Rex lays a hand on my back, pressing slightly to move me forward. "This way, darling."

"Wait." I stiffen my legs. "I need to get down to records

storage. There's an old case with similar details to the most recent murder."

Rex leans in, his expression intent. "You think it's him?" He keeps it vague because we're in public.

"It might be. Or it's related." The connection of the dead birds left at the scene is too important to ignore. "Either way, I need the murder book."

"One moment." Rex turns to George and murmurs to him. The man bobs his head so much he practically bows. Rex returns to my side. "We'll have them within the hour." His lips are close to my ear. "They'll be delivered to Hotel Magnifique by an NRPD records keeper."

I frown. Having a records keeper hand deliver a file is unheard of.

"There are perks to being a Roy," Rex tells me softly. And then he holds out his hand.

Feeling flutters in my core that have nothing to do with nerves. I take it and let him guide me to our first public appearance as a couple.

~

REX

OUR FIRST PRESS conference as a couple happens right on the City Hall steps. When I found out where Inara was, I worked with the head of my PR team, Nadia Jenkins, to plan the media event. We decided the classical architecture would make a beautiful backdrop for the world's first glimpse of Inara and me as a couple. Under Nadia's brilliant leadership, her team made it happen.

Events like these are a necessary evil. Better to craft a

juicy public persona and feed the sharks than have them rip into my private life.

But today, I feel a sense of triumph facing the crowd with Inara by my side. *Mine.*

My reluctant bride hangs back, so I step up to the microphone and give a wave, drawing the camera's attention. My security team—a long line of men and women in black suits —stand between us and the press.

In the past, I've dated a number of carefully vetted beautiful women. Mostly actresses or famous athletes, women comfortable with the spotlight. Our time together was more of a mutually beneficial business arrangement than anything else.

My relationship with Inara is different. I've never felt such strong emotions for anyone, both inside and outside of the bedroom. She's the only woman I've wanted to claim so completely. I couldn't wait another day without making it clear to everyone she belonged to me.

I hope St. James is watching.

"Dearly beloved," I say. "We are gathered here to witness this man and woman joined together in holy matrimony." I pause to wait for the joke to land. A grin stretches across my face, and cameras flash with a strobe effect. "It's true. Earlier today, I had the honor of making this woman my wife." I angle my body to include Inara. She takes a small step forward, raising her chin. She agreed to go through with this, and she's keeping her word.

I take a few steps toward her and hold out my hand again, inviting her to meet me halfway. A small pause, a sigh only I can hear, and she moves to my side. Her face tilts up to mine.

I only meant to give the cameras a good shot of us

together, but as I gaze at her, the world stops. Stills. I fall into her golden eyes.

Suddenly, there's only the two of us. Her complexion glows, her cheeks chafed by the chilly air. Her beauty stops my heart, even now.

The wind picks up, and I tuck her close, wanting to shield her from the cold. She relaxes against me. The only sign that she's out of her element is the way she bites her lip.

"All right?" I murmur to her. Press conferences are overwhelming if you're not used to them. But for someone as private as Inara, it must be hell.

She nods. She's strong and able to put on a bold front, as I knew she would.

I raise a gloved hand to her face, brushing back a few windswept strands of hair. "Can I kiss you?"

Her lips part, and her breath shudders out of her. In the distance, I hear reporters shouting my name, but there's only Inara. Only us.

I cup her cheek and lower my head. My lips brush hers, and I'm instantly, painfully hard. I was already aroused, bickering with her in the close quarters of the clerk's office. But now I'm ready to rip her clothes off and mark her here, in public.

I drop my hand, feeling as shaken as Inara looks.

And I realize why I was so quick to file marriage papers and mark her with my name. All my obsession, all my intense feelings add up to one thing.

Love.

It's not an emotion I've allowed myself to feel. All-consuming desire, yes. But the need to comfort, care for, and control her has alchemized and turned into something more.

I *love* Inara.

Have I told her yet? I almost want to shout it out now, shout it to the world.

"Mr. Roy!" Reporters are surging forward, shouting questions. Only the solid barrier of my security team holds them back.

I move back to the microphones, holding up my hands. "No questions today," I tell them. "Please respect our privacy. My media team will be in touch."

"Mr. Roy! Wait!" The press isn't taking no for an answer. Nadia is already striding toward me, ready to take over and rebuff all questions.

But one reporter calls out to Inara. "Mrs. Roy! Is it true the Bondage Killer killed your entire family?"

My head snaps back, searching for the speaker. It's a man's voice, but he's hidden in the crowd. "Who said that?" I bark before I can stop myself, and the mics pick up my question.

The reporters also look around, sensing blood in the water. "The Bondage Killer?" they mutter to each other. "Is it true?"

The same speaker calls out again, "What about reports that the serial killer is back and targeting you?"

I don't have to look back at Inara to know that she's gone still and stiff, shut down in the face of a threat.

I need to shut this down right now.

"Know this," my voice rings out. "I will not tolerate any attempts to pry into our private lives." A few reporters lower their arms, cowed. I glower at them and the cameras, giving them a glimpse of the monster I've worked so hard to hide. "And if anyone seeks to harm or threaten my wife, it'll be the last thing you do."

～

*I*NARA

"I DIDN'T DIRECTLY THREATEN ANYONE," Rex says.

"You didn't have to," Nadia replies. "You looked like you were about to leap off the stage and strangle someone with your bare hands."

We're in the back of a limo, riding to Hotel Magnifique. After the disaster of a press conference, Nadia took over. She ended the line of questions by announcing that she'd emailed them all detailed press kits. Reporters stopped shouting to check their inboxes then and there. She deftly dangled the possibility of private interviews to a few select news outlets, then bundled Rex and me into this car.

Now she's reprimanding Rex for bungling the statement she gave him. I've never seen anyone attempt to give Rex orders, much less dress him down, so this is kind of fun.

"It's not like I pointed at any of them and said outright that I would kill them."

"Good job," Nadia deadpans. "Do you want a cookie?"

I love this woman. If I weren't already married, I'd be tempted to see if she would top me sometime.

"Legal is shitting themselves," she says, swiping on her phone. "It's all hands on deck, trying to spin this."

"That's what I pay them for." Rex sounds like a sulky child. "Get my money's worth."

"Oh, you will, Mr. Roy. And we're billing overtime."

Rex doesn't bother to get the last word, and that's how I know he's shaken. As soon as we slid into our seats, he captured my right hand and kept it clasped between both of his.

"Is it bad?" I ask. My stomach is churning from the rollercoaster of the day. The last hour is still a blur. I remember the kiss, then a shadow falling over us—a psychic warning. "Is Rex in trouble?"

"It'll be alright," Rex assures me. "Nadia has fixed much worse."

Nadia snorts, and he adds, "If anything, I might have to pay a small fine."

"If the reporter sues, you could be out a couple million," she says.

"Like I said. Small."

Nadia shakes her head and looks at me like *You married him.* I squeeze Rex's hand. I don't know why I'm comforting him when he's responsible for this mess. I guess I can sense he's trying.

Please, Inara. Let me help. He keeps begging me to let him in. He's as damaged as I am, but he's trying.

Maybe I can try a little harder too. Let down my walls and stop shutting him out.

But I'm terrified, too. "It'll all be out now, won't it? Everything about my past."

Rex wraps an arm around me. We re-position so I'm leaning into him on the bench seat. A couple holding onto each other as we face the world.

Nadia's expression softens, but she doesn't shy away from answering. "It's out. But the press kit focuses on your exceptional career. We included statements from several officers from the LAPD, as well as Agent Larsen from the FBI. They all spoke very highly of your abilities as a detective."

Warmth floods through me. "Dirk did that for me?"

"Dirk? Who's that?" Rex stiffens beside me, and I soothe him with another squeeze of my hand.

"He said that you were the best profiler he ever had the

pleasure of working with. That you had, quote, 'A brilliant and unique mind.'"

"Oh." I fight a smile at the high praise. "That was kind of him."

"He didn't seem like the type prone to hyperbole. Or kindness. He meant every word."

"Yeah, that sounds like Dirk," I say, picturing the solemn agent who drove most of his team crazy with his meticulous nature and attention to detail. Beside me, Rex is bristling like an attack dog who senses an intruder.

"Dirk," he mutters the name like it's a curse word.

"Did you date him?" Nadia asks bluntly. Her no-nonsense professionalism is reassuring, and I can trust she'll tell me like it is.

"No. We just worked together. We made a good team," I add to rile up Rex.

"Maybe we'll invite him to the engagement ball," Nadia muses.

"Absolutely not," Rex interjects, then swears when we both grin at him.

What Nadia says suddenly penetrates. "Wait, what engagement ball?" I ask. "Isn't it a bit late for that?" We're already married.

"We're rich," Rex smirks. "We do what we want."

The limo is pulling around the back of the hotel. It rolls up to a gate and, after getting checked by a security guard, rolls through to the dark underbelly of a parking deck.

I have one more question. "What did the press kit say about how we met? Where we were. . ." I trail off. Nadia didn't mention Club Empire, did she? That would make the front page.

"At the NRPD Charity ball, of course," she says. "Chief

Jordan is already taking personal credit for introducing the two of you."

Rex scoffs, and I roll my eyes. The chief will be insufferable. It's going to take some getting used to being the center of attention and getting fawned over like this.

But I have Rex to shield me. I'm already getting used to the idea. Maybe that's what I'm craving—the feeling that someone has my back, no matter what. I can't trust Rex not to take the concept too far, but the primal part of me wants that level of devotion. He will stop at nothing to protect me. I know it in my bones, and it makes me feel safe.

The limo slows to drop us off at an elevator door.

"Okay, lovebirds, this is your stop," Nadia says. "Just lie low until I say so." She points a stern finger at Rex. "No more threatening the press."

He gives a grim nod, and then it's my turn to get lectured.

"And you," Nadia says, looking pointedly at my hand. "You need a ring."

I don't need a ring, but I'm not going to backtalk a domme. She turns back to Rex. "Get her a rock the size of Antarctica. Give people something to gossip about."

"Yes, ma'am," Rex says and half salutes her while helping me out.

"Is a ring really necessary?" I grumble.

Rex laughs. His hand skates down my back as he leads me into the elevator. "It is if Nadia says so. She's the best. She'll feed the rags a bunch of romantic nonsense, keep them speculating about our wedding colors—"

"There's going to be a wedding?" This whole thing is supposed to be fake!

"We might be able to avoid it if the engagement ball is

spectacular enough." He presses a button, and the elevator rises. "As for the ring, think of it as costume jewelry."

If I know Rex, he's going to get me something that costs more than a house. "Not as a tiny collar?"

He looks smug. "Not unless you want to."

I sigh. Once we're back in the hotel room, I turn on the TV. Every news channel is playing footage from the steps of City Hall.

I watch Rex cup my face and kiss me over and over again.

I replay the moment in my head. I was totally swept away by Rex's warmth, his touch. He looked at me like I was the most beautiful thing he'd ever seen. Like he never wants to look away.

Just watching it, I feel shaken to my core. I'm overflowing with feelings—fear, lust, acceptance, longing. All my emotions explode out of the box where I've kept them locked down.

And now I'll be on display.

"... is New Rome's most eligible bachelor settling down? Who is the lucky woman who tamed this notorious playboy?"

They show a picture of Rex on a red carpet, looking suave, then juxtapose that with a police academy picture of me in my dress uniform. I look like a kid playing dress up, clueless, impossibly young.

The news switches to pictures of Rex's glamorous ex-girlfriends, goddess after goddess with perfect skin and pouting lips like a slideshow on the screen. Women who deserve to stand on a red carpet with him. It's obvious the press thinks Rex should be with one of them.

But in every picture of Rex and one of his exes, he keeps a space between his body and theirs. In contrast, on the City

Hall steps, he crowded close to me and stared at me like we were the only two people on Earth. I'm not imagining this; it's clearly shown.

Our marriage doesn't look fake at all.

The chyron reads *Secret Wedding: Rex Roy married!*

Then it's back to footage of the press conference. They're not mentioning the Bondage Killer. Instead, the reporters are speculating about who will be in attendance at the engagement ball. They even include a quote from the chief, who is taking credit for our relationship. Nadia warned us he would, and she was right. And she must be good to be able to suppress the connection between the murders, the Bondage Killer, and me.

A click of ice in a whiskey glass warns me that Rex is approaching. "I'm sorry you had to go through that," he says.

I mute the TV. "Another perk of being a Roy?"

"The press will settle down. Nadia will reward the ones who behave and squash the others like a bug."

"I know." I face him, frowning. It feels like the ground is shifting beneath my feet, and I'm fighting to stay upright. At the same time, Rex is becoming the fixed point, my rock. He took control again and made himself a part of my world. But. . . I like it. And it's weirding me out.

"I'm going to find out who that reporter was. Bring him in for questioning."

I get a flash of insight—a greasy aura, nauseating green —but then it's gone. "Nadia won't like that."

"She won't ever know."

"Okay." I guess this is familiar ground for Rex, navigating between his public and private persona. I didn't realize how overwhelming it all would be.

It makes it that much more special that I'm the only one who sees all of him.

"You're upset." Rex moves closer, but there's still space between us, like the space he left between him and his ex-girlfriends.

Can I touch you? I smile to myself. He's being respectful. And now he's sensing me withdraw, as I always do in the face of strong feelings. But he can't stand it.

I have to be honest with him. It's hard, but I told myself I would try.

I motion to the TV, where an on-screen Rex cups my face over and over again. "I thought this was fake. You said it wasn't real."

"I lied."

My mouth falls open. He's half in shadow so I can't see his expression, but the way he sets down his drink makes me think he's getting ready to advance the offensive.

"I can't pretend it doesn't mean anything, Inara. It does mean something to me."

"You wanted to marry me," I whisper, testing it out. It feels like the Earth is shifting on its axis and Rex is keeping me grounded while everything else moves into place. "You wanted me as your wife. Admit it." It's half in hope, half a challenge.

"Gladly." He steps into the light, and I flinch at the savage yearning written on his face. "I want you any way I can get you. And if all I can do is mark you with my name, I'll do it."

He's not holding back, but I'm not afraid. "You meant every word of that threat. You'd kill anyone for me."

"Yes. If anyone seeks to harm you, their days are numbered." He reaches for me but doesn't let his hand cup my cheek. "I will protect you, and no power on Earth will stop me."

"Except me. I can stop you." I note his hand hovering in

the air. He's not touching me yet because I haven't given him permission.

He gives me a slow nod.

It's heady having this level of control over such a powerful man. "Because you want me. Not a controlled automaton version of me, a sex doll."

"Oh," he sighs, and I feel the full force of his longing. "I want to control you. I want to tie you up and feed you by hand. Fuck you hourly until you beg for relief, for an end to the orgasms, for a reprieve." We're facing each other, only a few inches between us, and I feel the heat of his desire. But I'm perfectly safe. He's taken all that glorious control and caged himself, all for me.

I lift a hand and let it hover in front of him. "Can I touch you?"

"Always. You don't need permission. Not with me."

I slide my hand over the expensive cotton of his shirt. He's removed his suit jacket, but the button-down does a good job of hiding the expanse of muscle underneath. The scars. "No one sees this side of you," I say mostly to myself. "No one but me. And that means something to you."

"Inara," he hesitates, but I catch it.

"Tell me."

"It's more than an obsession. What I feel for you." I sense that he's holding back, but not to hide from me. He doesn't want to scare me away.

"I feel it, too," I admit. "That's what scares me. That's why I run."

"I thought it was because you wanted me to chase you."

"Maybe I did." It's on the tip of my tongue to tell him that a part of me enjoyed being locked in his cage. "You were a good dom to me because you gave me what I needed. I need you to do that now."

His nostrils flare like a bull ready to charge. "I can do that. I can meet all of your needs. I want to. It's all I've ever wanted."

I remove my hand with a shaky sigh. This is what I want to hear, but I don't know.

"What do you need?" He's inviting me to let him in.

This is what I've been wondering since I escaped from Roy Manor. Is Rex capable of seeing me as an equal?

Am I just his possession? Or can we have a partnership?

Maybe the marriage was a declaration in more ways than one. To the world, it means he sees me as his, but he also sees me as someone worthy of the Roy name. He wants to be with me. That's why the marriage wasn't fake to him. He wants it to be forever.

He can't come right out and say how he feels. He has to show it through domination and control. But he does have feelings for me.

And I have feelings for him. He gives me everything I need. Safety, but a challenge. I even enjoy our fights. What did he say? *Arguing with you is better than fucking anyone else.* He gets the same thrill of the fight that I do.

Can we build a relationship on fights and sexy nights? Can the highs fix everything in between?

Can I take Rex Roy to be my lawfully wedded husband? Do I want to?

"I need to focus. I need you to help me catch the Bondage Killer." The question of not-so-fake marriage can wait until then.

"Then it's time for me to show you your wedding gift."

A gift? My heart lifts, even as I roll my eyes.

He goes to a door on the TV wall that I assumed was locked. He opens it and beckons for me to follow.

"What is this?" We enter a larger room, complete with

another lounge area and a minibar on the side. There's a huge entryway, an extra bathroom, and another bedroom beyond.

"Your rooms," he says. "If this is going to be your home base, you'll need the space." He glances back at me, his lips twisting into a smirk. "Or we can move to the honeymoon suite if you prefer." There's a mischievous twinkle in his dark eyes. "It is, after all, our honeymoon."

"Stop," I mutter, but the joke doesn't bother me. I feel lighter. "This will work. Thank you."

"Oh, this isn't your gift." He jerks his chin to another door, one that must lead to a bedroom. "Through there."

I pass him to open it. I have a psychic sense that something's waiting for me, something dangerous. A beast in a cave.

Then I open the door and see what Rex has done for me.

12

I *nara*

THE ROOM I enter isn't a bedroom. It's a situation room, complete with whiteboards, cork boards, and a state-of-the-art array of computers. In the center of the room, a round table holds stacks of files. There's one stamped "Confidential: Elyria Police Department."

"What is this?" I breathe. Rex hovers at my back.

"A place for you to work. Hamish had the original files couriered here."

I reach for the Elyria files and pause with my fingertips hovering over the folder. "NRPD needs these files."

"You can bring them in tomorrow morning if you wish. And there are the Blackbird files." He points to the murder book I requested at City Hall.

I'm looking at everything I need to put together the profile Bonds requested. This is huge.

I turn to Rex. He said I could touch him, but I'm still hesitant when I lay my hands on his chest. "You did all of this? For me?"

"I'd do anything for you." His face is a blank mask, but the heat smolders in his eyes.

I rise to tiptoe to touch my lips to his. He doesn't move except to lightly grip my elbows, steadying me. "Thank you," I whisper.

He kisses me back but lets me retreat. He's here to support me, protect me, but he's trying to give me space. Give me the freedom to fly.

My heart is soaring.

He inclines his head toward the table. "You want to catch him. Let's catch him."

My stomach turns over at the thought of the gruesome work ahead of me, but I nod. "Let's get to work."

REX

INARA PACES BACK AND FORTH. She's set up a wall of evidence by pinning things to the corkboard. We have the original files, but Hamish also had copies made of everything, and that's what Inara is putting on display. She'll bring the originals into the precinct tomorrow, but we'll have copies in this room.

I walk over to the wall and stare at the picture of the Bondage Killer. Dennis Bundy is a nondescript white male with a wiry but strong build.

"Alfie," I say, "give me the bio of Dennis Bundy."

The computer chimes and reads the file. Inara raises her head from her work when Alfie says, "Dennis Bundy worked in home security. He sold Guardian systems and oversaw their installation."

"That's how he cased his victim's homes," Inara puts in. "My father was worried about the recent murders in the area and called the security company for a consultation. That was the first time he was in our home." She's talking about her family, but her voice is as neutral as the computer's.

I've retreated to that cold space inside me, where nothing touches me. Most people wouldn't understand how I can compartmentalize like this. But Inara does because she's doing the same thing. We stare at the body of evidence like it's a thousand-piece puzzle we need to solve. Piecing together a picture we've never seen before.

"He was strong enough to overpower his victims," she continues. "And confident enough to put them on display."

"What else is in his profile?"

She reads from the document she's compiling. "White male, now aged sixty-two. No substance abuse. No mind altering drugs or medications. He was—is—intelligent and methodical. He loved the process. He took his time. He displays a psychopathic character style. What he lacks in empathy, he makes up for in narcissism. He believes he's better than others."

"Most serial killers have greater levels of narcissism," I say.

"Yes. Like most billionaires," she adds slyly.

My lips quirk, but now isn't the time for jokes. "His motivations?"

Inara lifts her head. "You've killed people. What do you think?"

I take her question in stride. "It's a compulsion. He was acting out a fantasy, one he'd rehearsed over and over." One board has a list of the Bondage Killer's original victims. "He was drawn to young girls or younger-looking women. He'd murder their parents or guardians and enact his sexual perversions on them."

Inara comes to stand beside me. "But not on me." Standing shoulder-to-shoulder with her feels right. Even though we're looking at the gruesome details of serial murder, it feels right.

"No. He spared you." I face her. "You have to acknowledge he's now fixated on you."

"The one that got away," she murmurs and moves to the next board. "In contrast, the Blackbird murders were simple. The killer isolated a single victim, incapacitated them, strangled them. No sexual contact, but he arranged the bodies afterward and left them on display along with a dead bird."

"Do you think Dennis Bundy also committed the Blackbird murders?"

She chews her lip. "I don't know. The timeline fits. But why would he change his MO so completely?" She murmurs the last part to herself, gazing off into the distance. "Death. Rebirth. BK was presumed dead in a fire that raged overnight. The warehouse was thought to have collapsed on him."

"How could he have survived?"

"There must have been a bolt hole of some sort. It would make sense for him to have an escape route planned. He knew the search was closing in. If he's alive, I want to know where he's been all this time."

"If he was wounded, he might have needed time to heal. Get medical care. Lie low."

"In addition to an escape route, he might have had friends. You know there are chat boards filled with his fans.

Sick minds, swapping fantasies."

"I do know," I say grimly. When I was a boy, I found those chat rooms and lurked long enough to learn a few things. I also worked on turning some of the worst offenders over to the authorities. I followed the cases and learned that money could buy a reduced sentence. After a few murderers proved to be so well-connected that they were let off without serving any hard time, I realized that there were better, more final ways to dispense justice.

I bow my head, reviewing the analysis Hamish sent over regarding the birds left at Inara's townhouse. Barn swallows, all of them. The same bird left at the last murder site.

And BK calls Inara *My Swallow.*

Inara is right. This is a clear tie to the Blackbird murders. But does that mean the Bondage Killer is Blackbird?

We need more evidence. The timeline fits; if BK survived the fire, he could have committed the Blackbird murders. Those murders all happened a few months after the warehouse fire. But then why did he stop killing for so many years? And why did he start again?

The hairs on the back of my neck prickle. I sense Inara staring at me and finally ask, "What is it?"

"Who was your first kill?" she blurts out.

I'M CAUGHT IN LIMBO, a place where time doesn't exist. This is how I get when I work on a case.

But Rex is here with me, and it occurs to me that if I

want to get into the mind of a murderer, I have one right here.

Rex raises his head to meet my stare. I sense the danger lurking in him, the violence barely leashed. "Who do you think?"

"The man who killed your family?" I guess.

"Actually, no, it wasn't the man who pulled the trigger. It was the man who ordered the hit. My father's business partner."

I come around the table to get closer to him. "What did you do to him?"

This is a strange conversation, but I don't know if Rex and I have ever had a normal one.

"Not much. I met him in an alleyway and shot him. Not my most satisfying kill."

"And not your last." I don't feel any pity for Rex's first victim. I'm guessing he was a wealthy man who thought himself above the law. "Did they tie you to the murder?"

"No. No one even knows he was behind the deaths. Back then, I was inexperienced. I lured him there with a text. I knew how to hide digital traces, even then. But I'd do it differently now."

I chew on this as he adds, "The man who pulled the trigger died in a gang altercation before I could get to him. In my search for him, I learned he was just a hired gun. He wasn't the mastermind. It wasn't until I killed the man behind the crime that justice was done."

Justice. Strange that Rex should use that word. We disagree on its meaning, which unsettles me, but not as much as the thought that by taking one life, he might have saved many.

People die in accidents every day. After my family died, I

tortured myself with what-ifs. What if Dennis Bundy had been hit by a drunk driver on his way to work before he became the Bondage Killer? Would his death result in the greater good? Would that absolve the drunk driver of manslaughter?

What is justice? What is its purpose? Is it better to kill one and save many, or better to avoid crossing that moral line?

Rex has made his choice. He's become a god, calling the shots. I don't like it, but I understand it. What better way to make sure nothing terrible ever happens to you again? You become all-powerful or as close to it as money and prestige can make you.

"Did it help?" I ask. Rex tilts his head, and I get the feeling that only he knows what I'm really asking.

What if the Bondage Killer was right here right now? Would I pull the trigger? Would I tell myself it's the best way of stopping him, of saving his future victims? Would I stick to my ideals, pull out my handcuffs and bring him in properly?

I can't even imagine touching him long enough to arrest him. But I can imagine standing over him once he's dead and reduced to a sack of meat.

It's horrifying and fascinating how quickly I can entertain thoughts of murder. I could blame it on Rex rubbing off on me, but my thoughts are my own, and if I'm honest, I've wished the gods had given me the power to strike a man dead on that fateful night BK came for my family. That's why I cling to the concept of justice. I know how easy it would be for me to cross a line.

"Did it help to kill the man who was behind my parents' murder?" Rex sounds thoughtful, like he's considering a hypothetical. "Yes, but not in the way you think. It helped to know that it would never happen again. But in some ways, it was worse."

"Why?"

"Because I learned something about myself in that alley. I enjoyed it, all of it. The hunt, the chase. The kill. I wanted to do it again." He pauses as if waiting on my reaction. Does he want me to act horrified?

When I simply nod, he asks, "Do you want to kill the Bondage Killer?"

Straight to the heart of the matter. I shift in my seat but stop when I realize I'm doing it and that it's giving away my unsettled state of mind. "I want justice."

Rex doesn't blink. "Do you want me to kill him?"

"I want him brought to justice," I reiterate, but at the moment, I can't tell him what that means. Rex narrows his eyes but says nothing. I have the uneasy feeling that he knows I want BK dead, but I can't bring myself to tell Rex not to kill him.

I return to my work. I'm trying to connect the Blackbird murders to the Bondage Killer, but it feels off. The Bondage Killer didn't select single victims. The Blackbird scenes were much more straightforward in composition.

I'm missing something.

I stand and stretch my aching back. In times like these, when I'm deep in a case and need release, I'd seek out a club and a scene partner. An anonymous meeting, a one-off to get me out of my head.

I can meet all of your needs. It's all I want. It's all I've ever wanted.

I can feel Rex's gaze on the back of my neck. He's been watching over me, vigilant as a dom. We're not in a scene, but Rex is so intense he probably thinks that every time we're together, it's a scene. He wants to exhort control over every moment.

And I want to let him.

I sigh and face him.

"What do you need?"

"I need a break," I say.

"Then let's take a break." He holds out a hand. He's been so careful to offer to lead rather than assume.

I take it and he leads me out of the dark situation room, back into the suite. I'm tense, waiting for him to snap and revert to the monster that wants to lock me away. So far, he's behaved himself, and I'm trying to give him a chance to earn back my trust.

The scent of butter and garlic hits me and makes my stomach gurgle. Rex must have called in someone to set up a table by the darkened windows. The food is ready, plated on fine china and covered by silver domes to keep it warm. Room service at its fanciest, except there are telltale red and white checkered placemats that tell me where the food is from.

"Oh my gods, you got Paisanos."

"Your favorite." He holds my chair out for me.

I waste no time digging into the food. Stuffed mushrooms, fresh rolls and bruschetta, fettuccine with prosciutto.

Rex inhales a huge steak and then sits back, watching me with a small smile on his face, as if it's satiating some need of his to watch me eat my food. My cheeks heat under the laser focus of his attention.

"You have to try this." I raise my fork, offering.

He leans in and lets me feed him a bite of pasta. His lips close over the fork, and I flush. Even though the act of feeding someone is dominant and the act of being fed submissive, I still feel like he's the one calling the shots, directing our roles. It makes me blush further.

His small smile says he notices my heated cheeks and knows the reason I'm blushing.

My phone vibrates, distracting me.

It's Silva.

Silva: Girl, you're married? To Rex Roy?

"Excuse me," I say to Rex and text Silva back.

Me: Long story

Silva: I heard Chief wants you to lead the 8 am debrief. Congrats

This is news to me. I check my email and sure enough, there's a summons for me to present my profile of the Bondage Killer at the early morning meeting. There's also an email from Bonds, gruffly welcoming me back to the case.

"What is it?" Rex asks, and I realize I'm grinning.

"I'm back on the case."

"Congratulations."

My smile fades when I realize my connection to Rex is what got me reinstated. "Nepotism at its finest, I guess."

"You earned it," he says, and he's right. I wish my own merits would have earned my place, but it's not a perfect world, and I'll take what I can get.

I imagine myself walking in tomorrow and swiping my badge that reads "Inara Roy." How is this my life?

Not to mention that I'll be dropped off by a personal driver and escorted to the door of the police station by two huge guys with skull rings.

Which reminds me of what Silva said earlier about Fraternitas.

"Do you have gang members guarding me?"

"I'm told that Kaiser and Jaeger are the best."

Kaiser and Jaeger must be the identical hulks. I make a note of their names. "Won't people be upset that an NRPD detective has criminals acting as her bodyguards?"

"The press knows not to talk about Fraternitas. No one will mention them at all."

I blanch. "Because they feel threatened?"

Rex shrugs. "Bribes, threats, favors, St. James deploys them all."

"Oh, that makes me feel better." I roll my eyes. "Wait, St. James is part of Fraternitas?"

Rex nods, and I throw up my hands. "Well, that's just wonderful."

Rex

I LEAN BACK in my chair, savoring the moment, drinking her in. I like that I'm the one to explain the intricacies of my city to her. "He doesn't wear his ring all the time because he's become the public face of the brotherhood. The business side, anyway."

"Good to know," she mutters, stabbing her fork into her pasta. "Now I know dwhy the ring looked familiar. I got a debrief about the criminal activity in NRPD as part of my orientation."

"Fraternitas is less a criminal organization and more an essential cog in the city's wheel that happens to step outside the bounds of the law from time to time."

"Like a corporation." She shoves a forkful of pasta into her mouth and chews, glaring at me balefully.

"Exactly."

She speaks with her mouth full, still glaring. "Like you."

"I'm more than just a cog."

"You're a pain in my ass," she mutters.

I tilt my head. "I can be. But I think you like pain in your ass."

"My gods," she mutters. I chuckle, and she grabs a dinner roll and throws it at my head. I catch it and take a bite so it doesn't go to waste.

She must be feeling better if she's goofing off like this. I love being silly with her. She seemed to have accepted her change in marital status. "This is nice, isn't it? Having dinner after work."

She grunts, unwilling to admit how much fun she's having. *Challenge accepted.* I reach for a final plate on the nearby rolling cart and present her with the last part of our meal—a large slice of tiramisu.

This turns out to be a mistake. Inara licking into a thick layer of mascarpone is more erotic than anything I've seen. I grip the edge of the table as she practically licks the plate clean. I display admirable restraint, but it takes all my control not to pounce on her.

Finally, she pushes her plate back with a sigh.

"Better?"

"Much. Thank you." One last swipe of her tongue over her plump lips. I have to turn away for a moment to get a hold of myself. My cock is painful in my pants.

I never knew a simple dinner with someone could feel like a rollercoaster, but this is as good as a scene. The high of connection. The lows of denial. The razor edge of need and the lightness when I hold the space for my partner to truly be herself.

I'm smiling when I face her again.

"What?" she asks, looking confused at my grin.

"Thank you for dining with me."

She looks uncertain. "I should be thanking you for feeding me."

My heart softens. She's trying to let me in. "My pleasure."

Her forehead wrinkles further like she's at war with herself. I stay silent, letting her wrestle with her feelings.

"Will you. . . will you stay with me? Spend the night, I mean."

Triumph. My patience and restraint paid off. "Always."

~

INARA

HE SLEEPS NAKED. Because, of course, he does.

After a shower to wash off the day, I come out of the bathroom wrapped in a towel, and he's already stretched out on the bed, lounging under the covers. He looks like the king of the castle, a warrior resting after winning the war.

He did win, I guess. And I'm okay with it because I'm aligning myself with him. Working with him instead of against him. It'll be nice to be on the winning team.

I return to the bathroom to dress in a short, navy blue nightgown trimmed with nude lace. I take the time to blow dry and brush my hair. I'm suddenly nervous about this. Like a virgin bride on her wedding night. I drop the brush and laugh at my reflection in the mirror.

It's just Rex. He's behaving. And it's more convenient to let him hang around than go out and seek a stranger.

I'm used to grueling nights like these. Working a case and handling the murder book and files always sends me to a dark place. That's why I would visit a sex club to break up the feelings. The impact play would give me the release I needed. Pain followed by an endorphin rush. It would be temporary, but it would help.

But whenever I'm in the thick of it, I can't escape the case. It would follow me home and haunt my dreams. It wasn't all bad. My subconscious would process the details and the answers could come to me in my dreams. More often than not, I've broken cases by waking up with the puzzle worked out.

Tonight will be no different, except this time, I won't be alone. It's a novel thought, one that makes me eager to climb into bed. I hesitate before sliding into the covers.

"I don't know if I'm up for anything tonight," I tell Rex.

"You should sleep," he murmurs. "You need rest."

He's right.

I curl up on my side, facing away from him. My back prickles. I'm acutely aware that there's a giant dom in my bed. My body is desperate for his warmth.

"Thank you for getting me Lacy's murder book," I say into the dark.

"You're welcome."

"I actually found it years ago when I was staying with Lacy. She was in the kitchen, and I snooped in her bookcases." I remember pulling the book onto my lap, and a loose piece of paper fluttered to the floor. It was a picture of my family. Teenage me had stopped breathing.

"That must have been hard."

I try to recall the feelings, but they're distant and muted

as if recalling the memories and talking about them put them firmly in the past. "It was, but I was also fascinated. I wanted to see how she solved the case. But it hurt, too. Like touching a live wire. It was a shock, but. . . I wanted it?" I don't know how to explain it, so I try again. "I wanted the pain."

"Like picking a scab. It hurts, but not as bad as the original wound. It's proof you survived."

"Yes," I say, smiling in surprise. It's amazing to have Rex understand me so perfectly. It unlocks something in me and makes me feel free. "That's exactly it. But then Lacy found me reading it and was horrified. She took it away."

"Is that when you wanted to become a detective?"

"I guess. I kept snooping. She wasn't supposed to bring those notes home, but she did. She worked on them constantly. And then, one day, I helped her solve a case."

"How?"

I grin to myself. I remember the moment so clearly. "I snooped again. It was a murder, and everyone thought the husband did it. He had no alibi. But then I—" My smile fades as I realize I'll have to tell him that I had a vision. I haven't told him about those yet.

I'm not ready to reveal that side of myself to him.

"I, uh, had a feeling that it was the neighbor. I told Lacy, and she followed my hunch and broke the case."

"How old were you?"

"Fifteen. I was in foster care at the time, but Lacy had me over for visits on the regular."

"She could tell you had a gift."

"Yes," I say carefully. Interesting choice of words, and too close to the truth for my comfort. "She got me a job with a private investigator she trusted, and I did so well that I decided to go to the Academy." I stop talking because

I've just told Rex more about my past than I've told anyone.

But somehow, it doesn't seem so heavy sharing secrets this way. They're just whispers in the dark.

I ponder this. It's nice to share things with Rex. Nicer than I thought it'd be. Especially because he's not pushing me to tell him more.

I hear him shifting in bed like he wants to reach for me, but he won't allow himself to transgress the boundaries he set between us. He's a tamed beast. Knowing that makes me want him more.

Finally, I give in. "You can touch me," I say, and smile when I hear him move. As soon as his arms close around me, I'm able to let go and drift.

Heat sears my face. I'm surrounded by a shower of sparks. An invisible wall of pressure hits me, and I'm falling into darkness. Someone's murmuring over me in a voice that sounds like Burgess.

"A shame," he says over and over again. "A shame about her. . ."

I come awake, still feeling like I'm falling. The dark bedroom is still, but shadows crawl in the corners of my vision.

I sit up, but it doesn't quite break the spell.

"Inara," Rex says. I feel his hand hover at my back. "I'm going to touch you."

I bob my head and relax against his hand. My muscles are tight, like I've been locked in a tight box. He rubs my back like a parent soothing a child who just had a nightmare.

"What do you need?" Rex rumbles.

This is about when I would do a scene. Something to bring me back to reality, to make me feel again. I wouldn't be able to cry, but hurting on the outside would be a relief and a release in itself.

But. . . I'm not ready for Rex to be completely in charge. I'm still afraid he'll consume me.

"Put your hands behind your back," I tell him, just to test him to see what he'd do. It's too dark to see more than the outline of him, but I sense his shifting movements. Very slowly, he puts his hand behind his back. The muscles of his shoulders bunch and then smooth.

He waits like that. I don't think anyone has ever seen him look so vulnerable. Maybe I really do have control over him.

"Now what?" he asks after a long pause.

"I'm not sure." We laugh together, and it's a soft, lovely sound.

"Lights on, lowest setting," he commands, and the lamps on either side of the bed brighten the barest amount.

"You can touch me," he says. I lean closer, intrigued. "Take your finger and trace my lips," he instructs. "Do it slowly."

"You can't dom me without touching me," I say, running my index finger over the shape of his mouth.

He raises a brow.

He's telling me what to do, but his hands are still behind his back, so I grow bolder, rubbing my thumb over his plush lips. His breathing grows heavy.

I sense the subtle changes in his body, too. A tautness to

his physique that wasn't there before. "Are you aroused just from this?"

"I'm always aroused around you."

I slide my hand down his chest, and his heavy muscles quiver under my palms. His body is a work of art. His abs are chiseled from concrete. I dip my hand under the covers to take him in hand, and he hisses. His cock swells in my grip.

"Do you want to come?"

"It's your decision," he whispers.

The power he's handing me is heady, but it feels wrong. I shake my head. "Tell me what to do."

"Is that an order?" There's a smile in his voice, and it annoys me. I want him to stop asking me things so I can relax.

"Yes."

"Then jack me off, slowly."

I wet my lips and obey.

REX

HER SLENDER FINGERS move up and down my shaft. In the low light, I can tell her eyes are heavy. She seemed frustrated when I tried to give her the reins, but the more I tell her what to do, the easier she breathes.

Her submission is heady. Blood pools in my groin, making it hard to think. "That's it, beautiful."

She licks her lips again, giving me another clue. "Do you want to taste me?"

A small nod.

"You'll have to be good and not use your hands."

Gods, she obeys so sweetly. Her mouth closes over me, and I grow light-headed with the sensation. Her breasts hang down, adorned with lace. She looks like a goddess, worthy of worship. It's overwhelming to watch her work to please me.

"You're being so good for me." I fight the urge to jerk my hips and thrust deeper into her mouth. "I'm going to touch you now." I pause, but she doesn't stop bobbing her head in an easy rhythm.

I gather her dark, silky hair away from her face. I can't help but control her head a little, increasing the speed, but she closes her eyes and sucks harder, so I know she's okay. I'm entering dom space, where I'm attuned to every flutter of her eyelashes, every deep inhale she takes through her nose. I want to continue this scene, coaxing her deeper until she's floating in subspace and I have total control.

She'll sleep well tonight. I'll make sure of it.

I tug her hair a little, enough to make her scalp sting. A little pressure on the back of her head and she takes my cock deeper. "Gods, you're perfect for me."

She shifts on the bed, growing restless.

"Are you wet for me, little sub? Do you need me to stroke you?"

Her lashes lift, and she pleads with me through her gaze.

I need to tread carefully. I don't want to take more than she wants to give. I've crossed too many lines. Going slowly now is how I regain her trust.

But then she curls her tongue around my shaft, and my hips rise. I fuck her mouth in short strokes, bringing myself to the edge. She's soft in my grip, letting me use her for my release.

So fucking beautiful.

I pull her off me before I come. Her mouth falls open, lax, and a string of saliva hangs from her puffy lower lip.

"My sweet submissive." I swipe my thumb over her mouth, collecting the spit. "You've earned a reward."

"You didn't come."

"You don't worry about that. I'll use you as I see fit." I fist her hair and draw her down where I want her, lying on her back, nestled in the pillows with her legs splayed.

I settle between them, lifting her foot to kiss the arch and make her toes curl. I kiss the inside of her knee and nuzzle my way up her inner thigh.

"Oh gods," she groans when I kiss her mons.

She's fresh and sweet and dripping for me. She shaved tonight, too. It might be her preference, but I'd like to think it was for me.

I settle in to lick her until she's squirming. Then I hold her thighs down and lick her some more. "So sweet." I want to live between her legs.

"Rex," she pants. Her feet scrabble on my back. I want her lost to reason, acting on instinct, wild. She's close but not there yet.

"Put your hands on my head. Pull my hair when you want to come." Her nails scrape against my scalp, and it's the best thing I've ever felt.

I push up the silky fabric of her night dress over her lower belly, sink two fingers deep into her channel, and tease her clit with my tongue. The perfume of her arousal rises around me. She loves this.

Her legs start to shake, and she's about to rip out my hair when I raise my head. "You don't come for me until I say."

"Oh," she sighs.

I spread her open further and drag my tongue lower down, teasing between her ass cheeks. My cock is pulsing with the need to be inside her, but the pain is its own sort of pleasure. A sign of my control.

I slow down, eating her more lazily until we're both covered in a fine sheen of sweat. Working us both up so the fall will be farther.

"I could do this all night," I murmur. "Would you like that? I could tie you down and eat you out until you're begging nonstop. Then make you come over and over until you're so sensitive, every orgasm is torture."

She moans, and I swirl my tongue around her engorged clit. "But not tonight. Tonight, I'll go easy on you. You're going to come for me, Inara, and then you're going to sleep." I need her to rest deeply, undisturbed by dreams. I'd give all my wealth to buy her a night of unbroken sleep.

I lick her until she's shaking. "Do you need a little pain?"

She nods.

"Ask me, then."

"Please. Please hurt me."

"Like this?" I slap her between her legs.

Her head jerks back, and her body writhes, tantalizing under her silk nightie. "Yes," she sighs to the ceiling.

My hand is wet from her sex. I use it to jerk off, stopping when the base of my spine tingles.

Then I slap her again. She rocks from side to side, keening.

Then I close my fingers around her clit and pinch it, hard. She almost levitates off the bed, but when I let go, she starts shaking.

"Come for me now." I thrust in three fingers this time, stretching her to the point of pain, and that does it. Her sex ripples around me. I could come from this alone. Only years of practiced control keep me from spurting onto the bedspread. "Oh, Inara. You're so beautiful when you take pain for me."

I lean in and lap up her essence. She reaches for me, and this time, I gather her wrists and pin them to the bed. More cream pours out of her, making me groan. I have to stop and rise to kneel over her, offering my cock to her mouth.

"I'm going to come." She takes me in, takes me deep.

She's so small under me, I have to be careful. But then she strokes her tongue on the underside of my dick, worshipping me. I release her wrists, and she raises her hands and grips my ass, urging me deeper. Her sharp little nails dig into my muscles, and I lose it. My climax ripples up my back, my body going numb with an overload of pleasure. I slide deeper into her mouth and give her my cum, spurt after spurt. I withdraw quickly so I don't choke her. But she swallows it all.

"Good girl. Such a good girl." I pull out and move back down her body, finding her hot, wet cunt and fastening my mouth over it, palming her ass and lifting her up so I can devour her. I want her to come a few more times until she's wrung out and half-conscious. Then I'll hold her in my arms and watch over her until morning, ready to soothe her if she has another bad dream.

13

I *nara*

What a difference a day makes. I walked into work this morning with a bounce to my step. Because of Rex, I'm well rested, and my sex is sated and only a little sore.

Today, my keycard works just fine. Chief Jordan is waiting to escort me to the situation room. Instead of feeling uncomfortable, I ignore the stares and walk to the front to present my profile. It doesn't matter how I got the attention; I have a platform, and I'm going to use it.

Bonds is in the far corner, studying me with narrowed eyes. I raise my chin and he gives me a wry smile.

Then, I present my findings. I cover the history of the Bondage Killer and his MO. "He's organized. Displays signs of psychopathy. He has no empathy for his victims. But he was regarded as competent by his coworkers." I outline his crimes in the barest of details. "He was presumed dead, but his body was never recovered. And I have reason to believe he's back."

I pause to click through a slide deck of the letters left at my townhouse. In the back of the room, Silva sidles in and salutes me with his to-go cup. His encouragement helps, and I breeze through the disturbing details of the Bondage Killer's obsession with me.

"I believe he was surveilling me." I pause on the letter that rants about how I belong to him. "He saw me interact with a male acquaintance," I recite dispassionately, "and wrote this letter in response." I take a sip of water and move on to show pictures of the dead birds left at my apartment.

The room is dead silent as I describe the scene findings by a "private contractor hired by the department to assess the scene." Rex and I already ran this past Chief Jordan and got permission retroactively.

"Now, there might be a link between two unsolved cases and BK's activity." I click through slides of the Blackbird murders. "The MO is different, but the unsub left the same signature—a dead bird—at the scene."

"You think Dennis Bundy was responsible for the Blackbird murders?" Bonds interrupts.

"I don't have any evidence to support this. But the timeline fits. He could've moved to New Rome after escaping the warehouse fire."

No one says the obvious. That he's killing women who look like me because he's hyper-focused on the one victim who got away.

I finish and let Bonds take over debriefing the room.

"How do we know this is the Bondage Killer?" Burgess pushes to the front of the room to ask. "Could be a copycat."

"We'll pursue all lines of inquiry, but for now, we're

going to operate as if it is him," Bonds deflects and gives us our orders. I note that Burgess is assigned a job, but I'm not.

After Bonds admonishes us not to leak anything to the press, the chief gives a few vague words meant to inspire or some shit, and then the meeting is adjourned.

I head out quickly, wanting to avoid Burgess.

Silva falls into step beside me. "Great job in there. But damn, chica, you're right in the middle of this again."

I shrug.

"At least you have a rich husband to soothe your pain." He winks at me.

"No comment." I bite back a smile.

"Ah, ah, not so fast. I suppose you think you can buy off my curiosity with this." He holds up his cup. "This morning, my favorite vendor told me I have unlimited chai. For life. And I know I have you to thank."

I can't suppress my grin any longer. "You're welcome."

"I knew it," he crows. "Apparently, the whole department is getting new computers. Someone has a black credit card and isn't afraid to use it. I figured it was you."

"Good sleuth work." Inara Ramos had nothing to her name, but Mrs. Roy does. I can pretend to be her long enough to spend some of those billions. If Rex has a problem with it, then he shouldn't have given me access to his fortune.

But the way he preened when he presented me with a new Roy Bank card this morning, I bet he likes it when I spend his money. Makes him feel like I'm accepting our marriage. He probably enjoys tracking every purchase I make. The megalomaniac.

Silva peels off, leaving me feeling good. I like being able to give gifts to the people in my life. I have something epic in mind for Mina, if only I can find her.

I take a moment to send messages to a few of Mina's handles on different chat forums we used to use. There's no answer, but one of them might reach her. I'm sure Rex kept his word and backed off from tormenting her, but I haven't heard from her since she went radio silent. I hope she's okay.

While I was leading the meeting, I missed a call from Lacy Collins.

I remember all the things I said to Rex about her last night and feel a little buzzed that she's called on the heels of that conversation. It's like I conjured her.

After a second of hesitation, I hit play on the voicemail she left. I haven't heard her voice in so long, and just the sound of her saying my name sends a pang through my heart.

"Inara, it's good to hear from you." There's no mention of how I've cut off contact for years. No guilt trip. I still feel the guilt, but it's muted because of her compassion. "After I got your message, I was contacted by a Hamish Hitchcock. I verified that he's acting on your behalf"—there's a touch of a smile in her voice, like she knows I'm married—"and sent him my case notes. I hope they're helping you." There's a pause, and her voice softens. "I'm sorry this is happening. I failed you." Her breathing catches, and my heart almost stops with the pain that underlies her words. Another pause, and her voice steadies, growing stronger. "But I know you'll make it right. You're going to nail him."

I clutch my phone to my chest, reeling. I should've listened to this voicemail at night, in private, when it'd be another secret in the dark. There are tears pricking my eyes, and I'm in the bullpen surrounded by hardened detectives who lost the ability to cry decades ago. I need to hold it together.

The pain in my chest expands, making it hard to breathe. I hunch over, willing myself to stay upright.

I failed you.

I know why she feels this way. I feel it, too.

It's the same way Rex feels about his own parents' murders. That he should've stopped it. We both should've been bigger, stronger, faster, smarter.

I should've done something that night to stop the Bondage Killer.

It doesn't make sense to feel this way, but I do.

You're going to nail him. She sounds so certain. She's always believed in me.

For some reason, that makes me want to cry even more.

I somehow make my way to my desk and sink into my chair. The room is busy with people, but only Burgess notices me. He frowns in my general direction but doesn't say anything before going back to his work.

I bow my head like I'm thinking and try to get a hold of myself. My psychic senses are screaming, trying to tell me something, so I dampen them a moment. I feel like I'm moving through water.

Breathe. Just breathe. The small, encouraging voice in my head sounds like Rex. It helps.

I'm going to nail him. My mentor is right. This time, the thought doesn't make me want to cry. It makes me want to work.

But then I look at my desk and realize what someone has left for me.

There's a worn book in front of me with a familiar image on the cover—a pattern of birds in flight. I haven't seen it in years and yet I recognize it right away. It's my journal from years ago. I know without looking that it's filled with my childish scrawl.

I remember my mother giving it to me, explaining the origins of my name.

Swallow. After she gave me the journal, I learned more about the birds. The knowledge stayed with me, lurking in my subconscious, so when it was time to choose a submissive moniker, I chose that word. *Little bird.*

My Swallow. This is why the Bondage Killer called me that in his letters to me. I can only hope he didn't discover my visits to Empire. Just thinking of him obsessing over my sex life makes me feel like I've bathed in a cesspit.

Don't spiral. Think. This is evidence. A clue. A sign the killer was able to infiltrate the department. His message is clear: nowhere is safe.

I have a sudden, wild thought: *I want Rex.* I imagine him here, standing with me, reminding me to breathe. He'd take over and eventually would go too far and annoy me, but he'd be a safe, solid presence. A powerful force on my side.

I look around, but there's no sign of anyone who might have left this.

"Burgess?" I call.

He raises his head so quickly that I get the feeling he was paying too close attention to me even before I called his name.

I point to the journal. "Do you know who put this on my desk?"

"Yeah, some guy from the press. He wanted to hang around to speak to you, but the desk sergeant made him leave. He said his name was Ted."

"When was this?"

He shrugs. "Half an hour ago."

This is it—confirmation that the Bondage Killer is responsible for the recent killings. He picked up this journal the night he came into my room. And now he's left it for me.

Slowly, gingerly, I pick up the journal, and a picture falls out.

It's a picture of my family. I stare at the smiling faces, and chills run through me. Every face has an X over it except one.

Mine.

~

REX

I'M BEGINNING to think that giving Inara her own private situation room was a mistake. Ever since Hamish delivered Detective Lacy Collins's notes, my beautiful wife has been holed up for days, staring at the walls of evidence for hours on end. She goes into the precinct for a few hours each day. Her team of bodyguards reports that she's visited the most recent crime scenes a few times, although the detail makes it difficult to do the sort of boots-on-the-ground police work she prefers.

I've stopped sending Jaeger and Kaiser out with her. I didn't tell her that St. James was the one who insisted on them being her main bodyguards rather than having a more traditional team. I think he was afraid I'd steal her away.

All that's changed now. As a Roy, Inara has a security detail a mile deep. Everywhere she goes, she gets media attention, which effectively restricts her movements as much as a cage.

Despite the police's best efforts, word got out about the connection between the recent murders and the ones in Elyria. The news has run constant stories about the Bondage Killer.

Nadia's been able to keep Inara out of the news. She's offered a bigger, better sacrifice: Me. There have been whole news spreads about "the last scion of the Roys." She even let them cover my threats to the press.

"Rex Roy billionaire shouts threats at press conference," read the headlines. One publication ran a long article on "the violent history of the Roy family" that included stories about my boot-legging great-grandfather and our warrior ancestors. Because Nadia gave them access to the Roy family records, it actually wasn't bad. Mostly accurate. I figure I can give it to Inara as an overview if she's ever curious about the family she married into.

If anything, painting me as a raging monster helps my image. Society allows all sorts of bad behavior from billionaires. Not that I give a damn. My reputation, my money, none of it matters. I only care about Inara.

And she's fading.

I've tried tempting her to leave the room for meals, sleep. . . a shower. Not even a tray of desserts delivered fresh from Paisanos was enough to get her to eat.

I've found her sleeping in the room, slumped over the table as if she'd worked so long her head was too heavy for her to hold up any longer. Each time, I've carried her to bed, but she's restless, tossing and turning.

Lack of sleep and not enough food has made her hollow-eyed. Lovely but haunted, a stunning statue worn by time.

I enter the situation room where she's hunched over the murder book Detective Collins sent her. The room seems too dark for her to read, so I command the lights to brighten.

Inara blinks and straightens but doesn't look at me.

I stand behind her, trying not to pace. I feel like a sailor's wife on a widow's walk, staring out to sea, hoping my loved one will come home.

"How's it going?" I ask, more to break the silence than anything.

"I'm close, Rex. He's taunting me."

"I know." I settle my hands on her shoulders, massaging them. I feel the same frustration. He's been here all this time, yet Fraternitas has turned up nothing. Neither has Victor, the silent assassin.

Her muscles are rocks under my hands. "We'll get him."

"Did you find Ted?"

"Not yet." Inara gave me a lead to track down, one that could lead us right to the killer.

Her partner Burgess told her a guy named Ted had delivered the latest evidence to her. When pressed, Burgess described the man as white, middle-aged, and skinny but with a gut. "A real 'loser' type, ya know?"

We've tracked down every reporter in the city named Theodore, Thaddeus, or just plain Ted and interviewed them. Even the ones that match the description claim that they've never seen the journal before. We've dug into their lives and studied their digital footprints and journalistic history, but so far, we've found nothing.

I tell Inara this, and she sighs. "I guess it was a long shot."

"Hamish is compiling a line-up of photos. We'll run it by Burgess and see if he can ID anyone."

She lets out a bleak laugh. "If he can, it'll be the first time he's ever helped on an investigation in his life."

I hate hearing her sound so defeated. "Do you want me to ruin his life? Drain his bank accounts, destroy his credit?"

"No. He's probably doing that all on his own."

I give a grim smile because Burgess does seem like the type whose karmic punishment is having to live his own life.

"What about the Blackbird murders? Any leads there?"

"No. I think it's a different killer, but I can't put my finger on it. The killer was careful. He left no DNA evidence, which makes me think he knew how to clean a crime scene. He wore gloves. He might have kept them on his person."

"Along with a dead bird."

She huffs. "I guess."

"Why birds?"

"I don't know. It could have religious or symbolic significance. But nothing else in the scene points to that." She worries her lip, lost in her thoughts.

I lay a hand on her shoulder, and my mood lifts when Inara turns toward me.

"Come. You need sleep."

"You're not going to threaten to tie me to the bed?"

It's a good sign that she's joking about this. "That can be arranged."

"I guess there are worse fates. It's not punishment if I like it, right?"

She lets me pull her out of the chair but curls into me. It's less of a hug and more of a collapse. I keep my touch light on her back, sensing how fragile she is. My little bird. I wonder if she'll ever allow me to call her that again.

"I'm missing something. I know it. Usually, I can see—" She cuts herself off. I wait, but she doesn't expound.

There's something she's not telling me. I want her to tell me, but I don't want to push it. Another thing for me to file under *Inara's Secrets.*

"I have instincts, I suppose," she says. "It's a part of profiling—getting inside the killer's head. But I don't want. . ."

It wasn't much of a guess to realize that part of Inara's gift is that she's able to sink into a madman's psyche. Drown in the darkness. I can understand why she wouldn't want to do that with the man who killed her family.

"It's all right. Let me help," I say. "I'll do anything to help."

"I wish you could. But. . ." She hesitates so long it's like she's gone somewhere else.

"Inara?"

She leans on me. "Just be with me. That'll be enough."

*I*NARA

REX IS WORRIED ABOUT ME. I know it.

I've retreated into myself, into that dark, solitary place where I've lived for so long.

He can't save me. No one can.

He doesn't know the secrets I've kept for my whole life. I long to tell him but can't get the words out. It's like I'm swimming in the ocean, getting plowed under the surf, but every time I break to the surface, I'm buried under another wave.

At least there have been no more deaths. Which also means no more clues, either. BK has a pattern of taking breaks between kills. At least according to the notes Lacy sent over. I pore over her murder book, practically memorizing each page.

The two most recent murders have different MOs, one in the BK style and one in the Blackbird style. Is it two serial killers? Or a copycat emulating both?

All I know is that BK is involved somehow, and he's not finished. There will be more bodies.

I'm holding my breath, waiting for the next horror to break. Meanwhile, for everyone else, life goes on. The papers are still covering Rex's secret nuptials. Fortunately, they seem to be more fixated on him and his wealthy family than me.

So far, being married to him hasn't been so bad. I'm under more scrutiny, but I have all the security money can buy. I can't move around as easily, but I don't want to, and until BK is behind bars, it would be wise for me to accept those extra layers of protection. I do feel safer.

And since we called a truce, Rex has done everything he can to support me. He gave me a situation room stocked with everything related to the case, a detective's dream. No criminal department is this well-funded.

We didn't say vows to each other, but he seems to be with me for better or worse. And right now, it's worse.

14

I *nara*

"I HAVE A SURPRISE FOR YOU," Rex tells me. We're in a limo, riding to our engagement ball. He's in a tux, and I'm in the most beautiful gown ever sewn.

"More jewelry?" I'm already wearing a fortune in yellow diamonds. One of the largest and rarest in the world is on display on the necklace around my neck. It's heavy. Feels like a leash more than anything.

"No. I think you'll like this surprise." He holds up a phone. A second later, it lights up, displaying an incoming call from *KittyBang*.

I grab the phone and answer it. "Mina?"

"Bitch, you got married?"

"Yes." My laugh is faint, but it is a laugh. It's so good to hear her voice. "How are you? Are you safe?"

"I'm good. Got your messages. But then *he* reached out."

The drop in the volume of her voice tells me she means Rex. "Is he there?"

"Yes. But don't worry. I'm not letting him listen in." I turn and narrow my eyes at Rex, warning him off. He raises a brow, looking suave in his tux.

"He's probably recording this call anyway." Mina doesn't sound fussed, though. She sounds almost. . . relaxed.

"I won't let him touch you," I say.

"You've got to tell me what is going on. I go on the run, and next thing I know, you're marrying the richest man on Earth. And then he's messaging me and offering me a position in cybersecurity—"

He what? This is news to me.

"And telling me you need my help tracking down a serial killer. He's already sent me files, and you know I'd do anything for you—"

"Mina," I interrupt, because when she gets like this, her mind racing like a runaway train, she doesn't take a breath. "Are you saying you're working for Rex?"

"I haven't taken the job. But if you vouch for him—"

"I do. And, yes, I do need your help with. . . everything."

"Then I'm your kitty. It's good to hear from you."

"You too." I don't want to stop talking, but we're almost to the grand building where we're hosting our ball.

"I'll be in touch. Strange, but not a stranger." Before I can say goodbye, she hangs up.

I give the phone back to Rex, noting that it's a high tech looking model but nondescript. Probably a burner. Mina would approve.

"Did you like your gift?" he purrs, pocketing the burner.

"I did, thank you. I was worried about her. She's. . ." *The closest thing I have to a friend.* "Important to me."

"I figured. You don't allow many people to get close to you."

"We're not close—"

He looks at me, and I squirm under his all-knowing gaze. I feel like I'm in therapy, getting dissected. "All right. She's. . . a friend." It's hard for me to say that word. I've taken pains to keep anyone I care about at arm's length and out of the danger zone. "We've never met in person, though." I felt safer connecting with Mina because she's also the private, standoffish sort.

"You can change that. When you're ready." He picks up my hand and kisses my knuckles. My heart warms. I like the idea of having friends. It's too dangerous to let someone in for long, but it's a nice thought, and the fact that Rex supports it makes me happy.

"What about you?" I ask. "Do you have any close friends?"

"Define 'close.' Define 'friend.'"

Good grief. Rex needs therapy as much as I do. We've both isolated ourselves.

I remember an article I read on friendship. "Someone you could get a beer with. Someone you'd allow to watch your puppy." The article said the closest friend would be someone who could do both.

"I drink whiskey. And I have staff overseeing my kennels."

I roll my eyes. "You know what I mean." I file away the fact that Roy Manor does have a dog house. Next time Rex annoys me, I'll tell him to go sleep there.

"I don't have friends; I have business partners. I drink with them."

"No one you'd go bowling with?" I tease. "Like St. James?"

"St. James and I have similar interests, but I'm not interested in him being present for my preferred hobby."

His dark eyes heat, and so do my cheeks. I press my thighs together, feeling the flush travel downwards as I think about the private room at Empire where Rex indulged in his preferred hobby with me.

The limo rounds a corner and pulls up to the front of the building. There's a crowd in front, held back from the red carpet by a long line of security.

"We're here." I square my shoulders like a soldier facing a line of enemy troops.

"Hey. Look at me." He doesn't use his dom voice, but he captures my full attention all the same. "I'm going to get you through this. We'll go inside, talk to some people, and drink champagne. None of this matters."

Staring into his beautiful face, I can almost believe him.

A shadow falls over the car door. A whole troop of security guards surround the limo, ready to escort us inside.

"One more thing." Rex doesn't seem to care that people are waiting for us and pulls a black velvet jewelry box out of his pocket. "You need this."

I know what's inside. *A rock the size of Antarctica.* But when he opens the box, I'm still dazzled. The ring is somehow delicate despite blazing with multiple gems. The center jewel is yellow, and it's surrounded by smaller diamonds and gold and shaped into a vine-like pattern. There's a floral quality to the design.

"What's this?" I touch the large yellow stone.

"It's a rare diamond. The color reminded me of jasmine." My favorite flower.

"Nadia will approve." I let him slide the ring onto my finger. The weight of it makes things feel more real.

"Ready, wife?"

I nod and let him guide me into the fray.

An hour later, I'm lurking in the shadows near the grand white columns that line the huge hall. A wallflower at my own party.

Nadia and her team outdid themselves. The ballroom looks like a garden. Huge, wild bouquets with plenty of yellow jasmine adorn the space. The Roy crest is everywhere. There are huge white plinths topped with statues of roaring lions, for the gods' sake. It's a spectacle, but somehow it all works.

I let Rex steer me around, greeting people. He knows everyone. He's pretty popular for someone who claims to have no friends.

Unfortunately, I understand why he wanted a detailed description of what I meant by 'friend.' Everyone here wants a piece of him because he's wealthy and powerful. Not because he's Rex.

Now he's holding court in the middle of the room, sipping whiskey and speaking in a booming voice loud enough to draw the attention of everyone in the room. I have a feeling he's doing it on purpose to let me slip away for a moment.

Gods, I hope I don't have to get used to occasions like this. I'm overwhelmed, surrounded by all the glitz and glamor of New Rome's upper crust. Fortunately, unless I'm on Rex's arm, no one notices me. If it weren't for the bodyguards shadowing my every move, I could slip away entirely. For now, standing behind a plinth is the best I can do.

I think I've successfully hidden when Hamish appears at my side.

"Detective," he greets me.

I'm not happy that I'm found, but at least it's Hamish and

not the chief of police. "Please, call me Inara. You might as well. We're practically related now."

"Inara, then. Welcome to the family. You look lovely."

"Thank you." My dress is custom, a shimmering gold fabric that makes my skin glow. Even I can admit that I look like a goddess. If I have to be stuck in a room full of the rich and famous, I'm grateful that Nadia's team and the designers dressed me in haute couture that feels like armor.

"Can I get you anything?"

"It's a party, Hamish. You can relax and enjoy yourself."

His mustache twitches. "Like you are?"

I let the fake smile slip from my face to give him a smirking grimace. "It's not really my type of party."

"Understandable. Myself, I'd rather have a cup of tea and a good book to read by the fire."

"That sounds lovely," I say. "I'm guessing Roy Manor has a beautiful library?"

"Several, in fact. I'm looking forward to giving you the full tour one day."

Across the ballroom, a tall, elegant figure materializes between the columns. I recognize that gray suit anywhere. St. James turns as if he senses me looking at him and raises his drink in a silent toast.

"Huh," I mutter, and when Hamish inclines his head, I explain, "I didn't realize he'd be here."

"You'll find that Rex's parties have quite a diverse guest list. But if Sebastian St. James wants to attend a gathering, the lack of invitation won't stop him."

Sebastian. I make a note of his first name. "He's all right." I wait for Hamish to disagree, and when he doesn't, a thought occurs to me. "Hamish, the morning I left Roy Manor. . ." And by that I mean the morning he helped me escape.

My train of thought slows. I can't believe I'm about to ask this, but I have a gut feeling and have to know. "Did you call St. James and ask him to help me?"

Hamish keeps a blank face. I bet he's amazing at poker. "Now, what makes you think that, I wonder?"

"I know you let me out." I'm not asking him to admit that, so I plow on. "But you knew Rex would be after me. That I'd need someone on my side, someone strong enough to stand up to him."

I knew St. James was a successful businessman, but now that I know he's part of the most powerful gang in New Rome, it makes sense that he's able to face off with Rex. He might be the only one who can.

"I'm afraid I can neither confirm nor deny your suspicions. Although I can compliment you on your deductive skills. It seems you're as talented a detective as they say."

"Thanks." I flush at the high praise. I was right. Hamish was the one to alert St. James that I was alone in the city and needed an ally. "I guess, I was wondering. . . how did you know you could trust him?" My instincts say that St. James is dangerous, but I can trust him. But my instincts thought that about Rex, too.

I guess I'm looking for proof that my instincts aren't fucked.

Hamish and I stand side by side, facing the ballroom. When his answer comes, it's almost too low to be heard. "I recognized a man who has condemned himself to being alone. Sacrificing himself in service for a cause. He sees himself as an island, married only to duty."

"Duty?" I blink. Are we talking about the same St. James? The man who's part of a notorious criminal gang and co-owner of a sex club?

"Yes, duty. He has a sense of honor. He is loyal to the brotherhood."

"You mean Fraternitas." I sound doubtful.

"For all their sins, the secret society is good for the city. Rex and I discovered they have a net positive return on reducing violent crime."

"Honor among murderers?" I murmur.

Hamish inclines his head. "Indeed."

"All right." Criminals, murderers, talking about a gang like it's a good investment? I can't take this anymore. "Excuse me." I flee to the restroom.

Two slim women in suits peel off from the wall and follow me. My bodyguards do a great impersonation of shadows. "Wait here," I order before entering the powder room. I just need a moment alone.

My reflection in the mirror shows a glamorous woman with a sleek updo. Diamonds sparkle at her neck and finger. But I don't recognize myself anymore. I'm beginning to realize that no one is what they seem.

I gaze longingly at a bathroom stall. I'm tempted to hide in there for the rest of the night.

Movement in the corner startles me a second before a male voice says, "Hello, Mrs. Roy. Or should I say, Swallow?"

I whirl, wishing I'd kept my purse with my handgun on me. "Who's there?"

A man emerges from the furthest stall from the door. He's sallow-skinned with deep circles under his eyes. The room takes on a chartreuse tinge, my psychic senses telling me something's off.

I hitch up my dress to run to the door and he holds up his hands. His left is empty, while his right holds a stained piece of paper. "Wait! I have something for you."

I pause, but only for a moment. The room tilts, disorienting me. I've been worried that my instincts are broken, but at the moment, they're shrieking like a siren. I won't ignore them again.

I'm not armed, and he might be. He went through all this trouble to corner me. I have self-defense training, but common sense says I get to safety as soon as possible.

I hit the door, shouting, "Help!" as I burst into the hall.

My bodyguards are quick to respond, whirling and surrounding me. "Ma'am? What is it?"

"In there," I gasp, "a man."

Both women hustle me down the hall.

"No, wait," I twist in their grip, "don't let him escape."

"On it, ma'am." One of the bodyguards releases me and darts back, her gun drawn. I wish I had my gun so I could follow. But my curiosity is outweighed by my sense of self-preservation, so I let the second bodyguard lead me into a private room. She's barking into her earpiece, "Intruder alert, I need backup—Mrs. Roy is secure—"

In less than a minute, Rex bursts through the door. "Inara! Are you hurt?" He runs his large hands up and down my arms. That's when I realize I'm shivering and cold.

"I'm fine. He just surprised me." It's on the tip of my tongue to ask for a gun, but Hamish has joined us, along with a few other bodyguards. It's getting cramped in this small, dark room.

"Get out there and find him," Rex orders them.

Hamish repeats the commands, leading most the security detail out of the room into the hall to assign them specific jobs. The more people leave, the more I relax.

"Here," Rex guides me to a chaise lounge and turns on a nearby lamp. "Tell me what happened."

I recite the scene, including a description. "White cis

male about five-eight, on the skinnier side. Maybe one sixty, one seventy . . . he said he had something for me—"

St. James appears at the door, flanked by Jaeger and Kaiser. "What's going on?"

"A man approached Inara in the bathroom," Rex repeats my description of the unsub and the identical twins lift their heads like bloodhounds sniffing a scent.

St. James turns to them, nods, and the blonds disappear, off to join the hunt.

St. James lingers. "Are you all right?" he asks, still hovering in the door.

Rex stiffens, but I put a hand on his shoulder to reassure him. I remember what Hamish said about St. James. "I'm fine. Thank you, Sebastian."

If my using his first name fazes him, St. James doesn't show it. "I'll alert my brothers to be on the lookout for a man of that description. Keep me informed," he orders Rex and disappears before Rex can bristle at being told what to do by his frenemy.

One of my bodyguards returns.

"No sign of him, sir," she reports. "But we found something."

Hamish enters, holding a familiar-looking piece of paper in his hands. He's wearing latex gloves, but I have no idea how he got them so fast. Does he carry them around in his pocket, like a handkerchief?

I shake my head to clear my wild thoughts.

"It's a letter," Hamish reports. "He left it on the sink."

Rex rises to look at it, but I stay seated. My nerves are raw. I don't know why I had such a strong reaction to the stranger when I'm trained for these situations, but the man's presence made me feel sick.

And then I realize that I've felt this way before. Long ago

when I was a little girl, huddling under the covers, listening to the creak of the floorboards outside my bedroom. I sensed the Bondage Killer's presence then as I do now.

"It's from him, isn't it?" I say right as Rex tells me, "It's from the Bondage Killer."

Hamish tilts the letter enough for me to see the opening line. *Dear Swallow—*

I don't want to look at it anymore. Not when I'm around so many strangers, exposed.

"Was it him? Was he here?" Rex demands. He's facing Hamish, but I answer, "No, that wasn't him. That was just a messenger."

My second bodyguard appears. "He's gone. He escaped through another exit and went through the kitchens and out the back door."

Rex swears.

"But he dropped this." They hand the badge to Rex, who holds it up so Hamish and I can see. "Ted Raider."

"Ted," I breathe. This must be the same Ted that Burgess told us about.

Rex grips the badge in his fist. "Got him."

15

New Rome: Midnight. The bright lights of the city blot out the stars and the moon. The suburbs are quiet and sleepy, but in midtown, it's as bustling as it is during the day.

A lone figure jogs away from a busy street and darts through a dark alleyway, running away from home to the soundtrack of sirens. He doesn't know where to go, but he can't go to his apartment. A man was waiting there for him. He's lucky he got away.

And now he's taking a shortcut to his favorite dive bar. He can hide out there. If he makes it.

There's something sinister about the shadows. Or maybe it's his own thoughts that color his surroundings. He's been on edge ever since the messages for the detective started coming to him.

He didn't mean to scare her earlier. He only wanted to give her the letter, as instructed. He knows why he was chosen—he has access as a member of the press. He doesn't know what will happen to him if he doesn't comply with the killer's requests, but he doesn't dare find out.

And now he can't go home. He's jumping at shadows, literally. He can't shake the feeling of being watched.

The pressure builds until he can't ignore it anymore. There's someone behind him—he can sense it.

He whirls around. "Who's there?"

But there's no one following him. And if there was, what would he do?

Better to keep moving, so that's what he does.

This is a mistake. If he looked up, he'd see a large shape rise from the roof and follow, stalking him from above.

The sound of motorcycles splits the night, and he freezes. A trio of bikes turn down the alleyway, blocking his exit. A street light illuminates two blond heads and one dark one. All three are wearing skull masks that cover the lower half of their faces.

"Ted Raider?" the closest one calls. The light glints on the silver skull ring he's wearing as he raises his hands to show he's unarmed. "We need to talk."

Ted doesn't wait to hear what they have to say. He turns and runs the other way. It's stupid to try to outrun bikers, but they don't follow, and he feels a little hope that he might escape his fate.

He's almost to the middle of the alleyway when something explodes in front of him. There's a flashbang of smoke, and he throws up his hands to ward off an attack, crying out.

Ears ringing, he staggers sideways. A large figure drops to the pavement in front of him. It's like something out of a video game —over six feet tall, bulky with black body armor and a helmet to hide their face. Ted doesn't need to see the dark figure's expression to know it's over for him. He's been caught. There's horror but also relief. No more dreading what's to come.

As the hunter reaches out a gloved hand, Ted gives up his shaky grasp on consciousness and slumps to the ground at the hunter's feet.

~

INARA

ON-SCREEN, Rex stalks toward Ted. In his body armor, he's both a futuristic soldier and a figure from a myth. An ancient warrior emerging from the mist.

"Wow," Mina says. "Men will literally dress up in a bulletproof suit and run around being a vigilante instead of going to therapy."

Ah, Mina, I missed you.

I'm back at Roy Manor, standing in front of the large array of screens in Rex's lair. After the ball, Rex asked me to return to the safety of the manor, and I was so shaken that I agreed.

I watch the action unfold from the screens, my heart racing like I'm standing in the alley with him. I smell the sharp, acrid funk of the gas. I've been Ted in this moment. I should be afraid for him, but for some reason, I'm not. I made Rex promise not to hurt him, and I guess I trust that he won't.

I should be appalled that Rex is out there, exercising his own form of vigilante justice to hunt down the mysterious Ted. But I'm not. And what does that say about me? I've lived my life by the law. Ted is a witness, and there are protocols. But here I am, rooting for Rex to trap Ted in any way he can.

"Can I get one of those suits?" Mina's disembodied voice echoes through the cave.

I don't know what possessed me to ask Rex if I could loop her in on this mission, but he agreed.

He probably hated seeing me so frightened and would've promised me the moon if he thought it would help. I needed someone familiar. I guess Mina is more of a friend than I thought.

Mina doesn't know I'm standing in a hi-tech lab in a cave attached to the Roy family mansion, but she can see the feed. "Are those gauntlets?" She sounds fascinated.

Reflected in multiple angles, Rex looms larger than life while Ted lies prone on the asphalt. Rex has gassed me before, so I know it won't hurt Ted. But my stomach twists at crossing this line.

I wanted to approach Ted and interview him the traditional way. But I was in no state to do that, no matter how much I wanted to, and Rex didn't offer me a choice. He was going to bring him in tonight. He sent Ivan to approach Ted at his apartment with money to bribe him. But when Ted ran, Rex chose to do things his way.

I wanted him to loop me in, but now I'm torn. I'm afraid for Rex, for what comes next. I'm afraid I've allowed things to go too far.

"Mission accomplished. Ending transmission." As one, all the screens go dark.

"No, wait," I say. "Mina, what's happening?"

"We lost the feed," Mina says.

"Mr. Roy ended the transmission," Hamish says quietly. I jump, not realizing he was standing so close.

"Can you get it back?"

He hesitates, and I get the sense he's wondering whether to lie to me. "I think it's better if we allow Rex to go dark."

"He doesn't want me to see what's next." I clench my fists hard enough to drive my nails into my palms. "He can't hurt him. He gave me his word."

"He won't injure him. Those weren't real grenades. Merely smoke bombs. Shock and awe go a long way to breaking a person."

Oh gods. Am I really allowing this?

"This is the best way," Hamish says. "He'll be ready to talk. We have less red tape than the police. They wouldn't have a reason to hold him."

"Hold him?"

"He'll be questioned," Hamish says. "We'll get to the bottom of why the Bondage Killer is using him as a delivery boy."

My stomach lurches with that sick feeling that overcame me when Ted first approached me.

"He's right, Inara, this is the best way to go," Mina says. "I've already looked into this guy. He's a sleazeball. Been in trouble before for trying to pick up underage girls."

"He still deserves due process." I press my fist to my mouth, biting the knuckle.

Mina snorts, but Hamish assures me, "Rex will handle him with care. He's our best lead in the case."

"And the sooner we get answers, the sooner we can catch BK," Mina says.

I hope she's right. This will get us closer to our goal. But I'm not okay with crossing this line. I wanted Rex's help, and I'm grateful for it, but that means doing things his way. I know how far he's willing to go. I don't want him to kill anymore, but in the heat of the moment, I don't think I'll be able to stop him.

"I'll message Rex for an update," Hamish says and heads off to his own computer console, leaving me alone with Mina on the line.

"How was the party?" she asks. "Other than the whole getting-another-letter-from-a-serial-killer thing."

"Fine. I'm glad it's over." She's trying to distract me, but I need to focus on the case. "What have you found out about Ted?"

"He's not a reporter. He freelances as a photographer for

the *New Rome Post*. You know, the sort of paper that publishes stories about alligators in the sewers."

I close my eyes. "Great."

"*The Post* is a sensational rag that barely rates being called a newspaper, and Ted isn't exactly a model employee, but it was enough to get him a press badge tonight."

Exhaustion hits me, and I sink into a swivel chair. I'm still in my gold dress but wrapped in Rex's suit jacket. I didn't take the time to change, claiming I wanted to get down to HQ right away. In truth, I wanted to keep wearing Rex's jacket. His scent surrounds me and might be the only thing holding me together. I couldn't think of a better excuse to keep wearing it and couldn't bear to give it up.

So much for me being a brilliant detective. I'm unraveling, barely able to do my job. I let my serial killer husband hunt down a prime witness while I clutch his suit jacket like a safety blanket.

Mina's still talking, giving me the rundown on Ted. "—a ton of debt. It'd be easy to bribe this guy or threaten him. He might not know anything. But then again, he might."

"Guess we'll find out." I can't stifle a yawn.

Mina hears it. "You should sleep. It's late."

"I'm good." I don't know if I can fall asleep. I miss Rex like a phantom limb. He's the only one who can comfort me. Not sure when that happened, but it has and it frightens me. It's not safe for me to need anyone. How did I get in so deep?

"I'll keep you company," Mina says. "You still haven't told me the whole story about why you got married."

I rub my eyes. "It was a spur-of-a-moment thing. He thought it would keep me safe."

"Huh. Ted still got close to you."

"Yeah, but it probably was a lot harder than it would have been a week ago." I hate having my movements constricted, but Rex has gone all out to make me safe. And I do feel safer. For the first time in my life, I'm able to fall asleep without checking the locks and security system twice.

"True. And now you have more resources to follow up on leads."

"A little-known perk of being a billionaire's wife."

"Speaking of perks, I have to thank you for my new digs."

I search my tired brain and then remember the gift I was going to use to lure Mina out of hiding before Rex beat me to it.

"How did you find it?" she asks. "It's seriously perfect."

"Hamish helped."

"Sexy moustache man?"

"Oh gods," I guffaw, looking around. Hamish isn't in my line of sight, but he's somewhere in this cave. "Mina, you're on speakerphone."

"I don't care if Butler Daddy hears me. He looks so deliciously stern in all his photos. Like he's the type to keep a stiff upper—"

"Mina!"

"Lip! I was going to say lip. And then I was going to wonder what else is stiff. Anyway, back to the lighthouse. It's awesome."

"I'm glad you like it. I know you always wanted one." She mentioned it during one of our rambling conversations.

"It's better than I imagined. There's no one around for a hundred miles. But it's completely modern inside. And you should see my computer room. All the latest tech."

"Good. You deserve it." Buying her a lighthouse was the least I could do after what Rex did to her.

"Best thing is, it's stocked with enough food for a year. I never have to leave my cave of wonders."

I smile. I'm half asleep, listening to Mina babble happily.

"And while we're on the topic, how does Rex like your cave of wonders?"

I come awake with a start. "What?" Is she talking about Rex's lair? Or is it meant to be a euphemism for my vagina? Either way, "No comment."

"The sex is that good, huh?"

I'm way too groggy to have this conversation. I tell her this, and she sniggers. "Go get some rest. I'm gonna keep digging, and I'll let you know as soon as I find anything."

I've already let my eyes close. I tell myself I'll only rest them for a moment—

$\sim$

REX

I'VE SPENT years hunting the men who've escaped justice, cockroaches who fall through the cracks of the law and the courts. Time and experience have taught me, again and again, that the most guilty escape justice.

Inara thinks the system works, but men like St. James and I know better. We are among the worst criminals.

But sometimes it takes a criminal to catch a criminal. And a murderer to execute justice. St. James and the Devil were kind enough to offer me a private space to question my victim.

Ted made the mistake of frightening my wife. What happens next will be up to him.

"We have him in a room." A Fraternitas member leads me down a set of stone steps. He has long, black hair tied back in a ponytail. There's little light in this gloomy, underground space, but when my guide walks under a hanging lantern, I recognize him from the drone footage—this is the biker who helped Inara escape me.

We reach an open door guarded by Kaiser and Jaeger, who greet me with a nod of their chins. When I look back, my long-haired guide has disappeared.

Kaiser notes the direction of my glare. "Do you have a problem with Asmodeus?"

"No, as long as he stays away from my wife."

"Asmodeus has an *elita* of his own," Jaeger tells me. "She is his sole obsession."

He's referring to the Fraternitas' tradition of claiming a "chosen one" or *elita*. An intriguing concept, but not one I want to learn more about right now.

I ignore him and enter the torture chamber.

While the stone walls of the hallway were a rough, gray-green stone, this room is made entirely of polished granite. It has a mausoleum-like look.

Ted is strapped to a gurney in the middle of the room. The gas still has him knocked out. My lip curls when I see him and take in his stench. We're all animals underneath our civilized trappings. And I'm an apex predator.

"We'll leave you to it," Kaiser says. "St. James wants us guarding the main door, but holler if you need us."

"Understood."

"Oh." He heads to the wall and plants a tattooed hand on the corner of a rectangular stone. With a strong push, a drawer pops out. I catch a metallic gleam inside. "You have full use of the room and everything in it."

"Thank you. And give my thanks to the Devil."

The twins leave without another word.

I circle around Ted. His mouth is slack, his pulse steady. I flick his ear to check if he's faking unconsciousness. He's still under, but the gas will wear off soon. His eyelids flutter like he's having bad dreams.

"I appreciate an invitation to the party," an accented voice announces as I sense Victor's arrival. The tall assassin slips in the door.

"Nice, very nice," he says, looking around the sinister room with satisfaction. "They have a good setup here. Everything we need." He sidles to the open drawer to examine the metal implements. "Good selection. And slick floors make it easy to mop up blood."

There's an incinerator down here, too, for easy disposal of remains, but we're not going to need it tonight.

"We're just going to ask him questions," I remind the white-blond assassin.

Victor pauses the dancing of his hands over the torturer's tools. "Just talk?"

"I promised my wife I wouldn't kill him."

"Pain doesn't have to equal death." Victor raises a bone saw.

"She won't like it."

"She'll never know." But he replaces the saw. "The things we do for love."

"Happy wife, happy life."

"So I have found," he agrees.

I didn't realize Victor was married, but now that he's let the information slip, I wonder if the dark-haired woman I saw him dancing with at our engagement ball was his wife. Hamish will know.

Ted groans and stirs.

"Shall we?" Victor holds up a black skull mask.

"I have my own." I turn the faceplate of my helmet opaque as Ted rouses. He winces and mumbles something.

He opens his eyes, squinting in the gloom. "What. . . where am I?"

I step into his line of vision, and he comes awake quickly, recoiling and thrashing in his restraints. "Who are you? What's going on?"

"Your worst nightmare," I snarl, the helmet speaker distorting my voice. "You're going to tell me everything you know about the Bondage Killer."

"Oh gods," Ted whimpers. "What is this place?"

Victor moves to stand beside me. The skull mask covers his face, but I can hear the glee in his voice as he says, "Welcome to the Abyss."

I *nara*

SOMETHING SOFT STROKES MY FACE. I sit up, and feathers fall from my body. I move and wince when something crunches underfoot. Feathers and fragile wings. Don't think about it. *I stagger forward into a small, dark room. The walls bow inward, covered with pictures of victims. One photo floats down and lands in front of me. It's the picture of my family, with every face crossed out. Including mine.*

Somewhere, I hear Burgess muttering, "Another body. . ."

"No," I gasp, shuddering awake.

"I've got you." It's Rex. I'm in his arms, still wearing my dress. I must have fallen asleep in the chair. I'm still half in the dream, feeling the broken feathers over my skin.

I rub my eyes, but it feels like there are grains of sand digging into my eyeballs. I blink, but it doesn't help.

Air wafts over my face. We're still in the cave, and he's carrying me to the elevator.

"What happened? What did you find?"

"I'll tell you in the morning."

He's taken off his helmet, but he's still in his body armor. I look him over. No blood, but the black surface might just hide it well.

"No, tell me now."

He doesn't answer.

"Sir," Hamish calls.

"Later," Rex answers and keeps walking. I hear and feel the whir of the elevator.

I must fall asleep again in the elevator because the next thing I know, I'm in bed in Rex's bedroom. I'm naked except for my panties, and the shower's running nearby.

When Rex walks out, he's in nothing but a towel. I search him for bruises but see none.

I scoot over to make room for him on the bed but put a hand on his shoulder before he can sink back into the bed. "Tell me. I won't be able to sleep until you do."

Rex's shoulders slump, and I know he wants to spare me from whatever he's about to say. "He started talking as soon as we secured him. But he didn't have much to say. He swears he's also a victim."

"What?" I try to reconcile that with the moment tonight when Ted approached me. His eager energy.

"The Bondage Killer sent him things with explicit instructions to deliver them to you. The first was the photo you found at your desk at work, which came to his work mailbox at the paper. The letter he had tonight was slid under his apartment door. He felt threatened, so he did BK's bidding and sought you out."

My brain is fuzzy, so it takes me some time to sort through this. "So he's innocent."

Rex's lip curls. "I wouldn't go that far."

"But he's a victim, like me."

"He seems to think so. He spent the rest of the time begging us to protect him from the serial killer."

The disdain in Rex's voice makes my stomach twist.

"Did you kill him?" I'm afraid of the answer but I ask anyway. Rex hasn't hidden his murderous side from me, and I won't shrink away from it.

"I wanted to. He has no business breathing the same air as the decent people of New Rome." He takes a strand of my hair into his fist and clenches it like he wants to absorb it into his palm. I wait for the painful tug on my scalp, but it never comes.

"But no, I didn't kill him."

My breath eases out of me.

"I have people watching him and his place to see if the Bondage Killer contacts him. But he's still breathing. We let him go."

"We?" I remember the bikers in the alley. It makes me uneasy that Rex is allied with a criminal gang.

"I had an audience. A few useful acquaintances."

"St. James?"

"Some of his brothers. Fraternitas loaned us a space to question him. Don't worry, we didn't torture him." A small smile touches his lips.

"Thank gods." I'm already wrestling with a crisis of conscience. I'm willing to bend protocol, but the ends don't justify all means.

Rex angles his body more to face me. "Why do you care about him?"

"He's innocent."

"He's sewage in human form. He was all too willing to do a murderer's bidding. The world would be a better place without him."

"You can't go around killing people who annoy you."

"Can't I?"

"Rex, I can't condone the way you're. . ." I don't even know how to describe what he did—chasing down Ted and gassing him. I give up trying and rub my mouth. "I'm already on the wrong side of the law."

"The world isn't so black and white."

"You don't live in the gray. You've embraced the darkness." I wait for him to argue, but he doesn't. He can't. "I've spent my whole life trying to uphold justice—"

"There is no justice. The concept you have, it's a fantasy. A fairytale. And you're not a child anymore."

I glare up at him, but he doesn't back down. "Justice may be blind, but wealth and power tip the scales. They always have."

"I guess you would know." There's no one more wealthy and powerful than Rex.

"I do know. Because I use mine to tip it back."

I shake my head. "I don't want to fight." I'm exhausted. I'm still piecing together everything that happened tonight.

"Tell me what you need." He uses his dom voice, and I relax immediately. It's heady, having such a powerful man willing to bend the world to my wishes.

"I need your help, Rex." I lean against him, and he tucks me close. "I need you on my side."

"Always." He murmurs into my hair. "I will always be on your side."

"Don't. . . don't kill anyone."

"I won't. But if the choice is between protecting you or upholding some limited law, I'll always choose you."

THE POLICE precinct roof is perfect for smoking, but few people know this, and Detective Bonds would like to keep it that way.

It's been a long weekend. He's spent every waking hour on the case.

Up here, it's peaceful for this desperate, dreary hour. He should go home and try to get some sleep.

But first, a smoke.

A shadow separates from the wall by the door and coalesces into a giant shape.

A flicker of movement out of the corner of his eyes makes Bonds turn. The figure looms over him, and he recoils.

"What the fuck?" He reaches for his gun, but it's not there. He didn't think he'd need it on his smoke break.

"It's me." The figure's deep voice sounds modulated somehow.

"Yeah, I got that," Bonds scowls and takes a drag on his cigarette to calm his racing heart.

The first time he got a visit from the warrior-like figure, he was on his balcony at home, having a smoke. He still doesn't understand how such a big guy can move so silently.

"This is a secure building," he adds, tapping ash onto the roof.

"Obviously."

The stranger's dry tone makes Bonds chuckle despite himself. He resents being surprised like this, especially by a freak dressed up like an action figure in body armor, but the dude does have his charm.

Bonds angles his head, squinting, but darkness shrouds the figure, like all the times before. The shadows embrace his form like the night wants to keep the figure's secrets all to itself.

"What do you want?"

"I have evidence for you."

This is why Bonds tolerates visits from the fiendish specter. He always comes with something to help a case.

The figure steps closer, and the ambient light slides off his giant form. He's in some sort of smooth body armor. Bonds wishes he could study the man's suit up close in better lighting. The black color makes the figure one with the night.

"Rex Roy sent me."

"The billionaire?"

"Yes. A man approached his wife last night and gave her another letter from the Bondage Killer."

The few half-awake brain cells fire and Bonds remembers his new single degree of separation from the famous Roy. "Inara?" It might be a trick of the light, but the figure seems to stiffen slightly. "I mean, Detective Ramos?"

"Yes. The man's name is Ted Raider. I've prepared a file on him." The figure points, looking so much like the specter of death that Bonds is reluctant to turn. But he does and sees a black case sitting on a nearby ledge. He picks it up and flips through it.

In his career, he's looked through thousands of case files. Habit allows him to scan for the pertinent details. "A photographer?"

"That's how he got access."

At the end of the stack is a stained letter in a plastic case. Bonds can smell the sour, smokey scent without even opening it. "This is what he gave her?"

"Yes."

After the greeting, "Dear Swallow," the writing degenerates so much that Bonds can barely read it. Only a few passages—"Your doom" and "Come to me"—are even legible.

"This is like the others."

"Yes."

Bonds tucks the letter back into the case. He's been staring at letters like this for so long, he's practically memorized them. It makes him sick, but he can't stop hoping they'll reveal more clues.

"The Bondage Killer sticks to his MO. But he's never used a delivery boy before."

"Raider swears he received these letters anonymously, with instructions to hand deliver them personally to Mrs. Roy."

"You've spoken to him?" Bonds looks up sharply.

"This is the third time Mrs. Roy has been personally targeted," the man continues without acknowledging the question.

"Well, he's fixated on her." Bonds can't keep the worry from his voice. Whatever he thinks about the enigmatic Detective Ramos, he feels protective of her. He tells himself he'd feel that way about any of his colleagues, but the truth is this detective is special. "What about this Ted Raider?"

"He claims he's never had personal contact with the Bondage Killer, that the serial killer left these things for him to deliver. He's scared out of his mind, afraid he's the Bondage Killer's next target. He'll insist on witness protection."

"Gods." Bonds' brain is skipping ahead, thinking about the next steps. Tracking down the potential witness, coaxing him in for an interview. It seems like this stranger—this warrior of the night or amateur detective—already shook Ted down. Bonds should be protesting the breach of protocol and harassment of a citizen, but practically, he knows that Ted will be spooked and ready to talk. It'll be easy to play good cop.

"He'll be delivered to you in thirty minutes. You can question him then."

The statement is so bizarre that Bonds' mouth goes slack and he almost loses his cigarette. This is the first time the figure has promised to deliver a witness along with evidence. "What the fuck is going on?"

"Rex Roy is personally interested in this investigation."

"He is, huh? I'm not in the business of bending to a billionaire's requests." Bonds knows the way the world works. He knows oligarchs rule, and the rest of humanity scrambles under the table for scraps. He's always tried to keep a low profile, but there are things he won't compromise on. "Tell him to keep out of my case."

"He only wants to help." There's a note of approval in the man's voice, but perhaps Bonds is imagining it. "Roy will do anything to protect his wife."

"And I want to solve this case. We want the same thing, right?" Bonds glances down at the file in his hand. He looks away for only a moment, but when he looks up, the figure is gone. Disappeared.

The hardened detective isn't unsettled by much, but this makes his mouth fall open. He turns in a circle, peering into the shadows to figure out which way the stranger went. He looks out onto the city, half-expecting to see a fleeing stranger racing over the roofs, but there's nothing but the tired glow of the city lights, the darkness before dawn.

~

SOMEWHERE ELSE IN THE CITY...

. . .

A MAN SITS in a room filled with photographs of the Blackbird murders. Carefully arranged limbs, naked in death, surrounded by feathers. The room has a sour, smokey smell. The man is a silent sentinel, sitting with his head bowed in an almost reverent state. The silence shrouding him is broken by an infrequent, hacking cough.

AN OLD-TIMER WAKES before dawn and rubs his bleary eyes. His dreams are a long parade of faces that belong to people now long gone. Old friends, victims in cases he never solved. But as sleep recedes, the vivid images fade to muted colors. By the time *he's walked from his bedroom to the kitchen to start making coffee, the memory of his dreams is all a muddle. Only the lingering sense of horror and sadness remains.*

THREE BIKERS in skull masks race up the road. They swerve toward the police precinct, and the middle rider dumps the bundle draped over his lap on the sidewalk before they all speed away.

Silva, walking in with his chai, hears the groans and rushes up to the writhing bundle. It's a man, bound and gagged. A press badge clipped to his shirt reads, "Ted Raider."

"Damn," Silva says and waves to a pair of uniforms to help him get the poor prisoner untied.

Rex

My car dashboard displays the feed from cameras in front of the police precinct. I watch Fraternitas dump Ted at the front doors, right on schedule. Satisfied that Bonds has his witness, I lean back to enjoy the ride back to the Manor.

"Call Hamish," I order.

"She's still sleeping," Hamish reports before I say anything. He knows this will reassure me, even though I have Alfie monitoring her. Still, I switch the camera feeds to show Inara's sleeping form.

"I'm on my way back."

"How did the meeting with the good detective go?"

I suppress a smile. I enjoyed the encounter more than I thought I would. The sneak approach, the disappearing act at the end. I have a touch of theater kid in me. "It went well."

Hamish says nothing for a moment. I've learned to parse his pauses like a language of their own. Sometimes, they're disapproving, and sometimes they're thoughtful. This time, I think it's the latter. "Do you think it's wise to involve him?"

I picture Bonds' weathered face, lit by the glow of his cigarette. "He's involved in the case. We need a way to loop him in." I know what Hamish is really asking. *Do I trust Bonds?* "I trust him to do his job. We need all the help we can get."

Hamish doesn't argue. He knows as well as I do that the killer's still out there, and he won't stop until he has Inara.

~

Inara

. . .

MONDAY, I drag myself to the police station. Rex told me that Bonds has already been brought up to speed on the whole Ted debacle, so I don't have to explain.

Bonds takes one look at me and sends me to my desk to follow up on random leads called into the department. He doesn't say that I look like crap. He doesn't have to.

I do my penance, reviewing the leads and returning calls to get the statements. Most of the "tips" are crank calls or useless leads from retirees who just want to report suspicious activity in their neighborhoods. By mid-afternoon, I'm finished, and my brain is soup. I could return to Bonds to get more work, but I know when I'm being banished.

I'm picking at my lunch when my phone rings.

Burgess, the screen reads, and I recoil. I saved my partner's phone number when we were assigned to each other, but I don't think he's ever called. He's been avoiding me, which suits me just fine. Technically, we're still partners, but we've come to a silent agreement that we both work better alone. If what Burgess does can be called work.

I take a deep breath and answer. "Ramos."

"Hey." It's Burgess. "I heard you found Ted."

"Yeah. Dead end."

"You busy?"

I don't bother lying. "No, what's up?"

"Got a call out. Someone called the station saying they found a dead body with a bird on display. I'm heading to the scene now if you want to come."

I rise from my chair, ready to leave, but darkness passes over my vision, leaving me dizzy. Something is coming. Another body, another clue, maybe even a break in the case. I need to be ready.

When the shadows clear, Burgess is still talking. "Ramos? You there?"

"Yeah, on my way. Where should we meet?"

"I'll pick you up." He names an intersection that's a few blocks away from the precinct. "Save me a wait in traffic."

I grab my coat but don't do anything to alert my body-guards. They've been lying low, but the department won't look too kindly on me taking them to a crime scene. I want to text Rex, but what would I even say? 'Hey, I have a feeling something big is about to happen. I actually have these feelings all the time, but I've been too afraid to tell you about them.'

No, I'm not going to share all that. But I do text Ivan that I'm headed out on police business and will be back by end of day.

Forty minutes later, I'm in the passenger seat of the department car Burgess got from the lot. There's a tension radiating from him, as if he's uncomfortable just being in my presence. He's barely looked at me, and I've kept quiet because I want as little to do with him as possible.

We pull into a deserted alley, and Burgess kills the engine.

"This it?" We're in the warehouse district. The alley is full of trash, but there's no sign of another cop car. "Where is everyone?"

"We're first on the scene." There's a distant wail of sirens, but they seem to be receding.

Something isn't right.

"Body was found in that building." Burgess points to the warehouse. He exits the car and I follow more slowly.

"Who called in the tip?" I ask.

"Anonymous call. Desk sergeant passed it to us." Burgess looks up and down the alley, muttering. "This place gives me the heebie-jeebies."

"Same." But I'm here, and I might as well do my job. I

search for an entrance to the warehouse. Finally, in between two stinking dumpsters, there's a solid metal door left cracked open.

"In here?" I ask but don't wait for an answer. I lean into the door, pushing it open. It yields with a ghastly creak, revealing a carpet of dead birds. There are too many here for it to be a coincidence.

Burgess sees and starts swearing.

"Shhh." I motion for him to shut up. "I think I heard something." It was faint, but it sounded like a bang from deep inside the building.

We wait in silence. A breeze sweeps past me, stirring the feathers.

Another banging sound. Like a door shutting.

I draw my gun and call, "Hello?" I signal to Burgess, who nods and readies his weapon.

"Police. Show yourself!" I shout. I move inside, leading with my gun, peering into corners. "Clear," I say and cover Burgess as he moves forward. We sweep through the dark warehouse, following the trail of dead birds. There's a faint sawdusty scent along with the smell of something rotting. Maybe it's the birds? Their tattered wings tell me they've been here a long time. But maybe it's something else.

I breathe through my mouth and move swiftly through the building, clearing each room. This warehouse hasn't been used in some time. There's still some machinery pushed into the corner like oversized insects. Everything is covered in a layer of dust.

The trail of birds ends at a three walled room, some sort of office cubby with a desk but no chair. It's open on one side, with a metal gate that serves as a door.

There's a dead bird on the desk, illuminated by a stream of light that comes from the narrow windows by the ceiling.

Because of the metal gate, the sunlight falls in a barred pattern, making the bird look like it's lying in a cell.

A cage.

"Any sign of the body?" Burgess asks.

I step inside to investigate. I check behind the desk, but there's no body. "No. Are you sure they said there was a body in here?"

A harsh clanging sound makes me turn. Burgess is behind me, sliding the metal gate shut and locking it.

17

I *nara*

"WHAT THE—?" I face Burgess, who's backed away from the metal gate. "What are you doing?" I grab the nearest bar and tug, but the metal gate is solidly shut. "Burgess, let me out."

"No can do. He wants you." Burgess's expression is flat, giving nothing away.

I get a flash of a vision—*birds flying in my face, descending, blotting out the sun*—but shake it off.

"You're not serious." I grab the bars again and throw my weight to the right in an attempt to open the door, but it doesn't budge. "What is going on?"

"He told me to trap you. So I did."

"Are you serious right now?" I stare at my so-called partner. Years ago, Detective Collins suspected the Bondage Killer might be working with someone in the department. Seems that's still his MO.

I grip my gun but hesitate. Burgess is just standing there. I could threaten to shoot him, but that feels like a last resort.

"How can you do this?" I ask, attempting to reason. If I can just get Burgess talking, maybe he'll drop some clues. "Did he threaten you?"

Burgess scoffs.

"Bribes? What did he offer you?"

"Not all of us can marry rich," he half-sneers, but his heart doesn't seem to be in it. The tension I felt in the car makes more sense.

He was planning to double-cross me this whole time. Not just double-cross but offer me up on a platter to the very person we're supposed to be investigating.

"How did he contact you?"

Burgess shakes his head, backing away. "Give it up, Inara. You won't win."

He's really going to leave me in here.

"You need to let me out." I raise my weapon, steadying it, and aim for his leg. "Unlock the door, or I'll shoot. Don't make me do this."

"You won't shoot me." Burgess keeps backing away. "You care way too much about the moral high ground."

"You're right, she does. But I don't." The voice comes from above.

"What?" Burgess looks up. A shadow falls over him.

Something falls and detonates.

Bang! Smoke explodes around Burgess, swallowing him whole.

My ears are ringing in the aftermath of the sound, but my training holds. I keep my grip on my gun, pointing it at the ground until I can figure out who I should shoot.

Burgess swears, stumbling amidst the smoke, disoriented. He's an easy target for the huge, helmeted figure who appears above him.

It's Rex. It has to be. My heart lifts.

But then Burgess raises his gun, firing wildly.

"No!" I scream. I bite back Rex's name before I blurt it out. I'm terrified that one of Burgess's shots will hit Rex. I raise my gun, aiming for Burgess, but hesitate.

The dark form leaps from above, landing in front of Burgess.

Burgess raises his gun, firing straight into the helmeted figure's chest. My shout is drowned out by the blasts of the gun. Bullets ricochet, and I flinch backward. I retreat deeper into the cell, but not so far that I can't watch what happens next.

The bullets seem to bounce off Rex's armored chest. In his suit, he's larger than life.

Burgess fires and fires as if he doesn't comprehend why his target hasn't dropped dead.

Eventually, he pulls the trigger and his gun clicks. Empty.

"You done?" Rex growls. "My turn." He lunges forward and grabs Burgess by the throat.

The detective is large but doesn't stand a chance. Rex lifts him off the ground. Burgess's face turns redder than usual. He claws at the gauntleted arm, his feet kicking, suspended.

"Rex!" I shout. "Stop."

It's too late.

Rex tosses Burgess to the ground. The detective crumples into a pile as I taste bile in the back of my throat.

Did Rex just murder my partner? A cop?

A dirty cop, but still.

I still hear the echo of gunshots firing over and over again. Or maybe it's my heartbeat.

"Inara." Rex whirls, striding to me. He grabs the bars. "Are you hurt? I'll get you out. Stand back."

I back away as he fixes a small black box to the bars.

"Cover your ears." I crouch behind the desk and avert my eyes, too. There's another bang and then a shrieking sound as Rex pulls the metal gate aside.

He doesn't waste any time slipping in and pulling me out. I shield my face from the smoke and let him guide me out. The place smells like burning metal.

My throat is gritty. I cough, blinking to clear my streaming eyes. "How did you know where I was?" I rasp.

"Tracker. Are you hurt?" He stops to check me over.

I click the safety on my gun and holster it in an automatic move. Then I cough again, doubling over.

Burgess' fallen form is nearby. My head throbs, and I decide I'm dealing with too much to think about him. I avert my eyes.

Rex must decide I'm unhurt because he takes my arm to raise me up. "Let's get out of here." He propels me through the warehouse and to the door.

"What about Burgess?"

"I'll send a clean-up crew," he remarks grimly, dragging me out of the building. He barely avoids stomping on the trail of dead birds. I stumble, trying to keep from stepping on any of them. It doesn't matter. My psychic senses torture me. I can hear their fragile bones breaking, the feathers crackling underfoot.

I'm grateful when Rex finally scoops me up, carrying me until we're in the alley. Outside, the fresh air is a welcome relief. I turn my face to the sun.

Rex sets me down but keeps pulling me along, away

from the warehouse. There's a huge black sports car idling close to the brown sedan Burgess borrowed from the lot. "We need to get out of here."

I wrench my arm out of his grip. I have to see if he was hurt. "He shot you." I'm panting with adrenaline. My eyes are still watering from the smoke, my ears still ringing. But I'm half sick with fear that, under all that black body armor, Rex is bleeding out. I know he was shot.

Except the armor is smooth. None of the bullets penetrated.

Impossible.

I run my hands over his chest, looking for dents in the thick armor. "How...?"

He retracts his faceplate, and suddenly, I'm staring at his face. "Bulletproof."

I've worn Kevlar plenty before. The material absorbs the bullet and mitigates the impact, but it doesn't repel bullets. No body armor is this good. What is this material? How did Rex survive a full round to the chest?

I shake my head, unable to speak.

"It's a new design," he says in answer to my unspoken questions. All I can see is Rex standing there while Burgess empties a clip into him.

Anger takes over. My hand curls to a fist, and I thump his chest. "You could've died." I beat his chest. "What the fuck is wrong with you?"

"Inara—" He catches my wrists, holding them lightly.

"You could've been hurt," I shout in his face.

He blinks in surprise. "Are you mad that I killed him? Or that I could've been killed?"

Oh gods, he killed Burgess. But that's not why I'm angry. Acid sloshes in my stomach, and my violent feelings give way to fear. "Both." I stop struggling, sagging against him. "Both."

His breath huffs out of him, blowing my hair back. I dig my nails into the strange surface of his body armor. He looks like a stranger, but he feels like home.

"I need you. I don't want you to die."

"Inara—" He pulls me close, cupping the side of my face. I'm winded, too overcome to say anything. I can only stare into his eyes. They're an open book of emotions—fear and grim determination giving way to confusion, then surprise and wonder. Hope.

Boom!

A blast of heat sears my skin. Rex barrels into me, enveloping me in his arms. His weight knocks the air out of my lungs and forces me to the ground. I scramble, panicked, until I'm able to suck in a breath.

The ground beneath me rocks like we're in an earthquake. Debris rains down, and I cry out, pressing my face to the smooth surface of Rex's protective gear. Rex covers me with his body as the world rumbles around us.

And then... silence.

My ears are ringing again, and I taste ash. Bright lights flash behind my eyes.

And then Rex is lifting me, carrying me to the car. I cling to him, half-hunched into a ball. The world has gone gray.

Rex bundles me into the back seat and slides in beside me. "Alfie, get us out of here."

I'm half in his lap. "What happened?"

"The warehouse. It exploded."

I manage to turn my head and see the plumes of smoke and ash filling what was once a clear blue sky. The warehouse walls are caved in, and whole sections have been turned to rubble.

My teeth start chattering, and I'm rocked with a whole-body shiver. My adrenaline crashing and the fear rolling through me are too much to contain.

"My gods, Rex. We almost died." A few minutes ago, Burgess had me locked in the warehouse. Now he's dead, and the warehouse is gone.

"I know." He squeezes me tight, and I'm relieved because his arms are the only thing holding me together.

Someone planted a bomb in the warehouse, enough to blow it sky-high. Was it the Bondage Killer? Was Burgess working with him this whole time?

My mind blanks. I can barely hold myself together, much less think of any answers. I lean into Rex, slumping against him as the car turns a corner and carries us away.

Rex

Sirens scream in the distance. I instruct Alfie to call the authorities and then Hamish to tell him we're okay. The car will take us to Hotel Magnifique, where we'll need to dig into Burgess and figure out his part in all this.

But all that can wait. I have Inara safe in my arms. She's curled into me, shivering like she just had a nightmare. I want to soothe her, but I'm fighting the urge to strip off her clothes and touch her everywhere and make sure she's real.

I was so close to losing her. If I hadn't found out about Burgess in time—

"How did you know I was in trouble?" she asks.

I press my lips to her temple, unable to keep from kissing her before answering, "We got evidence that Burgess was the one who left the birds in your apartment. A neighbor saw him leaving that night. One of my team canvassed the neighborhood and got her to make the ID." All my tech and an old-fashioned eyewitness broke the case. "Hamish reported it just as we realized you texted Ivan that you were headed to a crime scene with Burgess."

She coughs, and I fumble for a water bottle. This car is state-of-the-art, with turbo engines and anti-surveillance technology, but it needs more cup holders.

Once she drinks some water, I find wet wipes so we can clean some grit off our faces.

"I can't believe Burgess was involved in this. I should've known."

"We'll look into it." I tuck a strand of damp hair behind her ear and brush more debris off her head. I can't stop touching her.

"His body. . .?" she trails off.

"Gone." No need for a clean-up crew now. The explosions took care of that.

I'll still have to reckon with Inara's distress over killing a cop. I have zero moral qualms over Burgess's death. He threatened her. He professed to be working with the Bondage Killer. Whatever his plan, he had her locked up in a place rigged to explode.

"Burgess said, 'He wanted me to trap you.' He was talking about Dennis Bundy. Did the Bondage Killer set those bombs?"

"I don't know." I have the world's best explosives engineers working at Knight Corp, my PMC. I'll offer their expertise to the NRPD to make sure we get a thorough analysis of the scene. "We'll find out."

"Why would he make the building explode like that? All his kills have been up close and personal." Her teeth are chattering again. I instruct the car to increase the interior temperature.

"I'm usually able to hold it together better than this," Inara says between shivers.

Is she really beating herself up for having an emotional reaction to all this? "You were betrayed by a man you thought you could trust."

She snorts, and I amend my statement. "You thought he would have your back as a fellow cop."

"I always knew he was rotten. But this. . ."

"You couldn't have foreseen this."

She jolts as if unnerved. She licks her lips, her gaze darting to my face and then away. There's something she wants to tell me, but she's still holding back. . .

"You don't have to hide from me," I say. It addresses her earlier statement and applies to whatever she's reluctant to share with me now. "You don't have to hold yourself together. Not around me." Whatever she's feeling, I can hold the space for it. If she breaks down, I'll hold her tight and then help dry her tears. "I want to be here for you if you'll let me."

"Rex, I. . ." Once again, her voice trails off.

"It's okay. You don't have to say anything." And she doesn't. I'll wait as long as she lets me. "When you're ready, you can tell me what you need to." As long as I can hold her, I have everything I could ever want, right here.

∼

*I*NARA

·   ·   ·

I'M FALLING from a great height. The blast seared me, but now the air is soft and sweet, embracing my face.

Death is calling me. "Inara. . ."

"Inara," Rex snarls. He's gripping both my arms, his eyes wild. Water is streaming down both our faces.

We're in the shower, washing the grit of the explosion off each other.

I've had visions during the day before, but only in the most tense moments of a case. I guess surviving an explosion is as intense as it gets.

"I'm here," I say. I find Rex's hands and grip them.

"You went somewhere." He fumbles for the shower handle, and it takes a few tries for him to turn off the water. I've never seen him so clumsy.

"I'm okay." The words are heavy on my tongue. I'm not okay. I haven't been for a long time. But at this moment, with Rex, I feel more stable.

"I'll call the doctor back." After the explosion, Rex took me straight back to the hotel. We entered via the private elevator, as usual, and a doctor named Atticus met us in our private rooms. Rex had contacted him, and he insisted on looking us over immediately to check for signs of a concussion.

"No. . . it's not that. I'm fine." It's not a head injury. It's my visions, intruding in my waking moments. I need to tell him about them. I'm ready, but I can't find the words.

"Okay. But the next time it happens, I'm calling Atticus." He cups my cheeks in his calloused hands, looking grim. I try to force a smile, but it drops away.

"We almost died," I say instead. We're naked in the shower together, with nothing between us. More than that, we've connected in so many ways.

He's shown me all of him.

I want to show him all of me.

"I know." Water drips from his brow, sliding down his cheeks like a tear. His face is a harsh but cold composition, his incredible beauty another sort of armor. But the more he looks at me, the softer his gaze becomes.

"It was so close."

"Inara..."

"I don't want you to die." There's a knife driving down my breastbone, opening me up. The water sliding down my face is real tears. "I—"

"Shhh, I know." A smile breaks over his face, pure joy like a brilliant sunrise lighting up the heavens. He thumbs what he just knows are tears from my cheeks. "I know. But I was grateful for one thing."

"What?"

"If the explosion had happened when we were both inside. . ." His head drops under the weight of what he's about to say. "We would've gone together."

My mouth opens, and I shake on a silent sob.

"I would've been with you. And that's all I want. To be with you."

I lean into him, sobbing full out now, and he bows further, pressing his temple to mine. He holds me close, gentle, treating me like I'm delicate. And I am.

I'm so fragile, so broken, but this? This makes me feel real. Maybe the pain inside won't poison me fully. Maybe I can let it out while he holds me together.

"I feel so weak," I whisper.

"No. You're the strongest person I know."

And then I surge to my tiptoes, pressing against the strong wall of his chest. I find his lips, needing more connection. His mouth meets mine, but instead of consuming me, he sips, tasting my watered-down tears. It's not enough and I grow frantic, clawing at his shoulders, trying to climb him.

"I need you," I gasp into his mouth.

"I know." He lifts me up but keeps kissing me gently. Passion claws at my throat, but it's not for sex. It's for this, the closeness. His palms cup my ass, and I twine my legs around him, but he just holds me up. Holds me against him so I feel all of him. "I have you."

I let my head fall to the crook of his neck and shoulder. He rocks me a little.

"I have you, Inara." And he does. I am lifted and loved.

Life is so hard. We're born out of darkness and struggle in the sun until it's time to die. There's so much suffering, so much pain.

But there's also love. And that can be enough. Even when the night comes, love will be enough.

"Please... call me 'little bird' again."

His shoulders and head relax, collapsing toward me even as his arms remain strong. I let myself go limp, too. I don't need to carry anything.

"I want to be with you," I tell him, and it's so easy. It's the easiest thing I've done. "By your side. I can't lose you, either."

"You won't, little bird. You won't."

REX

I FEEL like I'm flying. I carry Inara from the shower to the bedroom. We're soaking wet, but I want to lay her out, examine her for myself. Kiss every bruise, reassure myself that her heart beats and her lungs breathe. Worship her as she deserves.

She looks at me like she's seeing me for the first time. Her fingers dig into my hair, pushing it back from my face. "My king."

I almost fall to my knees. I'm so overcome with everything I'm feeling, everything she is.

"Little bird." I stagger to the bed and sink down, keeping her in my lap. I'm hard, aching to be inside her, but I don't need sex right now. I need to hold her. "My Inara."

She's still crying but somehow smiling. I grip her tighter when she begins to shake, but she lets her head fall back, laughing. "Oh, gods." She straddles me, still combing her fingers through my hair, gazing down at me like she's content to simply marvel that I'm here. My dick is folded between us, and it's painful, but the pain feels good. Desire's like a shot of whiskey burning down my throat, reminding me I'm alive.

I wait for her to kiss me, but she cups me close and wrinkles her nose when she looks at the bed. "We made a wet spot."

"First of many." I grin and nuzzle her jaw. We're going to wreck the whole bed together as soon as I'm sure she's steady. She's gone from crying to laughing in mere seconds, and I want to make sure she's okay. I'll wait for her to confess what she's feeling and get what she needs off her chest. I'll wait forever. It's enough to hold her like this.

She glances to the side and sees my phone lighting up. "Someone's calling you."

"Doesn't matter." Let the world fall apart. I'll just keep holding her.

"You should probably get it. We just survived an explosion. There's going to be questions." I see the moment reality creeps in. She sobers, but her face is still lighter. Unburdened. "Repercussions."

I run through the list in my head. Burgess—dead. The Bondage Killer—still out there. Hotel room—secure. Inara—with me.

She's with me. Finally. Nothing else matters. "We'll deal with them. Together."

"I know." She touches her fingers to either side of my chin. The lightest of touches that coaxes my face up to hers. She doesn't kiss me, just hovers close, letting her breath mingle with mine. "We have to figure out what to do."

"We will," I say to reassure her. Then I surge up, flipping her over. I lay her out on a dry part of the bed and stretch over her, planting a knee on either side of her legs. "But I know what I want to do right now."

"Mmmm." She reaches down, and her fingertips brush the head of my cock. My groin tightens, and I groan but hold back from pouncing on her completely.

"Say it again," I growl through gritted teeth.

Her eyes glitter like she knows the power she has over me. "My king," she breathes. Her fingers close around me, and I bow forward, desire like a punch in my gut.

"Little bird." I'm lightheaded, ready to pump into her fist and spill my seed over her glowing skin. "I love you."

She gasps and releases me. Thank the gods. I don't want to come before she does.

"I love you." I grasp her hair and hold her immobile for my kiss. I drag my lips down her throat, licking, kissing, even scraping my teeth over her shuddering skin. I spend some time at her breasts, lapping at her nipples while she pants and wriggles. But the siren scent of her cunt calls to me, and I nestle myself between her legs. I could live here. I can see everything—her sweet folds, already wet with desire, her lithe body laid out on the bed. Her fingers dig into the bedspread, and her heels kick when I kiss her inner thigh. I pin her hips and plant kisses on her sex.

She's so soft and sweet under my mouth. I sweep my tongue into her, chasing the flavor. She writhes like she might try to escape, so I palm her ass and pull her onto my face. I thrust my tongue into her, fucking her with it while my neglected cock weeps onto the carpet. My own pleasure is an afterthought because I don't want to leave this space between her legs. I'm right where I want to be.

"Oh gods, Rex—" Her abs tighten, and color floods her face as she comes. I gentle my hands on her, stroking her lightly as she relaxes into the afterglow. Her delicate muscles twitch, sensitive after the rush of pleasure. I place two fingers at her entrance, watching for when she comes down so I can stimulate her again. Her juices glaze my fingertips, and I can't help bringing them to my lips to suck her off my skin.

"I'm going to worship you all night," I tell her, and she moans. "Until you know to your bones how I feel."

A shy smile curves on her lips. "You love me."

"Yes." I let her sit up and touch my cheeks with tentative fingers. "You love me," she whispers in wonder. "My king."

My cock jerks painfully, but I don't move. I don't want this moment to end.

There's a harsh rapping at the door. Inara flinches, twisting away.

"No..." I reach for her, and she grabs my wrists. "Rex—"

More knocking. Whoever is at the door is insistent.

They're going to have to get a fucking battering ram. I've got my little bird naked under me, calling me her king, and I'm going to give her the royal treatment.

"Sir, I need to talk to you," the person at the door calls.

Inara stills. "Is that Hamish?"

It is Hamish. "Go away," I call.

Inara shakes her head. "We should talk to him."

"It's urgent," Hamish says. He's no longer knocking, and there's a sound I don't want to hear—the beep of an electronic keypad. Of course Hamish has the master key to any door in my own hotel. "I'm coming in."

"No—" I bark, but Inara shrieks and rolls away before I can grab her. I watch her gorgeous backside as she runs and disappears into the bathroom.

The door opens, and I rise to my feet to face Hamish. If he's surprised that I'm giving him the full Monty, he doesn't show it. His stone face doesn't crack.

I cross my arms over my chest. Hamish wanted to see me, so now he can see all of me. "What?"

"You're alive."

"And well."

He shuts the door behind him. I shift on my feet, willing my dick to soften faster. I was excited to be with Inara, but this is weird.

"The news is reporting an explosion."

"I sent you a message that we're fine." I had Alfie do it, but still, I gave him an update.

"Both of you?"

"Thank the gods." Now he does look relieved. "I had to see it with my own eyes."

"Well, now you have." I spread my hands as if to say, "Here I am." All of me.

I cross to the closet and pull out something for Inara to wear, grabbing a pair of slacks while I'm at it.

Inara opens the bathroom door enough for me to hand her the lounge set, thanking me. I grunt. My dick perks up at the sight of her but withers again when I turn back to Hamish.

"Does anyone else know Inara is alive?" Hamish is intent on something, but I'm not sure what.

"Just Atticus. I had him check us over a few hours ago. But no one else has seen us." No one in the hotel would have spotted us entering because we used the private elevator. My car has tinted windows, so no one could see us from the street.

"Thank the gods," he mutters again, and I raise a brow. He's not particularly religious.

"What's going on?" Inara emerges, looking calm in a loose black sweater and joggers. Her hair's freshly combed back from her face. I can't stop myself from reaching for her and pulling her to my side. She lets me, and we face Hamish together.

"What's going on is that a major explosion rocked the warehouse district, and you were reported to be on site. Not to mention, your partner, Detective Burgess, is now dead."

"By my hand," I say.

Hamish's brows rise. "Perhaps you'd better tell me the whole story."

I give him the highlights. I trust him with the truth, and he'll need it to spin this story to the police and the press the way we want it.

"Does anyone know Rex killed Burgess?" Inara asks as she chews on her lip.

"No, he's presumed dead from the explosion," Hamish says. "The police will investigate, but they have no reason to suspect his betrayal. Meanwhile, we've already looked into Burgess's accounts and found three equal payments of twenty grand. That's all it took to turn him."

Disgust turns my stomach. Burgess got what was coming to him. "Any luck tracing the payments?" I ask.

"Not yet. The payments were made in cash. Burgess deposited them in his personal checking." Hamish doesn't outright call Burgess a fool, but his tone suggests it.

"He didn't expect to get caught," Inara says.

I drape an arm over her shoulder, inhaling her floral scent. It calms and arouses me at the same time.

"The Bondage Killer was behind this. I know it. Burgess said as much." Inara stares into the distance, her detective mind working on the case.

I wish I could take her far away from New Rome, hide her away to keep her safe. But she'd never forgive me.

"Has he ever used explosive material before?" I ask.

"The warehouse fire that supposedly claimed his life," Hamish says. "There were traces of accelerant, but it was thought to be a coincidence."

"Let's revisit the evidence." If BK was really behind the events of today, it's a break from his usual modus operandi. But so is his new habit of leaving dead birds.

Inara's voice drops to a hush. "This was meant to trap me once and for all. He's fixated on me and won't be happy to be deprived of his prey."

"Which is why I came to you immediately," Hamish says. "I have a plan. But I need both of you to agree."

INARA

"WHAT PLAN?" Rex growls at my side. I'm glad he's here. My head is full of puzzle pieces—Burgess, the path of dead birds, the explosion—and I don't know how to sort them so I can think. I know I'm being too hard on myself. I'm not alone anymore. Rex is on my side. He doesn't have to carry me forever, but the fact that he can is a relief, a safety net I didn't know I needed. Right now, I'm content to remain silent and lean on him.

"The explosion is an opportunity," Hamish says. "The department-owned vehicle Burgess was driving has already been found at the scene and linked back to him. Eventually, they might discover that he invited you to ride along with him."

"He did," I say. "But he made sure to pick me up off-site. No one at the department saw me leave with him." I'm sure that was part of Burgess's plan—deliver me to the Bondage Killer and leave the site unscathed. I can't say I'm sorry he's dead. "No one will know exactly what happened."

"Unless we tell them. We can leak that you were there with him and did not survive."

I blink, trying to follow.

"You want to spread the news that Inara is dead," Rex says. His muscles tighten as if the mere thought causes him stress.

I can pretend I'm dead. Go into hiding, lay low. The idea takes hold, and suddenly, it all makes sense.

A laugh bubbles up my throat. I try to stop it and end up wheezing. Which only makes me laugh more.

Rex and Hamish stare at me, but I can't stop my hysterical outburst. My head grows light with a rush of relief.

I've dreamed of my death, but maybe this is it. I don't have to *actually* die. I just have to fake it.

"I'm all right." I press my hands over my face, trying to get myself together. For a moment, I get a brief vision of black feathers covering my face and the sense of falling, but as soon as I drop my hands, I'm back in the room with Rex. Both he and Hamish have somber expressions I read as worried. "I'm okay," I reassure them. "It's a brilliant idea, Hamish, thank you. I'm in. How do we do this?"

"I've taken the liberty of turning off your cell phone," Hamish says. "Any calls will go straight to voicemail, and texts will read as undelivered. You'll still be able to see them. . . but I recommend you do not respond. We'll need you to keep up the ruse."

"Got it." I sober, realizing how this will play out. My contacts, my colleagues at the department? Everyone in the world will need to believe that I'm gone.

"Why would we do this?" Rex asks. "You'll have no outside contact. And then what?"

"That's how we catch him." I face him so he can see my determination. "We find a way to lure him out and catch him. And maybe he'll stop killing because he thinks he's won."

18

I *nara*

I SIT in my situation room with Lacy Collins's old murder book in front of me. Rex and Hamish are holed up nearby in a makeshift office, dealing with the details of our plan. My role is done, so I'm paging through Lacy's notes, still unable to focus.

I'm in the first few hours of being a dead person, and it's both a relief and a burden. My phone's blown up with messages from colleagues. I can see them come through, although I can't answer because the official story is that my phone was destroyed in the explosion. The frantic phone calls from Diego Silva and Agent Larsen are the hardest to ignore, even though it's necessary. Even Bonds called twice but left no message. At least Hamish and Rex agreed to loop Mina in. It's a relief not to have to lie to everyone and worry about how Mina might feel.

To pull off Hamish's plan, Rex went ahead and released preliminary data that I was seen in Burgess's vehicle. The news is speculating that we both were there to investigate a lead in a murder case when a "terrible tragedy" took place.

Unfortunately, this requires Rex to play a shocked and grieving widower. He's been on the phone with his staff ever since. I'm trying to give him space, although I'm wondering if that's a mistake. He's roleplaying his worst nightmare.

I'm twisting the ring on my finger, fiddling with the giant rock he gave me, when the vision rocks me.

Smoke billows around me. My eyes sting with it. I taste ash, flinching as the sparks fly in my face and burning flecks bite my skin.

"Inara!" Someone is shouting. It's Rex, and I'm seized with incredible terror. Not for myself, but for him. Death is coming for one of us, and I have a choice to make.

I open my arms and let myself fall.

My hand slaps the table in front of me, and the vision clears. I feel like I'm still falling, the sensation strong enough that I needed to catch myself before I face-planted on the files I was reading.

My visions are coming faster. They're a warning, and I have the sinking feeling that they're heralding my doom.

"Detective," Hamish says from behind me.

I fumble to close the murder book as if I'm a school child caught daydreaming, then realize how ridiculous this is and turn towards him.

He holds up his cell phone. "I have Detective Lacy Collins on the line."

I can't talk to her because I have to pretend I'm dead.

I must look confused because he explains, "She's been fully vetted, so I've been keeping her abreast of the situation. We connected when I requested her notes and have kept in touch ever since. She heard about the explosion, but I was able to reach her before she called your cell."

What is he saying? "So she knows?"

"She knows everything I know," Hamish says, and a flood of relief weakens my limbs to the point where I slump in the chair. "I think it's wise to keep her informed. I believe we can count on her discretion." Is that a hint of warmth and respect in Hamish's normally stuffy tone?

I nod. Lacy is a steel trap. She was the only woman detective in her department for a decade, and based on the stories she told me, she learned the hard way to keep her own counsel. I trust her.

"She'd like to speak to you if that's all right. She might be able to tell us more about the accelerants found in the rubble of the Bondage Killer's last hideout."

Right. She's still a key part of this case. But my hand trembles when I reach for Hamish's phone. I haven't spoken to her in so long.

"Inara?" I don't know what I was expecting, but hearing her familiar deep voice is like coming home.

I splay a hand over her notes as if touching them will connect me to her. "I'm here." My throat is closing. There's so much I want to say—*I'm sorry, I'm okay, please understand what I've done*—but I'm too overwhelmed.

"Thank goodness you're okay." Lacy is normally very stoic, unfazed by the decades of horrible cases she's worked on, but I can hear the relief in her tone. "Hamish told me about your partner."

No one knows about Burgess's betrayal. Not anyone in the department or the news. There's no proof other than my testimony, and I'm happy to let people think he died in the warehouse tracking the Bondage Killer.

"He filled me in and gave me his private number, and I called him after I heard about the explosion."

"You were right. He had an in with the cops." I don't have to say who *he* is. "Just like before."

"Any leads?"

I close my eyes. "No. He's still a ghost."

"He's not. He's a man, and he makes mistakes."

I want to believe her. BK looms large in my nightmares and seems omniscient. Always several steps ahead of even Rex.

He almost killed us.

"Inara. Listen to me." My mentor's voice is as steely as it's ever been. "You can't blame yourself."

"It is my fault. I should've seen it coming." I did. I had glimpses of Burgess in my visions, I just didn't put it together.

"No, it's not. You have to believe me when I tell you it's not." Her voice softens. "I know why you're a detective. I know that you've been trying to atone for your family's deaths all this time. I know because I was the same." Lacy signed up to be a policewoman after her friend died in a brutal assault. "But you can't let guilt drive you. It's a distraction. It will steal your sleep and your sanity if you let it. You help people better when you're healed. When you're thinking clearly."

I stay silent because she's making sense. I haven't been able to sleep through the night, and it's affecting everything.

"You're beating yourself up because you think it might do some good. But it doesn't. And even if it did, you're worth the healing." She sighs. "It took me a long time to let go of my own shit. I'm sorry I wasn't able to teach you to do the same."

She's teaching me now, I realize, and it might be enough.

"Promise me that you won't spend one more second in guilt if you can help it. The faster you release it, the better your life will be."

I can tell Lacy imagines a long life for me. I don't know how to tell her I haven't considered that I might live for much longer.

"You're going to get this guy. It's only a matter of time. But you know how to get revenge? You live, Inara. You live long and you live well. That's what your family would want. That's what I want for you." Her voice cracks, and I choke back my own emotions. I can imagine her here, her graying hair pulled back in a bun, her blue eyes intent on mine. "We're all rooting for you. And. . . you're so precious to me. You were a gift, and I'm sorry if I didn't tell you that sooner."

My sinuses are tight with oncoming tears. I cover my mouth to keep in a sob.

"You did," I say when I can speak without fear of losing it. "You didn't have to say it; you showed it. You saved me."

"I could've told you," she says briskly. "I was too much of a hard ass."

I gasp out a laugh. "You were not." She could be stern and closed off, but that was just her way of dealing with the horrors of her career. She'd seen things that would give grown men nightmares.

"I was. But now I'm in therapy and think you should be too."

"Noted." My eyes tingle, but I'm smiling. "I'm sorry I didn't stay in touch."

"I understand. You probably had your own reasons. But don't do it again."

"I won't." On impulse, I add, "I'm married now."

"I heard," she says drily. "I assume my invitation got lost in the mail."

"We didn't have a wedding. But, if we do in the future, I'd like you to come."

"I'll be there. Now, I'll let you go. I know you're busy."

"I'll be in touch," I promise, and I intend to keep it. We end the call, and I hand Hamish's phone back, savoring the warmth that's flooding through me.

I thought I had to keep my distance to keep my loved ones safe. But maybe I was wrong. Maybe I can let people in. Maybe it'll turn out all right.

There's a noise behind me, and I turn, expecting to see Hamish. Instead, it's Rex. His face is a study of shadow, harsh planes like the craggy, uncompromising face of a mountain.

He needs me, I realize. He needs me as much as I need him.

"Come to bed with me." I hold out my hand. He comes over and takes it, his huge hand swallowing mine. Something settles between us. We're in this together, and no matter what, we'll be okay.

A BLAST OF EXCRUCIATING HEAT, *strong enough to sear my flesh from my bones. I whirl and spread my arms like wings and leap into the cool air.*

I'm falling from a great height. There's no sound, only the sensation of surrender. Everything will be over soon—

I flail, jerking upright out of the dream. Rex is right next to me, sitting up and turning to comfort me.

I cringe away from him at first, not wanting him to touch me. I've seen the same thing over and over, and I'm afraid of what it means.

I just got him. I just realized I could allow myself to be with someone. Please. I pray to the gods who have never listened and never will. My fate was woven from the start, and it seems I'm headed to my death.

"Another dream?" Rex asks.

"No. . ." I need to tell him about my visions. It's not fair. I almost died and almost lost him. That sacrifice should be enough. "It was more than that."

He waits for me to explain, opening his arms when I turn to him. My limbs are chilled and clammy with sweat. His heat surrounds me and draws me further into the room, out of the dream.

I'm safe here. Rex is here. His presence makes the darkness a gentle comfort.

"I need to tell you something. Something I've never told anyone." There are so many reasons I've hidden this part of myself. It's a curse and makes me feel like a freak. "But I don't want to burden you."

"I want it all." He means it.

There's a long silence, but I don't feel afraid. Telling him everything feels right, like everything's sliding into place. "Okay. I'll tell you. But I have to start at the beginning."

I shift in his arms, turning to face him. He rests his hands on my back. "I see things. Visions. I told you I have. . . instincts, but it's more than that. I get glimpses of what happened at a crime scene. But not only that." I've spent so long keeping this secret locked away. It's hard to continue, but his quiet attention compels me. "I'll see visions of the future sometimes. The way a crime will unfold. It's almost like I'm being given the vision so I can stop it from happening."

"That's incredible."

"No, it's not. Because I can't. I fail." I clench my teeth.

"Shhh," he brushes a hand over my hair. "It's all right."

"No, it's not. It's not. They started the night. . ." I can't say it.

"*The* night," he says for me. He knows the night I'm referring to.

"Yes. The night. . . he came." Shards of glass line my throat, but I make myself say it. "The night my family died."

19

I *nara*

REX and I stare at each other. Our faces are inches away. I've told him a secret I've carried for years, one he seems to know. "How did you know?"

"Because." He toys with my hair, slow to answer. I sense this is as hard for him to share as it is for me. "I know what it's like to look in the face of evil. To have it change the course of your life. To unlock something inside of you, something you have to keep hidden because no one else will understand."

I understand him perfectly. Our families' deaths broke something. Our lives continued but were forever changed.

"You have a gift."

I shake my head. "A curse."

"It's a gift," he insists.

"No, you don't understand." I fight to sit up. He rises with me but doesn't let me out of the circle of his arms. "It was my fault. I dreamed their deaths." I've opened the well of secrets, and now the poison bubbles out. "He killed them as I lay there. I did nothing!"

"You were a child—"

"I knew." I thump his chest with my fists. "I knew, and I did nothing."

"You did. You survived. It was all you could do."

I'm back there, in my ten-year-old bedroom, hearing the creak of the floorboards. Watching the blood drip from the knife.

"Inara," Rex calls me back to him. "It was his fault. He's the monster who came for your family—"

"I could've stopped it. I was supposed to stop it." I bury my face in my hands. "I saw the Green Street Murders before they happened. The same with Emily Rodriguez. I've dreamed of all the victims. It's my fault that they're dead. My fault." Telling this to Rex feels like carving open my chest with a knife. There's nothing but air between him and my beating heart. All he has to do is reach out and crush it in his fist.

But he doesn't. He closes his fingers around my wrists and draws my hands down. "No, little bird. It was him. It was not you. It was never you. You have nothing to apologize for. Whatever younger Inara did, it was what she needed to do. Whatever she said, whatever she did or didn't do, it was right."

I answer with a sob.

"Feel your pulse." He guides my fingers to a spot under my jaw. "Feel that? That means you won."

I let my hand slip away. "I don't want to feel this way anymore."

"Then give it to me. Give it all to me. Let me take it. I'm strong enough, little bird. I'm strong enough to carry it."

Oh, how I want that. I want to give in to him fully. It's so tempting. I could lay all my burdens on him and live freely in his dark control.

"You lived through it." I squint at him. It's dark, but I can see his aura, the infinite blackness like a midnight sky. "You know what it's like." I sense the truth he's hiding, and it tumbles out of me like I'm an oracle channeling a message from the beyond. "You think it's your fault your parents died. You think you could've stopped it."

His silence tells me I'm correct.

"You were a little boy," I tell him.

"You were a little girl," he reminds me.

I have a flash of memory. The old journals in his room—the ones I found where he wrote about me. "Is this why you wanted to find me?"

He tilts his head up to the ceiling. What little light there is in the room caresses his handsome face. "You understand." He blows out a breath. He doesn't want to share the way I'm sharing, but his truth is the price for mine. "It started as a childhood obsession. I was caught in a world of pain and fear. I knew you'd understand my pain as I understood yours." He cups my face. All my life, I've longed for someone to hold me just like this. And now he's here, and my heart is cracking open. "I'm here for you, Inara. For your pleasure and your pain. I want it all."

All those years he spent searching for me. It's come to this moment. I believe everything he says.

But there's more to tell him.

"I see death before it happens." This is it, the moment we break from each other forever. "I saw my family's death. My mother and father, my two brothers. But after. . . after. . .

I also saw my grandmother's death. I went to stay with her, and I saw her in a dream. One day, I went to school, and when I came home. . . she was there at the table, clutching her heart."

"A heart attack."

"That's when I knew I was different. I saw death, and it happened."

"You have a gift."

"It's a curse. I don't just see death. I am death." This is why I've built myself a fortress of solitude and hidden behind its walls. Why I've been careful not to allow anyone to touch me. Why I don't let anyone in. I can't allow anyone to see me or know me.

Rex opens his mouth, and I continue again in a rush. I need to get this out before I break down. "It happened again with my aunt. I saw the poisoned darkness spreading through her. I tried to tell her." I shake my head. "She went to the doctor, and they found it. Cancer, spread everywhere. But it was already over. Again, I was too late." I swallow around my shame. I'm that little girl again, trying to explain what her dreams impressed upon her. Trying and failing until the horror dawned, and it was always too late.

"After my aunt died, her husband didn't want anything to do with me. 'You're not mine,' he said. 'Your family is all gone.' He told me I was cursed."

Rex sucks in a breath, but I'm not seeing him. I'm seeing my uncle's pain-stricken face. I smell my aunt, the jasmine she grew on a trellis off the back porch. The chance at love and a home ripped from me for the third time.

"He said I was meant to die that night with my family, but I didn't, and now I was spreading the curse around." My throat has closed, making it painful to speak. Tears fill my eyes, but I hold them back. I don't deserve them. "He was right."

Rex's face comes into focus. I'm afraid to look at him in case he recoils from me, but I have to. He's my lifeline to the present. I sink into his dark eyes.

"And then. . . I ran. I stole a coat that belonged to my aunt, stuffed my pockets with granola bars, and left. I had to. I was cursed. Death followed me. It would visit anyone I loved."

"It wasn't you." Rex squeezes my hand.

"I would have a vision of someone dying, and then it would happen. What was I supposed to think?"

He squeezes my hand again, and it gives me the strength to continue. "I lived in a park. I found food in dumpsters. I was gone for weeks, even as the leaves turned and it got cold."

"How old were you?"

I have to think. It was years after my parents died, during a dark time unmarred by holidays or birthdays. "Twelve."

He sighs. "I was searching for you."

I squint at him, unable to understand. Then it dawns on me—the journals in his childhood bedroom. The ones I didn't get a chance to ask him about. It feels like I found them ages ago.

"I was trying to find you. The papers originally printed your name wrong. It took me weeks to work that out. Hamish didn't understand. He resisted, but I kept going. Finally, he saw how much it meant to me and gave in. We could contact you. Help you. I just knew. . . you were like me. You would understand."

"I wish you had found me. I was so alone." I stare into the distance, remembering the dread that would fill me as the sunset crept over the park each night. I would retreat into the shadows of the trees, but not so far that the wild animals would find me. I stayed on the boundary between the woods and the lights and noise of humanity, but not so close that someone could see me. There was a bare sliver of space I could exist in.

He strokes my cheek, and it brings me back. "What happened? What got you off the streets?"

"Lacy Collins happened." I remember her appearing on the edge of the parking lot where I was dumpster diving for moldy bread. "After working on my family's case, she kept in touch. She would come and check on me from time to time, especially after my aunt died and my uncle told her I'd run away. He made it clear he wouldn't be my guardian. She searched until she found me. Just in time, too. The night she took me in, the ground froze. My aunt's coat wouldn't have been enough." I shiver, and Rex moves, tucking the blanket around me. "She got me into a group home. I'd run away, and she'd find me again."

"I remember. Hamish hired a private detective who got close to finding you, but the trail ended with Lacy Collins, and she blocked him at every turn."

That sounds so much like Lacy that I have to smile. "She checked me into the group home under a false name. She was protective."

He strokes my hair. "She helped you. That's what's important."

"She saved my life. She got me a roof over my head, gave me a chance to finish school. I graduated early and went to work for a PI friend of hers. She's the reason I survived and why I use my abilities to solve crimes. And then I stopped speaking to her because I didn't think I could let her in. I can't get close to anyone." I pull away from Rex, scrambling back on the bed. Rex reaches for me, but I avoid his touch. "Everyone I've ever loved has died. Being close to me is a death sentence, and it is absolute."

REX

SHE STARES at me so solemnly. The tear tracks under her eyes glitter.

This is it. She's confessing everything now. She's giving me everything, even though she's afraid. She's trying to scare me off, but one thing I heard rises above the rest.

I grip her hair in my fist, squeezing but not pulling. "Are you saying you love me?"

She doesn't have to say it. The way she's looking at me. . . I know.

"Little bird—"

"We can't be together. It's impossible."

"You think that will stop me?" I lean in. "There is nothing that will keep me from possessing you."

"It's been so hard, going through life alone."

"I know." I draw her into my arms. She pushes against my chest, but not hard enough to keep me from hugging her close. "I was so lonely until I found you."

She hides her face against my shoulder. "I can't have this," she whispers.

I cup the back of her head, unwilling to let her pull away. "You're so afraid. Give your fears to me."

"You don't know what you're asking for."

"Oh, but I do. I've been waiting all my life for you. You are everything to me."

"Rex, are you hearing me?" She digs her nails into my

biceps, but the bite of pain only makes my cock harden. Maybe I like it to hurt a little, too. "It's not safe for you to be with me. Everyone who gets close to me dies."

I draw her head back by her hair, forcing her to face me. "I'm not afraid. If being with you is a death sentence, so be it. I'd rather die than live without you."

"You don't mean that." Her gaze darts between my eyes, her breath coming in pants like she's ready to run.

"I do." I rub my cheek along hers, drawing her focus with a touch. "Will you be with me?" My lips find her ear. "Be with me, Inara."

A jolt runs through her, and she pushes at me. I don't give her an inch. I wrap my arms around her, rolling us so she's under me. "Be with me," I order because she loves to be a good girl and do what she's told. "Please?" I add, because I want all of her. I've had her reluctance, and now I want her to come to me willingly.

"I'm so scared."

"I know, my love. I know. But I'm here."

"What if we don't get to have good things?" Fear is written on her face, and I feel it like a punch in my gut. We're both afraid of the same thing—that childhood tragedy will mark our lives forever. When the worst thing that could ever happen to a kid happens to you, how do you believe there's good in the world?

I squeeze her tighter. If she feels fear, I'll share it with her. I'll take the burden gladly. "I don't know what tomorrow will bring. If I could control it, I would." I've spent many years trying to exert control over every part of my life. I failed, but it doesn't matter because it led me to her. "But. . . I have you now. And you have me. If all we have is this moment, it would be enough."

"Rex," she's crying now.

"Inara, please." It's a special kind of hell watching my wife cry.

"I'm here. I'm with you. Don't let me go."

"Never," I whisper.

Her eyes are wet, pleading. She needs me to keep me with her. Present with me. I set my hand on the back of her neck and clamp down. Nothing focuses the mind more than the threat of a constricted airway. "And when you leave this Earth, I'll chase you. I'll follow you into the darkness, and we'll be together."

She shudders with a sob. I move my hand around to the front of her throat, collaring her. "You are mine." I increase the pressure of my fingers and watch her mouth go lax as she calms under my dominating touch.

"Yes," she whispers. I squeeze her neck tighter and shift my position so I can reach down and plunge the fingers of my free hand into her sex.

Her body bows upward, and her pupils bloom. She's wet, wetter than I've ever known her to be. My fingers are drenched.

"My gods, you're beautiful. Come for me."

Her muscles squeeze my fingers, and I groan, imagining that vice grip on my cock. Later. This is for her.

"Come for me, now," I growl, and like the good girl she is, she breaks apart around my fingers. I pin her down by her neck and sex, keeping her grounded when she'd fly off the bed. She seems to love the force of my control, writhing with a round of aftershocks. Her pussy milks my fingers. "Good girl," I praise her. "My good girl. I love how you come for me and me alone."

I wait until her eyes find me and pull my dripping

fingers out of her. I suck her essence off my hand. Her taste is sweet and tart, addictive. My arousal kicks into overdrive, making me dizzy. Making my body throb with wanting.

I'm drunk on desire just from dominating her. "Thank me for letting you come," I order.

She licks her lips before she obeys. "Thank you, sir."

Sir. She called me sir. I don't deserve the gift she's giving me, but I'll take it, selfish sinner that I am. I growl again, clamping my hand on the back of her neck and pulling her up for a kiss. I force my tongue into her mouth, making her taste herself, and she opens for me, allowing me access. It makes me wild.

I'm shaking with need and violent urges when I lay her out in front of me. I kiss down her body to lap up her orgasm. I want to drink her down. It's not enough to make her come and submit to me. I want to consume her.

She cries out when I thrust my tongue into her cleft. Reaching down, she seizes my hair and tugs like she will rip it out from the root.

"No, it's too much—"

"I'll say when it's too much." I shackle her legs and hold them apart, wide enough to hurt. It makes her gush all the more.

Pain and submission. My perfect girl.

And she's giving me all of her. Everything I wanted and chased for so long. She's giving me something only she can give, and I feel like the king of the world.

I have to be careful; I have to go slow. Otherwise, neither of us will survive this night.

She allows my violence, even feeds off of it. I nip at her labia, then lash her poor clit until her knees lock around my head and she screams.

And then I can't take it anymore. I rise over her and line

up my cock at her dripping sex. Her body accepts mine, even though I punch my hips into hers, thrust after brutal thrust.

And she takes it. She takes my possession and brutality and transforms it into something beautiful. She takes all of me, and I didn't know I was craving that until now.

And as we come together, sweat gilding our skin and sealing us together, we become one and it feels like love. I love her, and I know she loves me. If I have to wait forever until she admits it, I will.

All that matters is that she's mine.

*I*NARA

I WAKE UP A NEW WOMAN. I lie in the circle of Rex's arms, marveling at the lightness I feel. Rex exorcised something from me. I feel sore and hollowed out but also loved. It's like he lanced the wound, and now I can heal.

A thought intrudes—a tiny shadow in my happy glow. There's one thing I didn't tell him, one part of my visions I didn't explain: the death I've been seeing in my dreams was mine.

But I don't want to think about that right now.

I try to leave the bed and don't get very far. Rex tightens his arm around me and drapes his heavy leg over both of mine, mumbling something like, "No, don't go."

"What time is it?" It feels like dawn, but it could be any time. Midday or still the middle of the night. The hotel has excellent blackout curtains.

"Doesn't matter," Rex murmurs into my hair. "I don't have to go anywhere until tonight."

"I have to use the bathroom," I say primly and wriggle until he lets me go with a growl. In the bathroom, I take inventory of the redness Rex imprinted on my skin. There's some lingering soreness, a bite mark or two, but not as many marks as I'd like.

I tell Rex this when I return to the bed, and he opens his arms. "Let me fix it."

We snuggle together for I don't know how long. At some point, it turns to slow, languorous kissing. I wait for Rex to twist my hair into a leash and force me to go down on him, but his kisses remain sweet. Almost chaste, except we're both naked. His hands roam up and down, stroking my back and bottom lightly but never venturing further.

"I could do this all day," he murmurs against my mouth.

I'm squirming again, this time with arousal. "Hmmm, I want more."

"Too bad. You have to lie here and take it." He moves his big body over me, pinning my limbs with his muscled bulk.

I pout up at him. "Not fair."

"Who's in charge?"

"You are."

"Say it again."

"You are, my king."

Turns out those are the magic words. His eyes darken, and his chest rumbles with a satisfied hum.

I end up with my hands bound wrist to elbow behind me with one of Rex's silk ties. He sits me on his lap and props my legs over his. The position puts my breasts and sex on display.

He leans me back against him and slaps my inner thighs, spanking them red. My breasts get a few swats, and the pain feels like bliss. It's a beautiful alchemy, how he hurts me so I feel good. I'm high from just that.

"Is this what you wanted? For me to treat you like my little pain slut?" He punctuates each word with a swat.

My breasts throb, and each pulse of pain takes me higher. "Yes."

He slaps my pussy. I groan at the sensation and the wet sound it makes. I'm filthy, soaking wet. My abs tighten reflexively, but I can't close my legs because they're propped over his. "Yes, what?" His hand hovers over my sex in silent threat.

"Yes, sir."

His hand wavers, and I flinch, then make myself relax and remain open for him.

"Good girl."

The words warm me through. But then he adds, "Now beg me to spank your pussy until you come."

"Oh, gods." Hot liquid pools in my belly, threatening to spill over. I'm close, just from the thought of coming from this. "Please, sir, spank my pussy. I need it."

"With pleasure."

He lets his hand fall, lightly at first, a tease, but then with more force, until sparks fly from my clit and I know one more blow will send me over.

"Please," I whisper, "Please, please, please—"

"My gods." His cock is rock hard under my ass. "I can't deny you anything. Come for me, Inara."

His hand falls, jarring me into a place of anticipation. The pain rushes in a second later, and my orgasm explodes.

He rolls, planting me face down in the bed and spreading my legs. He spanks my bottom next, each slap sending me higher.

Then he's pushing into me, and oh, it's so good. He's

rough, his fingers biting into my hips, thrusting hard enough to make the movements make my clit rub against the bed, and I scream, thrashing. He pins me and makes me take it.

And then we do it again. We spend the day in a scene, napping and cuddling when we need to. Twilight finds me soaking in the bath. Rex ordered all manner of bath salts for me to sample. I tried to get him to join me, but he refused.

He comes in now, dressed in his business suit, knotting his tie.

"I have to go. Press conference."

I lay my head on the rim of the bathtub, trying not to pout and burden him with my reluctance to let him leave. I know being Rex Roy in public sucks for him. "Or you could stay here with me. . ."

"I need to go play the part of grieving widower in public. Really sell this."

Ugh, that's going to be awful. I'm glad I get to play dead. "You could be the sort of billionaire who becomes a recluse. Someone who retreats from all human contact."

"Tempting. But not tonight. Nadia will have my head."

I sink into the bubbles to hide my smile. It's nice to know there's someone my husband will obey.

"I'll be back as soon as I can." He says it like a vow, and I nod. I believe him.

"Will you be okay?"

"Of course." I wave a hand, flicking scented bubbles down the bath.

"All right. I love you."

I suck in a breath. It's still a shock to hear it. He hasn't insisted I say it back, but I want to. At the right time.

There is something I can give him. "Rex. . . when this is all over. I'd like a wedding."

He tilts his head. "A ceremony?"

"Let's make it official. I'd like to invite Lacy. And Mina," I add. It's about time I met my online friend in real life.

"Done. We can do it at the house."

My mouth falls open, but I get an instant flash of the future—me in a white dress, holding a bouquet of yellow roses under a trellis of jasmine vines, Roy Manor looming in the background. "I was thinking of something small. . ."

"You're married to a Roy. We don't do small." He leans down and kisses my forehead. "I accept your proposal, wife."

I roll my eyes. Of course he'd take my request as a win. Proof that I want to stay married.

"It might be difficult because I'm supposed to be dead."

"We'll figure all that out. After."

After BK is behind bars, he means.

"Come back soon," I call. I should be grateful to get some time alone with the case, but a sense of foreboding comes over me. Not a premonition, just a feeling that I want him by my side.

He pauses at the door, his body cut through, half in light, half in shadow. "I will."

He leaves, and I take my time getting out of the bath. This time, Rex left a number of marks on my skin, and I get to catalog them at my leisure.

I dress in jeans and a sweater and head to my situation room. Rex already ordered room service, so I eat while I go back to working on the case. I chomp on a burger and switch on the TV, thinking I'll put on Rex's press conference but just leave it on mute. I want to see him, but the notion of me being dead is more depressing than I thought it would be.

I'm immersed in Lacy's murder book when a phone rings, interrupting my focus.

It's my cell. I reach for it automatically, but it cuts off after one strangled ring, and I remember I'm not supposed to answer. Once the news announced my demise, the wave of calls from people checking on me died away.

The phone lights up again with another call. I check the screen to see who's so insistent.

Burgess calling.

The room spins around me, and I blink against the vertigo. Chills go up and down my arms.

It's not him. Burgess died. I can still see Rex lifting my former partner up by the neck. And even if he did survive that, he was then blown to bits. Right?

The phone goes silent, then lights up again. *Burgess calling.*

My thumb hovers over the button to answer, but I hesitate too long. The call ends.

But I have to know who's calling. I hit redial and wait.

"Hello?" It's a man's voice, and for a disorienting second, I think it's Burgess.

"Who's this?" I make my voice harsh.

"It's Ted."

"Ted?" I scrape my memory and finally remember—the man in the bathroom at the ball. So much has happened between now and then. "How did you get this number?"

"He gave it to me." He, meaning the Bondage Killer. "He said the man who had it let him down."

The man would be Burgess. Burgess was working with the Bondage Killer. But now BK has Burgess's phone, which means. . .

He was there. At the warehouse.

"He said I needed to call Detective Ramos. Are you her?"

I take a chance. I have a connection to BK and need to follow it as much as I can. "Yes."

"Oh, thank gods." Ted sounds like he's about to cry. "I thought it was all over for me. The news said you'd died."

I lick my lips, trying to think of an explanation, but Ted doesn't stop talking. "He's got my family. He said you have to come, or he'll kill them."

20

He's *got my family*. Ted's panic reverberates through me, turning my stomach. My mouth fills with saliva, the burger threatening to come back up, but I can't vomit now. This isn't the worst moment of my life, but it's up there. Top ten, maybe top three.

Think, Inara. I need to remain calm and clear-headed. Imagining the worst won't help. "Where are they?"

"He gave me an address. You're supposed to meet me there, and then he'll tell you where my family is. But he said you have to come alone." Ted's voice wavers, then rises as he starts to lose it. "He's watching to make sure it's just you and me and no one else. That's what he said. No cops or he'll kill them, even the kids—"

"Okay. Okay." This is it. The moment I've been waiting for. The Bondage Killer must have seen me and Rex leaving the warehouse or guessed that I was still alive. And now he's going to lure me in, using this innocent family. "I'm coming." I'm already in the bedroom closet, reaching for my leather jacket. I leave it and take a hoodie instead. "Tell me where to meet you."

"No one can know," Ted's voice thickens as he responds, and he chokes. He sounds like he's crying. "Or I'll never see them again. Oh, gods."

"Ted? Deep breaths. Focus on my voice. He doesn't want your family; he wants me. And I'm coming." I will save this family if it's the last thing I do.

And it might be.

"He took them," Ted is mumbling, crying. He sniffles. "You're coming?"

"I'm on my way." I head out of my room toward the private elevator. I need to slip out of the hotel. Rex's wardrobe for me didn't include any baseball caps, so I flip up the hood. I need to look as anonymous as possible so the press won't clock me. Or my bodyguards, who I'm more concerned with avoiding.

"Give me the address so I can take a taxi."

"Okay." Ted sounds calmer. "Okay."

I feel a pang of regret. All the beautiful things Rex and I spoke to each other last night, all the love we have for each other, and I'm abandoning it. Abandoning him. But if there's a chance I can save this family, I have to try. He'll understand that, right?

It won't be easy staying under Rex's radar. But that's what I'm counting on. I need him to spot me and bring the cavalry.

THE ADDRESS TED gives me is a deserted corner at the opposite end of the city from the warehouse BK blew up. But it's still another commercial district, this one even more derelict than the last.

The sun set hours ago and the night is dark and cold. A feeling of hopelessness rises in me.

I hope I can get to the family before it's too late.

The taxi leaves, and I step into the street, searching for Ted. "Hello?"

"I'm here." A lanky figure in jeans and a stained khaki-colored jacket steps out of the shadows. I startle and force myself not to run, even though I was expecting him.

Ted looks a million times worse than he did at the ball, like he hasn't slept a wink for a week. Exhaustion has carved chasms into his gaunt face.

"I came alone," I tell him.

"Thank you." He steps closer, and I balk at his sour smell. His sallow skin is streaked with tears. "It's this way." He hunches and starts walking without watching to see if I follow. "He just gave me the exact address."

"I need you to tell me what happened."

"There's no time."

"Please, Ted, I need to know what I'm walking into. For your family."

"I fucked up. I told him I didn't want to do his work anymore. And then I went to my brother's house for dinner and found that he'd taken them. This phone was on the table and started ringing."

Tingles spread over my body. I'm closing in on BK; I know it. "Did you speak to him?"

"He told me to follow his instructions or else. No police." His brow furrows as if he's concentrating on repeating everything verbatim. "Call Inara Ramos. Tell her to meet you at the corner of 29th and Williamson. I'll give you further instructions from there. Do it, or your family dies. And then he texted me that he's watching."

I hold out my hand. "Can I see it?"

His hand shakes as he holds up the phone in front of me. There's an unknown contact texting in all caps.

I'M WATCHING.

The last text came through minutes ago.

13056 WILLIAMSON

SEND IN MY SPARROW

ALONE

I bite down, tasting metal. That's BK, all right.

"He means you, right?"

"Yes. What's that address?"

"Here. . ." Ted fumbles with the phone. "I put it into Maps." He peers at his screen, then looks around and points down the block. "I think it's that building." He's pointing to a square brick building that takes up the rest of the block.

We walk toward it slowly, but after a few feet, Ted halts. "Do you think they're inside?" He nods to the warehouse door. It's so much like the warehouse where Burgess tried to trap me that my gut twists. But I won't chicken out now.

"We'll see."

"I'm not supposed to go in." He wavers as if he wants to. If it were my family, I'd be charging in, instructions be damned.

The phone in his hand buzzes, and he jolts like he's been electrocuted.

"Is that him?" I can guess who's texting.

"Yeah. I'm supposed to take your phone," Ted mumbles but keeps his hands at his sides. His head hangs, and I feel a stab of pity. He's trapped in a nightmare I understand all too well.

"Take it." I offer it to him. Rex will be tracking it. I turn to face Ted fully. Even if BK is watching, he won't be able to see or hear me murmur. "As soon as I'm in, call for help."

He looks up, a dash of hope breaking his fearful expression. "But—he said—"

"If he's watching, he'll know you followed instructions. I'll get him to let your family go. He wants me." I press my phone into his unwilling hand. He almost drops it. "But I'll need help getting them out safely. So call for help."

"All right."

I don't know if Ted can pull himself together long enough to be useful, but it's worth a shot.

I turn from him and square my shoulders. The real challenge will be getting BK to give me a chance to talk to him before he does what he did at the last warehouse and detonates a bomb to send us to our deaths.

This is the end game. Chances are, my vision is real, and I'm going to die.

But if I can save this family before I go, it will be worth it.

The steps I take toward the warehouse are the longest of my life. I get deja vu from the last time I entered a warehouse, but this time is worse because what Rex told me last night is playing on repeat in my head.

I've been waiting for you all my life. You are everything to me.

I'm sorry, Rex. I draw my gun and push the door open, and it swings out of my way with a creaking whine.

I step in to face my fate.

21

This warehouse is smaller. Older.

The first thing I do is kick something. It goes skittering across the floor, rolling into a patch of light. A flashlight.

Did BK leave it for me? I clear the area and keep my head up when I crouch to pick the flashlight up. I deliberate for a moment. Should I keep it off and try to sneak around in here, or use it even though it leaves me without a free hand?

In the end, I flick it on and blink to adjust my eyes to its full brightness. I swing the beam in a circle, feeling braver. Normally, I'd use the flashlight on my phone, but BK made me surrender it.

The beam illuminates the far brick walls, stained black with soot. There are a few scattered feathers on the concrete floor.

I pace onwards, scanning for any movement with my gun at ready. If I'm going to die, I'll take BK with me.

But I can't kill BK without saving the family first.

I find them in the middle of the warehouse. Their bodies

are lying in a circle, tied together. A brunette woman and two school-age children. Beyond them, a lanky, balding man is stretched out. I can't see clearly, but he looks a lot like Ted. Must be his brother.

I shine the light on each face, but no one moves. My breath shorts out, but I push down my panic and focus on the mother. She's alive. I let the light linger on the rise and fall of her chest long enough to make sure. She's breathing. They all are. They're not dead, only unconscious.

The family is surrounded by barbed wire. And worse, there are small cardboard boxes with wires spiraling out of them, duct-taped together and placed inside the barbed wire barrier near the family. These have to be explosive devices.

I approach slowly but keep my distance. The family is right there, and I can't even touch them. Can't shake them awake or drag them out to save them from their doom.

BK knew I would come to save them. He made it so I couldn't do it.

It's so evil that it takes my breath away. How many families has he terrorized?

It ends tonight. One way or another.

Without moving, I use the flashlight to search every square inch of the space around the family. There's no movement. No one else is here.

But I know this isn't over. He won't be content with blowing the building now. He'll want to see my face and know my torment.

There's a crackling sound, and I jerk, raising my gun in that direction.

Someone taped a walkie-talkie to a metal post near the family. They used the same silver tape that they used to secure the explosives. I pace toward it, shining the light around it as if a bogeyman might be hiding in the shadows around the post.

BK doesn't appear, but my sense of dread increases. I circle the post and end up facing the walkie-talkie, checking for any loose wires that might hint at an explosive device near it.

The walkie crackles again, and I almost leap out of my skin. Acid pools in my stomach. I point the gun at the radio, even though I know it's only the voice of evil and not the whole man.

Another crackle, and this time, I can make out a word.

"Inara." It might be the walkie-talkie distorting the man's voice, but I recognize that flat tone from when I heard it years ago in my childhood bedroom.

I tuck the flashlight under my arm so I can grab the radio without holstering my gun. I rip it off the wall, duct tape and all, and stare down at it, breathing hard.

"You came," the Bondage Killer says.

I don't reply. He wanted me here, and I'm here. I need to say something, but I can't force the words out of my throat.

It's hard enough to hold it together.

And it doesn't matter, because this is the Bondage Killer's show. "Take the stairs."

I have my gun in one hand and the walkie-talkie in the other. I clip the walkie to my belt and swing the flashlight around to find the stairs he's talking about. They're in the middle of the room, zigzagging up several stories.

I don't know how long I hesitate before BK radios again. "Do it, or they die. Now."

I really am going to be sick. Saliva pools in my mouth. I take a deep breath in through my nose and spit into the dust at my feet. *Gotta hold it together.* I can't wig out now. Ted is counting on me.

It takes everything to leave the family and walk to the metal stairs.

I can only hope Ted called for help. I can't get the family out, not with them rigged to explode. After Burgess and the warehouse, I know BK isn't bluffing. He'll blow us all sky-high. I've got one shot to do this right. If I can distract him long enough for help to arrive, the family might make it out of here alive.

I probably won't walk out of here, but they will, and it'll be enough.

It takes forever for me to climb the stairs. I do it slowly, hoping to give the cavalry more time to arrive. I don't like relying on Ted, but I do have faith that Rex will do what it takes to find me.

I could've called Rex immediately, and he'd be at my back now. Scratch that; he wouldn't have let me come at all, and Ted's family would suffer the same fate that Burgess did.

No, I made the right choice. I had to come alone.

I pause on the landing at the second floor, shining the flashlight around the abandoned space. The light catches on a set of glittering eyes in the corner. Some sort of vermin has made its home here and disappears with a scuttling sound.

The walkie at my collarbone comes alive. "Keep climbing," BK rasps, and my body physically recoils. I want to rip this thing off of me and never hear BK's voice again. "All the way to the roof."

I crane my head upwards. There are several more stories before I reach the top of the building. I'd rather stay down here with the rats.

"I'm waiting for you," BK singsongs. "Come to me, my Swallow."

Bile spurts into my mouth and galvanizes me into action.

I press and hold down the largest button and snap out a "Fuck you" into the walkie-talkie. It's not a good idea to antagonize the serial killer who holds more than my life in his hands, but seriously, fuck him. If I'm going out, I'm going on my terms. "You don't get to call me that," I tell him and use the surge of energy that anger gives me to power up another set of steps.

I pause on the next landing. BK holds the cards, but I have something he wants. "Let the family go."

"They're free to leave at any time." He sniggers, knowing full well the family is unconscious and tied up. I grit my teeth so hard my jaw aches.

His laughing turns into a coughing fit, and the transmission cuts out. I wait, but he doesn't say anything more, even though I've stalled on the steps.

"You've already won," I tell him. "You have me. You don't even want them, so why not let them go?"

No answer. I keep climbing, moving slowly but steadily. "I surrendered my cell phone, but you can call the police."

He's still silent, but I bet he's listening. I pace around another corner, sending the flashlight's searching light over every inch of the next flight of stairs before continuing my ascent.

"You have all the power. You can call for help. You'll still have me." I'll gladly trade myself for the family. "And I'm who you really want, right?"

Still no answer, but there's some movement down below. A shadow darting across the ground floor. Is it Ted, finding his courage to creep inside and free his family?

Or did Rex find me?

I wait, watching for more clues, but there's no more movement. But it gives me hope that someone is down there, helping Ted's family.

With that thought energizing me, I finish my climb. I can stall for time and keep BK distracted.

I press the PTT button and say, "Hello? Are you still there?"

"Keep climbing. All the way to the roof."

Was that a flicker of light on the ground floor? It gives me the courage to try something,

"Not until you admit that I'm the one you want," I test. "Not them. Me." Maybe if I act possessive of him, it'll surprise and excite him.

The silence stretches long enough that I worry I've put him off. Maybe he won't like me jostling for control of the situation? I'm supposed to be the victim, after all.

But something tells me he wants a worthy adversary. Someone worth all the trouble he's gone through to haunt me.

"All right," he sounds pleased. "You're the one I want."

He's in a good mood; I can use that to my advantage.

"I'm coming," I tell him.

The stairwell ends at an open door. The night air is cool on my face as I step onto the gravel-covered roof.

There's no sign of BK. I set down the flashlight. I don't need it, not with the ambient light of the city.

"Hello?" I call. "Dennis?" I use BK's first name. He's spent all these years obsessed with me and probably feels close to me. I'll do my best to encourage that.

I let my gun precede me and start clearing the roof. Multiple large HVAC units block my view of the entire surface.

I'm halfway across the roof when I get a sense that someone is behind me. I whirl, gun raised, but there's nothing but shadows.

"Hello?" I call again. I want to call Rex's name, but I'm not going to clue BK in that I have help. *Please let it be him.*

"This way," BK calls from the opposite direction, the one that will lead me further out on the roof.

I keep walking, inching around a large metal AC unit, and there he is. A slumped form in a chair, shrouded in a dark coat. I can't see his face, only the top of his head, and even that is in shadow.

I stare at him, my gun raised.

"Put down your gun," he orders.

"No." I grip it tighter, aiming for his torso. "I'm here. Just like you wanted. And you're under arrest."

He starts laughing, and once again, it ends in a wheezing cough. Even from a distance, I can tell that a sour smell hangs around him. But I don't know if it's real or my psychic impression.

"It's no use," he says and raises his head out of the shadow. I flinch at what I see. There are patches of shiny skin-like scar tissue mottling his face. Like he's been badly burned.

He didn't have those scars the last time I saw him.

But the eyes are the same. Flat and dead.

Then he flicks open his coat, and I see why my gun would be of no use. His torso is wrapped in duct tape, with the same makeshift incendiary devices that I saw downstairs all over his body. The wires wind down his right arm.

He lifts his hand to show me he's holding the trigger.

"Put down your gun, or we all die."

~

Rex

. . .

THE PRESS CONFERENCE TAKES FOREVER. Nadia walks me out, and finally, I sink into the back seat of the car and wave at Ivan to start driving. I can't wait to get back to Inara.

Alfie alerts me that Hamish is trying to reach me and connects the call.

"Hamish?" I ask.

"Victor has urgent news for us." Hamish's voice is tight and strained.

I sit up in the seat. "Victor?" The assassin I hired has been quiet, only checking in with sporadic reports.

"He got a lead that put him on Ted Raider, the photographer, and followed him tonight. There's something you should see."

My phone screen lights up with footage of Inara entering the building and Ted hovering in the back.

No. "Get me eyes on that building. *Now.*"

INARA

CHECKMATE. BK's done it. He's lured me out alone, and now I know his plan. If I shoot him, it'll trigger the explosion. If I don't, he'll probably do it anyway.

We're going to die together. The only question is if I can stall him long enough for Ted to save his family.

I raise my hands in the air to show I'm complying, then slowly set the gun on the ground.

When I straighten, I raise my face to the sky. *Come on, Rex.* One thing I know is that he's got this whole city surveilled. He might be watching us, even now.

I don't want him to see me like this, but I don't want to

die alone. So it's a comfort, knowing he might have eyes on me.

A tiny part of me holds out hope that he'll come for me. I try not to dwell on it, but the more I push it away, the stronger it becomes. I even sense someone behind me again.

Don't think about it. Focus.

"Come closer," BK says.

Adrenaline races down my arms. I want to snatch up my gun and shoot. *Remember the family. Stay strong.* "Promise me the family will live."

"Just the family? Not you?" He coughs a few times.

I say nothing. We both know my life is a lost cause. I'm not going to beg for it.

"I've been waiting for you."

"Why?"

"It was always going to end like this. You and me, together."

Ugh, I hate this. I don't know if I can do this.

As soon as I think that, I hear Lacy telling me, *He's a man, and he makes mistakes.*

What would she do if she were here? She'd rely on her training.

I know BK's profile. He thinks of himself as extraordinary and better than everyone. He liked our small town because he blended in. He was able to move from home to home freely, finding his victims. He seemed ordinary in every way, a wolf in sheep's clothing.

He thinks he's smarter than everyone else. Even now, he thinks he has the upper hand.

I can work with that.

"That's why you've done all this?" I ask. "Killing victims, entire families? You could've just asked me to come to you."

"Would you have traded yourself for them?"

"I'm here now, aren't I?" I'm tempted to rush him and get this part over with. Let him blow us both. Relieve the intense pressure.

But then—there's a flicker of something from the corner of my eye.

This time, I know there's movement behind me.

BK mumbles something, but I'm only half listening. Is that a crunch of gravel under a booted foot?

It takes everything not to turn and run toward help. I don't need help, but the family does.

"The family on the first floor—you need to let them go," I say loudly to cover any other sounds of my backup. *Go downstairs,* I think, as if I could connect telepathically with them. *Don't try to save me. Get the family out.* "They're innocent. They've done nothing to deserve this."

"No one is innocent," BK says, but I'm not focused on him. I'm watching the shadow. *Please, Rex. Please.* If it is him, I'm hoping he'll get the message. I need him to get the family out.

I need to keep BK talking.

"I was," I say. "So was my family."

"They would've kept you from me. I watched you in the park but couldn't get close. Your parents were protective."

"Is that why you killed them?" It's breaking my heart to talk about this, but I'll do anything to distract him. If I have to use my pain as bait, so be it.

The shadow moves away. Hopefully, they got the message to focus on saving the family downstairs.

My work is almost done.

I can hear Lacy Collins saying, *You're going to nail him.*

BK is coughing again, a hacking sound that doesn't sound good.

"Are you alright? You sound like you're sick." I concentrate on the conversation but keep an eye out for any more movement. Whoever was behind me is gone. I can sense it.

Maybe the family will be okay.

"The after-effects of smoke inhalation."

"Smoke inhalation?" *Keep him talking. Give Rex time.*

"The fire in Elyria."

I shudder when he says my town's name.

"It almost took my life. Collins made sure of that, the bitch."

"Lacy?" I try to follow.

"She found me out. I had to blow the building early, and I almost didn't escape."

"We all thought you'd died."

"I nearly did."

"And then what?"

"I hid out. Healed best I could. Reached out to a friend to help nurse me back to health."

"A friend?"

"A protégé of sorts." He says it with such pride that I get a hit of insight.

"Protege. The Blackbird Killer?"

"Yes." Now, he does sound smug. Like a proud papa talking about his son making the honor roll.

"Who is the Blackbird Killer?" Even though I'm about to die, I want to know.

"My student."

"Who are they? Give me a name." I take another small step forward but stop when he raises the trigger.

"Ah, ah."

Shit, I pushed too hard. I need to have more finesse. But I'm wired, my whole body buzzing with adrenaline and my senses heightened. Suddenly, the lights from the glittering city and the sound of my own heartbeat are all too loud, too bright.

"This isn't about them," BK says. "It's about us."

"Us?" I can't keep the disgust out of my tone. "There is no us."

"Ah, but there is." His rasp grows softer, more intimate. "That's why I had to find you. We're meant to be together."

The sour taste is back in my mouth.

"Only you can heal me."

I shake my head. I shouldn't deny it; I should feed his delusion, feed his fantasy. But I can feel his darkness threatening to pull me under, and if I go down, I'll drown. "I don't understand."

"You know what you said to me? The first night I came for you?"

He means the night he killed my family. "I don't remember." I do; I just don't want to.

"You said you saw me die. In an explosion, in a fire."

That was the first night my visions came to me. It would be harder now to hear this if I hadn't told everything to Rex last night.

I'll let him boast and relive that night. The night of his triumph and my suffering. I'll give him the fantasy and let him wallow in it.

Only I can do this. Only I can give him what he needs.

"You were so young. So wise. You knew that I had killed them," BK says. "I didn't have to tell you. You knew everything."

I was a child, I want to scream. My body aches like he's beaten me. "Why did you kill my family? Why did you spare me?"

"I came for you. You were special," he says now.

I swallow. I'm not a little girl anymore, trapped. I'm a

grown woman with a gun nearby. I can take control of this situation at any time because I'm not afraid to die. "That's why you killed them all?"

"We were supposed to be together."

"So it is my fault." I knew it. This is the guilt I've carried all along. "You killed them so you could have me."

"Yes," he says softly, and it hurts so badly knowing the truth. I'm the reason BK murdered them.

"We have a connection," he says, and I want to deny it. But I know it's true. We're connected in so many ways. He was there when my psychic ability awakened. He was the reason I am who I am today.

And now we're going to die together. I couldn't kill him the night he first came to me, but I can now.

Before I can grab my gun and rush him to end this, a new voice rings out.

"No, Inara is mine." And Rex steps out from the shadows.

The gravel crunches under his boots. He looks larger than life in his dark suit, but all I can think of is how he's bulletproof but not bombproof.

"No, please." I hold out a hand to stop Rex from moving forward. "Wait," I say to BK as much as I do to Rex. I step between them, like I'm protecting one from the other. I'm not sure who I'm protecting from whom.

Rex speaks over my head. "It's over, Dennis. You've lost."

BK tries to say something and starts wheezing instead. His hand trembles around the trigger.

"Stay back," I say to Rex. "He's rigged to blow."

"It's okay," he says to me. "We got the family out."

Relief weakens me, making me bow forward. *I did it. They're safe.*

Rex looks back at BK. "The only victim tonight will be him." He makes a move toward BK, and I panic.

Rex is going to try and take BK down, but BK isn't bluffing. Rex will get blown to bits.

I can't let that happen.

I have to stop it.

And I know how.

"This ends now," I say to them both. Before they can react, I stride to the edge of the roof and jump onto the ledge. The wind whips up from several stories below. I don't look down, though, because I'll get dizzy.

"Inara, no—"

BK wheezes something. He lifts his hand, wiggling the trigger at us. He's seconds away from killing us all, I can feel it.

It's now or never.

I face Rex. "I love you," I mouth to him and leap into the night.

22

I*nara*

I'M FALLING from a great height. There's no sound, only the sensation of surrender. Everything will be over soon—

A blast of excruciating heat hits me. I scream, feeling like it's searing my skin from my bones.

My eyes are closed against the stinging. This isn't a dream. It's happening. It's real.

"Inara!" someone shouts. Something hits me hard enough to knock the air from my lungs. I wheeze, choking, but the arms around me squeeze tighter.

"I've got you," Rex growls in my ear. His grip is painful, and it feels so good. I'm alive. So is he.

I crane my head. Behind us, fire blooms, eating into the night.

The Bondage Killer blew the roof.

I'm with Rex, and we're flying through the air somehow.

"Hang on," Rex says.

There's a jolt, and my heart flips with a swooping sensation. Whatever's keeping us in the air adjusts. Rex and I drop together, but then he gets one arm under my legs while his other arm cradles my back, carrying me bridal style. There's a dark shape overhead—wings, maybe—and a whirring sound that tells me this is another expensive bit of tech.

Behind us, the warehouse is gone, collapsing in on itself. The sight makes me gasp, but I remember what Rex said. He got the family out. He saved me, and now we're airborne, soaring over the city.

I glance down and grow dizzy at the sight of rooftops and streets below. My stomach catches up to all the jerking movements of the last few seconds, and I clutch Rex's neck, seeking something stable to lock onto. BK is gone and his answers with him. I wish I could've gotten more out of him, but I never expected to survive.

The helmet's faceplate retracts, and Rex's breath hits my cheek. "Inara?"

"I'm all right," I find my voice. It's scratchy from the ashy air. "I knew you'd catch me. You'd never let me fall."

"Never," he tells me. The vow reverberates through me, warming me to my toes.

We're alive, and we're together. That's all that matters.

Fresh air streams over our faces. I breathe it in along with Rex's scent, clearing my lungs.

The city lights glitter like jewels. From this vantage point, New Rome is so beautiful. There's even a glimmer of gold on the horizon, although I might be imagining that. Even if I am, I know the sun will eventually rise.

I switch my gaze to Rex. His jaw is clenched, his eyes fixed ahead, and there's no softness in the sober angles of his expression. But his face is the most beautiful thing I've ever seen.

I reach up and trail my fingers over his cheek.

He glances at me, eyes questioning.

"Take me home," I tell him.

"Where is home?"

"Wherever you take me." I tuck my head against his chest and close my eyes, content to let him fly us toward the dawn.

HOME TURNS out to be Roy Manor.

While Rex debriefs Hamish and Mina, I take a shower. There will be press conferences, stories to be told to the command staff, and procedures to be followed. But I'm happy to let Rex handle it while I take a moment alone. I stand under the spray, imagining the night's events washing down the drain. There might be a few tears escaping along with the water, but when I turn off the tap, I feel lighter.

It's over. I am at peace.

Rex told me that he had hired an assassin named Victor to help hunt BK. Victor happened to be tailing Ted to see if BK would reach out to him again.

I felt like someone was following me up the stairs in the warehouse. It must have been Victor. He assessed the situation, phoned Rex, and focused on freeing the family. Hamish and a team of explosive experts were en route and on call the whole time, but once the family was safe, they made the decision to stay clear.

I could be angry that Rex hired a criminal to do his dirty work, but one thing I've learned is that Rex is going to Rex. His sense of justice is warped, but he's also going to throw all his money, time, and energy at a project until he gets his way. The result was that Ted's family was saved. I'm not going to bitch about the means. For now.

There is someone I want to talk with, but I don't have my phone back yet; I left it with Ted earlier. It feels like a lifetime ago.

"Alfie," I call while I'm towel-drying my hair. From what I can tell, the AI assistant is always listening.

"Can I help you, Detective?" Alfie answers politely.

"Can you call Lacy Collins?"

"Dialing Lacy Collins."

I smirk at the mirror. I could get used to having this kind of assistant.

"Lacy Collins is unavailable. Do you want to leave a message?"

"Yes, thank you," I say, and Alfie cues me to leave a message at the beep.

"It's me," I say. I imagine Lacy's face. In my mind's eye she has more gray hair and deeper wrinkles around her eyes. I'll have to tell her that in the heat of the moment when I faced BK, her advice saw me through.

Later. I can't get through that right now. I still have to process everything I felt on that roof. For now, I tell her, "It's done. He's gone. Forever." Simple, but it'll get the message across. I wonder if she'll be able to hear the emotion in my voice. Am I upset that I didn't get to arrest BK for his crimes?

Not at all. I feel lighter, like the weight of the world has fallen off my shoulders. A burden I took on when I found Lacy's murder book all those years ago.

Or maybe it was earlier, from the night BK came to murder my family. I think of that moment and what BK said about it on the roof, but the poison is gone, leached away.

Because I survived. I went through hell, but I survived. And what's more, I'll be able to thrive.

The worst moments of our lives shape us but also fuel us. What happened to me made me develop my psychic abilities. What happened to Rex drove him to become a warrior. Tragedy shaped us, but because we are who we are, we've used it to fuel our growth. We were forged in fire and came out stronger. When the pain is gone, only the power remains.

When I step outside the bedroom, Alfie's waiting.

"Take me to Rex," I tell the little robot.

He leads me to Rex's office.

Rex is there, leaning against his desk. He's removed his body armor. His dark hair hangs spiky over his forehead, so he must have taken his own quick shower.

This is our first moment alone since yesterday. The flight here—first on the dark wings of Rex's glider, then in a helicopter to the mansion—didn't afford us much time to talk.

He doesn't look up when I approach. He must still be processing. But I feel giddy, so I sidle up to him with a smile.

"We did it," I say.

He's got a hand over his mouth, rubbing as if in thought. It's as if I'm not even here.

"Rex? Why won't you look at me?"

He raises his head, and I see why. He's furious. The heat of his anger hits me like the blast of a bomb.

"You left me," he says. His voice is cold and dark, but I hear the sad little boy he was in his accusation.

He's right. I did leave him. I shrug, accepting his censure. "I had to. I had to save them."

"I—" He cuts himself off, looking away. The muscles in his jaw jump as he chews on what he wants to say.

I move in front of him. For such a big man, he can be

fragile. I need to remember that just because someone looks big and bad doesn't mean they don't have feelings or can't have their feelings hurt.

And Rex is hurting. He might not know how to say it, but I can tell.

"Talk to me," I prompt softly and get another glare from under his thick brows. Then the mask slips, and he looks down at the ground.

"You didn't even tell me."

"I knew you'd be tracking me."

His wet hair makes him look like a schoolboy. I want to stroke it back from his face.

So I do.

"I knew you'd be watching. Somehow, someway. That you would find me."

"When you jumped off the roof ledge, my heart stopped."

"I knew you wouldn't let me fall."

His breath gusts my hair, and he finally relaxes and leans into my palm.

"Inara." His tone is broken, pleading. I feel each heave of his chest like it's an earthquake. "You can't. . . I can't." He closes his eyes as if he's angry and can't articulate what he's feeling. Or maybe he's angry at the feelings themselves.

I understand that completely. I've spent a lifetime shackling my feelings, only allowing myself a release with pain. But now I have someone to share things with, and that alone is so freeing.

I want Rex to find that same freedom, so I let him struggle with his feelings. But I keep holding him. *I'm here.*

When he looks at me again, he's accusing and pleading, all at the same time. "You alone hold the power to destroy me."

I can't say anything, so I push my tiptoes and press my lips to his. Just a quick kiss. *I'm still here. I'm with you.*

I love you.

He shudders under my palms and hesitates, then wraps his arms around me and pulls me to his chest. This time he grasps my chin and guides our kiss. It's deeper but sweeter somehow.

"You can't just leave me." His voice is muffled because his face is buried in my hair.

"I'm not," I whisper back. "I'm here with you. I'm not leaving, Rex. I'm here."

"Gods," he chokes out, and I relive that moment when I stood on the ledge of the roof, my fear overcome by the need to save him.

"I'm here, Rex." I tease his hair with the tips of my fingers, grounding myself with touch.

"I almost lost you. Again."

"You can punish me. If you want."

His laugh is broken, but his fingers dig into my hair. "You'll like it too much." His grip tightens, and the stinging on my scalp feels like home.

"Is that so wrong?"

"It's not punishment if you like it." He growls deep in his throat and draws my head back to kiss my neck. His lips hover over my pulse as if he's reassuring himself I'm alive. "I want you in my dungeon. I want to tie you down so you can't breathe without feeling my bondage. I want to mark you with the tawse, the whip, the cane. Stripe you until you sing for me." He hesitates, as if reluctant to admit the rest. I press myself against him, and his control snaps. He makes my back bow with my hair. "I want to cage you so you can never fly away."

"Yes," I gasp as the bite of pain sends me higher. "I want that too."

"Fuck," he snarls and pulls me back up, controlling my movements, holding me still for his kiss. His lips drag down from my mouth as he scrapes his teeth against my neck. I push my hips against him. I could orgasm like this.

We're both breathing hard when he lifts his head. I meet his gaze, and there's no more anger in his eyes. Nothing but desire.

"Please," I mouth, awash in happy neurochemicals. I'm sinking fast into subspace. His control makes me weak. The strength leaves my legs until only his grip is keeping me upright.

"Please, what?" His voice cracks like a whip.

"Please, sir." I arch in his hold, letting myself go soft with surrender. My eyelashes flutter. "Take me to the dungeon."

~

Rex

She wanted the darkness? She's going to get it.

But now, riding a vibrating saddle that tortures her clit, she might be having second thoughts.

Too late. Her arms are bound behind her in a reverse prayer position. She's flexible, but after a few minutes, the strain will have set in, and her shoulders will be screaming for release.

I've gagged her with a rope winding around her beautiful face, and she groans into the knots at her mouth. I like it when she begs me, but I'll enjoy that later. For now, I'm riding high on the desperation in her eyes.

She has a fat dildo wedged inside her—only her pussy. I still need to train her ass to take me.

Her legs shake, and she rises off the saddle, straining for a respite.

"Ah, ah." I flog her ass. It's already flushed red, a prepared canvas for more of my marks. She'll be taking the cane and the whip today, but first, I'm going to flog her a bit more. Make the blood rise to the skin so she feels everything that much more. "Get back down on that dildo."

She makes a distressed noise but sinks down like a good girl. She's so wet, it's no hardship to slide right on.

Damn, she's perfect. Tied up and in distress and wet as a raging river.

I pace around to her front to flog her chest. Her eyes are half-lidded, pleading.

"I'll let you off when it's time to cane you," I tell her. "But first, I want you to orgasm a few more times for me."

She groans behind the gag, eyes wild. I step close to stroke her sweaty hair back from her face.

"This is how you please me," I tell her quietly. She nods and closes her eyes, giving up her will. It's a heady power trip when a goddess like Inara gives over control. It turns me into a god. My muscles swell, and I move through the room like I'm ten feet tall.

Her body rocks on the saddle, and she moans through her orgasm. Her skin is slick with sweat. She's still soaking the saddle, but her front isn't as nearly as red as her backside. Time to rectify that.

I rock back and forth, letting the flogger swing easily, letting my feet do the work. St. James taught me the dance of a dom. It's all about the footwork. The leather tails rain down. I beat her breasts until her head is tipped back and she's leaning into each blow. She's riding high on a wave of bliss.

This is supposed to be punishment. Punishment and a renewal of our connection. A baptism by fire. A start to our new lives.

I trade the flogger for a whip. "Ready?" I crack it next to her head. Her eyes fly open at the sound.

She stares up at me, fear and lust warring in her eyes. Her chest heaves.

Then she nods. The trust she gives me triggers a feeling so powerful that I feel like I'm floating. Like I could drift up to the sun.

It's not easy to be with me. I require nothing less than all of her. But then I'll give her all of me, too. Love and trust in an infinite loop. There's nothing between us now.

The whip licks her torso. She'll feel like I'm flaying the skin from ribs, but I'm being careful. The marks won't last long. Which is fine. Once they heal, I'll get to whip her all over again.

I pause to cut off the gag and free her mouth. "I want to hear you scream."

She gives the screams to me, the sweetest music. Her poor breasts are mottled red. I even whip her nipples. That sends her over the edge again. More screams.

When her head droops like she's too wrung out to hold it up, I put down the whip and cut the power to the vibration saddle. I cup her face, making sure she's still with me.

"Did I do good for you?" she murmurs, and my heart cracks open.

"So good, little bird. You just need a break and some water, and then you can take more."

"Okay," she murmurs, drowsy with endorphins. I kiss her sweet face and steady her as I lift her off the dildo.

She shudders like it kicked off another round of aftershocks.

She's too limp to stand, so I take her weight while I admire the shining dildo.

"Gods, you soaked the floor. You're going to lick that up for me later."

That makes her moan again.

I put her on her knees on a platform in front of me. She's still in tight bondage, but it'll be a mercy for her to be off that vibrating saddle. Those last few orgasms must have been painful.

Her lips are dry from the adrenaline. I hold her chin and give her water, a few sips at a time.

Halfway through the bottle, she closes her eyes and leans into my hand.

"You're doing so well," I tell her. "My sweet little sub. I know you want to please me."

She nuzzles my palm and kisses it. So damn sweet.

I can't take it anymore. My cock is about to burst from my pants.

"I was going to cane you next, but first, you're going to take care of this."

I unzip myself and step close. She's positioned on the platform at the perfect height for me to play with, so I cup the back of her head to guide her closer, and she gets to work.

The first press of her lips to my erection sends me shuddering.

"I'll have to whip you more often," I say. She moans and takes me into her throat, either to placate me so I don't punish her or encourage me to whip her harder. Probably both. The submissive and the masochist, holding hands and skipping along in her psyche.

I let her do the work until my balls tingle and I have to take over. I pull out and order her to breathe. She gulps air like she's going to dive deep.

I'll have to take her in the pool again. The breath play we experimented with there was fun.

Although there are ways to do breath play on land. St. James once mummified a partner in plastic wrap. He covered their nostrils so the only way they could breathe was through a straw in their mouth. And then he would cover the straw and watch the panic rise in their eyes.

Thinking about Sebastian is a boner killer, so I turn my attention back to my little bird—tied up tight, on her knees, working to please me.

She swallows me down again, and my control snaps. I fuck her face with abandon, driving my dick into her hot little mouth. I'm lightheaded, a man possessed, and my orgasm blows up from the base of my spine. I erupt into her mouth, bowing over her head as I pump into her.

When I pull back, her hair's mussed and her lips are puffy from the abuse, but she looks peaceful. She opens her mouth to show me my gift, and gods, if that doesn't make my cock jump like it's ready to come again.

"Swallow," I order her, and after she does, she opens her mouth to show me it's gone. I stroke her face to reward her.

"You did so good for me. Just a little more punishment, and then it's over."

I release her arms and check her over. More water, more caresses. Her skin is sensitive from the impact play, so I soothe the soft welts the whip made and then scratch them lightly to make her squirm. The marks are proof of my power over her, and I'm going to enjoy them.

All the boundaries between us are gone. There's nothing but us. "I'm going to make you feel your love for me. Write it on your skin." Pain is a brand that proves I own her fully.

"Yes, sir. Please."

"This won't be easy," I warn.

She smiles and keeps smiling as I use her braided hair like a leash to guide her to crawl to the cross. I allow her to stand on her own to tie her to it, secure her arms overhead, and tuck her braid out of the way, leaving her back as a bare canvas for me to paint.

She's standing on blocks so she's the right height for me to fuck her from behind. Her body is at an angle, too, her ass sticking out so I can see her puffy pussy, beckoning me.

"Soon," I say and stroke her lower lips in promise. Inara sighs and presses her torso into the cross, even though it must be painful. Goosebumps rise on her back.

It feels right to be back where we started—her tied to the cross and me drinking in her lovely form, reveling in her submission.

So much has changed. So much is still the same.

"I'm going to love you now," I say, stroking her bottom. She arches further to press her buttock into my palm. Her skin has a rosy glow, ready for welts and cane stripes.

"But first... tell me this. Who owns you?"

"You do," she sighs. "You do, my king."

INARA

I LOSE myself in the rollercoaster, the highs and lows the pain brings. The pride and excitement that I've reached a deeper level of submission.

I want to be perfect and pleasing to him. The thought that I can serve him so fully fills me with warmth. I want to be put through my paces, made to writhe and cry out and surrender. I want to be brought low by his dominance until my whole self is obliterated. There will be no Inara and no Rex, either. We've become something else, something more. A push and pull, a giving and receiving. An inhale and exhale. Pain and bliss in one perfect body.

He lays love on my skin. Each lash becomes a caress. Each welt is the result of the most intense, all-consuming kiss. It's the most extreme proof of connection. I feel so close to Rex. So loved. The feeling sends me flying high. I'm no longer myself. I have no identity. I'm free, made new. I'm his, and he is mine.

And we are one.

It's heaven, and it's hell. Or it's all hell, but it's a wonderful place. With Rex, I can descend into the darkest places of need. My shadow self that craves the lowest places. He breaks me down so beautifully, and I trust him. Gods help me, but I trust him to walk through the darkness with me.

It makes me so happy, I could weep. I am weeping. I am undone.

"You're doing so well for me," he praises me between whip cracks. "You take what I give you so beautifully. You are perfect when you're falling apart."

I'm addicted to these sweet nothings earned with sweat and pain. Rex leans close, and he's breathing hard, too. He's working hard to bring me to that place of ecstasy, and I love him for it.

"I bet you could come like this." He runs a hand down my back, re-igniting the fiery sensation. "From just the touch of my whip."

I moan. I want that.

"Do you want me to do it? Do you want me to whip your clit until you come?"

I have a flash of terror. Not fear that he will hurt me, but fear that he will and I'll let him down.

"I don't know. What if I can't."

"You will. I won't let you fail."

No, he won't. He will never let me fail or fall.

I weep then because I'm so happy. I was so afraid, but he took that fear, consumed it, and turned it into something else. There's no more danger. Only ecstasy.

I tug on my bindings just to make sure they're there. When I'm sure I'm held fast, I lean into the cross and smile. "Please."

"I'll give it to you. . . on one condition. You don't ever leave me again."

I shake my head frantically.

"You'll be with me forever. Whether or not you wear my collar, you're mine."

"Yes." I'm sobbing. "Yes."

"Okay, little bird. I'll give you what you need."

The whip crashes down, sparking an explosion inside me. A white hot, searing pain. And then I fly like a bird, traveling safely home.

23

F *aded photographs, peeling from the moldy walls. Feathers crushing underfoot. BK's scarred face, telling me, "It's over," before the flames engulf us all—*

I WAKE DISORIENTED, my instincts screaming at me. *Something's wrong, something's wrong!*

I'm in our dark bedroom. The pillow is soft under my cheek, but Rex's side of the bed is empty. I grope the rumpled covers. They're still warm, but Rex is gone.

I have a vague memory of him cutting the ropes and letting me down from the cross. *It's okay. You did so well. Just be with me.* He must have cleaned me up and carried me to the bedroom. I was too deliciously limp to do anything but allow it.

A few hours later, I remember him rising and waking me. He kissed my head and told me to go back to sleep. I was still drunk from orgasms and pain.

I make a move to get up, and my muscles start screaming, too. My sex is raw, and my abdominal muscles ache. Forced orgasms hurt.

Muscles I didn't know existed cry out. They're overextended from me clenching so hard and so often for so long.

I push through the pain and rise. I want Rex. He should be here. It feels wrong that he's not. He wouldn't leave me unless it was important.

"Alfie," I say. "Where's Rex?"

I expect it to say the cave lab or his office, but it tells me, "En route to New Rome."

"What?" There's a fog in my head, and I'm fighting it to clear it and make sense of what Alfie is telling me.

"There was a report from the morgue. The body of Emily Rodriguez went missing. Mr. Roy went to investigate."

Emily Rodriguez was the last Blackbird victim. How does a morgue misplace a body? Between this unsettling news and my dream, I'm officially freaked out.

"Call Rex."

"Calling."

While Alfie's trying to reach Rex, I scramble out of bed. There's a shock of pain, like jumping into cold water, but the more I move, the easier it gets. I push through the stiffness and throw on some clothes. I'm still chilly, so I find Rex's bathrobe and drape it around me. The weight grounds me into the room, allowing me to shake off the lingering ick of the dream. The robe even smells like Rex. I press my face into the plush lapel and inhale.

"No answer," Alfie reports, and my nerves start to jangle. I'm awake now.

"Is that typical?"

"No. Mr. Roy has orders to put your calls through no matter what. Re-dialing now."

I can't just sit here while Alfie rings Rex. "Is Hamish awake?"

Ten minutes later, I'm in Rex's office, watching Hamish commandeer the console behind Rex's desk to check on his whereabouts. The Scotsman looks a bit rumpled in a tartan dressing gown, but he's wide awake.

"He didn't want to wake you," Hamish explains. "He thought he'd be back before dawn."

This is exactly what I did when Ted called me on Burgess's number. Now I'm the one left behind, and I hate it.

I'm chewing my lip. "I have a bad feeling."

Hamish nods as he types. His focus on the computer screen reminds me of Mina. "I've contacted Rex's network. Including his more. . . nocturnal acquaintances."

"Fraternitas?"

"Yes."

That reminds me. . . "Hamish, there was someone Rex told me about. The—" Do I just blurt 'the assassin?'

"Killer-for-hire?" Hamish says for me.

"Um, yes." I guess Hamish is used to conversations about hitmen.

"His name is Victor. I've left a message for him as well."

"Rex says Victor was following Ted."

"Ah, yes. Victor had a theory that Dennis used Ted as an errand boy. Ted might have delivered the cash payments to Burgess."

"Ted definitely delivered the photo of my family to my desk," I say, shuddering at the memory. "Or Burgess did it and pinned it on Ted. Either way, Ted was involved from the beginning."

"Indeed." Hamish opens his mouth to say more, but Alfie interrupts.

"Incoming message from KittyBang."

"Mina," I say, straightening in my chair. It's a bit early in the morning for Mina to be awake.

Scratch that. She probably never went to sleep.

"Message as follows: Is Rex okay?"

"Why?" I ask out loud, knowing Alfie will convey my message to Mina. "What have you heard?"

Alfie puts Mina on speaker, and she says, "Turn on the news."

~

REX

HEAD, foggy. Pain pulses through me with every heartbeat.

Someone's hot breath hits my cheek. I try to jerk away from their sour stench but can't move.

I'm propped up on some sort of hospital bed with my limbs and torso tied down. I'm naked, and my head feels like I've been drugged.

"Not so big and strong now, are you?" my captor taunts.

My tongue is swollen, too big for my mouth. There's no moisture so I fight to speak. "Who are you?"

"Question is. . . who are you? Rex Roy or something more?" He's gloating. He's learned my secret. "I bet Inara knows."

At the sound of her name, I go wild. My muscles bunch, and I strain against the cords holding me.

"Oh, does that upset you? Me talking about that bitch?"

Red bursts in my eyelids. I'm fighting whatever knockout drug they used, clawing to the surface.

Then, something presses to my chest, and electricity

crackles through my limbs. My lungs seize along with my muscles.

My captor's voice comes from far away. "Settle down now, settle down."

The pain ends, but I feel like I took a punch from a gorilla. While I fight to breathe, my captor says, "She ruined everything. He was obsessed with her, never looked at me."

What is he talking about? *Think, Rex, think. Your body is bound, but your mind is coming back online.*

Just have to fight the fog. . .

"Maybe I'll deliver you to her in pieces," the man sniggers.

Who is he? The answer's close, but then I'm falling back under. . .

~

INARA

THE NEWS SHOWS a sky full of smoke against a backdrop of high rises. The remnants of a helicopter that exploded mid-flight litter the ground. Not only did it explode, but it showered the ground with feathers as if it were full of birds.

The silent TV screen shows black feathers raining down from the sky.

I'm supposed to panic.

I'm supposed to think that Rex was in that helicopter and that he's dead.

But he's not. I can feel it. When I close my eyes, I see a dark space. A room with no windows and photographs on the wall. Rex is there with the killer.

I need to trust my instincts to see this through. I need to figure this out in time to save him.

Think! What are my clues?

There was an explosion, like the ones caused by the bombs strapped to BK.

Feathers, like the birds left at my townhome and the trail of feathers in each warehouse.

"This is the Blackbird Killer. He's the one who likes explosives." My mind is working, putting things together. "He's the protégé BK told me about. Both times, it was him rigging the warehouses to blow."

"You're sure?" Mina asks.

I close my eyes and feel the situation. "BK had help. Not just Burgess. Someone else. His student." BK is dead, but there's still a second killer out there.

I open my eyes to find Hamish peering at me, his eyes dark under his bushy brows.

"This is a message to me," I say. "We have to find Rex."

"We have contacts in the morgue," Hamish says. "I've checked with them. There's no sign of Rex."

"He's not there?" I ask.

"He got there around two a.m. but left soon after."

Rex went to the morgue to track down the missing body. If he had a lead, he'd follow it. So where did he end up? What clues would he have found?

"I'll keep digging," Mina says, and I thank her.

Hamish is on the call with someone, barking orders.

I stare at the TV screen, letting my thoughts wander. I keep thinking about the warehouse where I faced BK. The first floor, where he tied up the family.

The family...

"Hamish," I ask suddenly. "How is Ted's family?"

He looks puzzled.

"The family that was tied up?" I explain. "The ones Victor got out."

"The Walker family? They're safe. They were admitted to New Rome Central Hospital and are staying in the private Roy wing there. Rex ordered them to be provided with bodyguards and access to excellent psychiatric care. There seem to be no lingering physical effects."

"How were they drugged?"

"Some sort of gas."

Gas is what Rex liked to use to incapacitate his victims.

Something else nags at me. "Did you say the Walker family?"

"Yes."

"I thought Ted said it was his brother? Wouldn't they have the same last name?"

Hamish frowns. "I could be wrong, but I don't believe Ted is a relative at all."

My insides quake. This is a lead, and I'm afraid of where it will take us. "We need to find out."

We recontact Mina, who confirms it. "No relation between Ted Raider and the Walker family. No obvious contact between them, either."

"But. . ." My thoughts are coming slowly. It feels like I'm moving through murky water, swimming toward the light. "Ted told me BK had taken his family. That's why I snuck out of the hotel in the first place. Why else would he try to lure me out?"

Hamish visibly recoils.

"Holy Sith," Mina breathes.

We're all coming to the same conclusion. I feel it like a weight in my bones.

Ted lied to me. It wasn't his family at risk. And he had no reason to lure me out unless. . .

He was working with the Bondage Killer the whole time.

I remember the details of being with BK on the roof. "On the roof, BK was having trouble breathing. He was older, not as mobile. He had to have help capturing the family and tying them up."

"A partner," Hamish says.

"A protégé," I correct. "Someone he mentored." The Blackbird murders were homework. "But then, yes, they partnered together. BK saw him as a sidekick, but now BK is gone."

The weight in my body lifts. I break through the surface and breathe the sweet air.

I've got it.

I turn to Hamish. "I know where Rex is. I'm going to rescue him, and I'm going to need help."

24

I *nara*

I CAN DIVIDE my life into a series of before and afters.

Before my family was murdered, I had a happy childhood. After their deaths, I felt alone. Before Lacy found me, I lived on the street. After she took me in, I decided to become a detective.

Before Rex. . . everything was different. There's so much that's changed. Before him, I was closed off. I clung to a cold concept of justice, keeping a moat between me and the rest of humanity. I saw myself as a warrior priestess, someone who would go to the dark places to keep innocent children safe. I refused any human contact and condemned myself to be alone.

Rex was the only one who could break through. He refused to let me be and rudely trampled on my boundaries because he's a fucking psycho who needs a few decades of therapy, but he's the psycho I need. I needed someone to rescue me from myself.

He's the master of my afters, and I know he wouldn't have it any other way.

Before Rex, I did things by the book. I'd never think of heading an investigation with a team made up not of detectives, uniforms, or SWAT members but criminals. The blond twin enforcers are at my back, and a tall, lean assassin with white-blond hair is helping me break into Ted's squalid apartment.

"You're sure about this?" Hamish murmurs in my ear. I'm linked to him and Mina by an earpiece.

He's giving me an out. I can still go to Bonds or even the chief and conduct this investigation the legal way.

But there's no time. The wheel of justice turns too slowly, which is fine for the victims who are dead. But while Rex is still alive, I'm not waiting.

I guess I agree with Rex now. Walking a moral line is a luxury I can't afford. Sometimes, you have to descend into the darkness to fight monsters. Sometimes, you become a monster yourself.

"I'm sure," I tell them, then signal my teammates.

Victor steps back and allows one of the scary twins to kick in the door. The two of them rush inside, guns in hand.

I hang back, my heart pounding. I'm wearing what feels like seven hundred pounds of body armor. I'm even in a Rex-style helmet that Hamish found in my size.

"Clear," Scary Twin One calls out.

"He's not here," Victor says.

"All right." I step inside Ted's bachelor pad. I didn't expect him to make it easy. "I can still look for clues."

Victor joins me in tossing Ted's apartment.

"We've searched his place before," Hamish says, "when we first suspected Ted. I'm reviewing those notes now."

There's a corner of his tiny living room that holds a hospital bed and medical equipment, including a breathing apparatus and an oxygen tank. I report this to Hamish. "Was all this equipment here, then?"

"Yes, Ted claimed it belonged to an infirm uncle who was now deceased. We are still in the process of confirming this."

I remember BK's coughing and his raspy voice. "Is it possible Ted's 'uncle' was the Bondage Killer?" I ask my team. "BK had definite respiratory issues on the roof. This medical equipment could be his."

"It's possible. We'll keep digging." Hamish sounds grim.

"Don't beat yourself up for missing it," I say. "Ted could've stashed BK somewhere before you searched here."

"You think Ted was taking care of BK while they planned and executed the final showdown?" Victor asks. "Or was it Ted who decided it was time for BK to die and set up the explosives?"

I imagine the second scenario, and bile rises in my throat. I don't want to think of BK as a helpless old man, so it's possible Ted was calling all the shots in the end. "We'll never know."

To distract myself, I grab the TV remote and turn it on to a news channel. On-screen, the helicopter explodes over and over.

We find photography equipment in Ted's bedroom, along with some notes.

I read one aloud, "'Pool cleaner, fuel oil, duct tape, zip ties.' He used the last two to tie up the Walkers."

"The first two are useful for creating explosive devices,"

Victor says coolly. More evidence that Ted was rigging the explosions.

We finish tossing the room, but I don't find anything of use. No journals laying out his master plan or any dead birds. He must keep them offsite.

"Look for keys," I tell Victor. "Or bills with another address that he might be using as a hideout." I head to the kitchen to give it another pass.

"Mina, is there any property in Ted's name? Even a storage unit?" I keep seeing Rex held in a dark room with photographs taped to the walls. But there's no room like that here.

"When we dug into him earlier, there was nothing like that," Hamish says. "But we must have missed it. Perhaps he has access to someplace through his work?"

"On it," Mina says.

I find a set of keys in a junk drawer and go out to the hall to try them in the front door. The twins hover close, keeping guard.

One of the keys works, but the other doesn't. What door does it open?

The neighboring door opens, and a stooped senior lady appears, holding a white bag of trash. Her eyes fall on the twins and she jerks back, her hand grasping for the doorknob.

"Excuse me," I call to the neighbor.

One of the twins catches the door before it closes. The lady cries out, looking terrified.

"It's okay," the twin says in a kinder voice than I expected. "We won't hurt you."

The lady doesn't look convinced.

"We don't mean any harm," I say, stretching out a hand. "We're just looking for Ted."

"I don't know any Ted!"

"Your neighbor," I correct. My guess is Ted was antisocial. "You might have seen him with a camera? He's a photographer."

Camera. Dark room. No windows. . . Photographers sometimes use dark rooms, right?

"Is there any storage space available in this building?" I hold up the keys.

"Basement," the lady says and points toward the stairwell.

Yes! That must be it.

"Thank you," I say. Twin One sticks his head into Ted's apartment and whistles for Victor to join us.

"Is this trash for the dumpster?" Twin Two asks the lady. When she nods, he lifts the bag out of her arms. "We'll take it for you. You stay inside for a bit, okay?"

The lady blinks but nods. He lets her shut her door and turns to catch the rest of us staring at him.

"What?" he shrugs.

"Aren't you just a good boy?" Victor purrs. "By all means, let's take out the trash."

The men close around me as we head downstairs. Each step I take jostles my sore muscles, but the pain carries me forward, singing sweetly with every step, and it's like Rex is with me.

Then we hit the bottom of the stairs, and it's like I've stepped into a cloud of black, acrid smoke. I hold my breath, trying not to cough out the stinking miasma stinging my eyes. It feels like ashes are coating my throat.

"He's here," I whisper.

The twins box me in. Twin Two must have set down the trash bag because he's got his gun out. I draw my weapon and flick the safety off. Victor goes first, a long knife glittering in his hand. We all move quietly into the basement.

We pass several wire cages containing dusty furniture and long-forgotten exercise equipment. My helmet shifts to night vision, and I can see the shapes outlined in green.

Victor stops, and we stop with him. He crouches down to pick something up. When he rises, he holds it out for us to see.

It's a black feather.

We've found Ted's lair. But where is he? And where is Rex?

Victor points out a room in the corner. The closer we get, the louder someone speaking gets.

Ted.

I reaffirm my grip on my gun and move closer.

"—never respected me." He's raving. "He was obsessed with her."

In my mind's eye, I can see the room through the dark haze. The walls are covered in faded photographs. Rex is there, sitting restrained on a hospital gurney, his clothes gone, his arms pinioned with cords.

He's straining against his bonds, his muscles bulging until blood runs down his bare chest.

Ted hovers close, livid and holding a knife. "I'm going to carve you up. Then I'll call her down here and kill her, too."

Ted wants me? I'm here, and I'm pissed.

I signal to the men surrounding me. "I'm going in."

One of the twins puts out a hand to stop me, and I shake my head at him. I'm wearing a helmet and armor. I'm as protected as I can be. Plus, I'm armed. Ted won't know what hit him.

Before Rex, justice was an abstract concept, but now, faced with a threat to the man I love, I'm not waiting to do things the right way. There's no justice on a battlefield. If saving Rex means spilling the blood of my enemy, I'm not just willing to spill blood; I'm willing to bathe in it.

When you love someone, you don't hold back. Rex taught me that.

The guys pause in silent deliberation. I make a move toward the door, and Victor signals his surrender. He crouches by the door and pulls out a pick for the lock. I let him break in for me.

I raise my gun. I don't need the door to open to know where Ted will be. I can sense him. My gifts crystalize the scene, and I know just where to aim.

Victor stands to the side, his hand on the doorknob. He counts me down—three, two, one—and throws the door open.

I step forward, and the scene I saw in my mind is there, laid out in shapes of black and green.

Ted turns toward me, his mouth falling slack in surprise.

And I blow him away.

***

~

REX

ONE SECOND, I'm fighting for oxygen while Ted taunts me, and the next, I'm showered with his blood.

A short, helmeted figure steps into the dark space. "He wasn't wearing body armor," a feminine voice says, observing Ted's body. "That was a mistake."

Gun drawn, she scopes out each corner of the room. "Clear," she calls, and whoever was backing her up rushes in to help me while she covers them.

I blink back a sense of deja vu. It feels like I'm back in the Abyss with Jaeger and Kaiser. Only this time, I'm in the victim's place. Ted's place.

The woman steps in front of me, and my grasp on reality shifts. Maybe I'm imagining this, but I've seen the way I look when I'm in my body armor, and the small figure looks a lot like a mini-me.

I have to be hallucinating this.

The cords binding me loosen and fall away. The men on either side of me continue to work to free me, but I have eyes only for her.

Someone hands her a water bottle, and she holsters her weapon so she can hold it to my lips. *An angel. She's an angel.*

I tip my head back and let the water relieve my parched throat. I shake my head when she offers me more.

"You okay?" she asks. I don't recognize her voice until she pulls off her helmet.

"Inara," I snarl. This is real. This is happening. *She's here. I can't believe she put herself in danger again.*

There are still remnants of the knock-out drug in my system that make the edges of my vision foggy, but fresh adrenaline pumps through me, clearing the cobwebs away.

"I'm here." She moves to put a gloved hand on my shoulder but stops when she notices the blood covering my torso.

I'm lightheaded with relief and rage. "You shouldn't be here!" I left her sleeping in our bed while I went out chasing monsters. I wouldn't have left her if I wasn't sure that she'd be safe.

"You left me," she retorts. "You went to the morgue and then went missing."

I gnash my teeth. I hate that Ted got the jump on me, but I refuse to let her shift the focus to me. "I left you at home, where you were safe. Who gave you that suit?"

"Hamish. He said this was a prototype. We had to retrofit it to my frame a bit, but it works." She sees me seething and lays a hand on her chest. "Rex, I was perfectly safe."

I can't look at her, so I glare at the men beside me. Jaeger, Kaiser, and Victor.

I'm going to kill them. They were meant to keep Inara safe, not let her go gallivanting around the city in body armor. "You," I snarl at Victor. "You let her come here—"

"They couldn't stop me," she says.

Now that I'm not tied to the bed, I should be able to rise. But I'm still feeling weak, like my limbs aren't mine to control. I should be familiar with this from watching my victims struggle with this partial paralysis enough times.

"Rex." Inara stoops so I have to look at her. "It's okay. It's over, and it's going to be okay."

"You shouldn't have come."

"What, you can save me, but I can't save you? I only did what you would do."

She has a point, but I hate it. I'm too disoriented to argue my position, so I'm reduced to threats. "There aren't enough whips in the world," I grind out and stop when Victor's head snaps in our direction.

"Don't mind me," he says with glee. "Please continue."

"Later," I grumble to Inara. Victor is kinky as hell. I'm pretty sure he tied his bride up in his own private dungeon and tortured her as part of their courtship. He doesn't need any ideas, and I don't want to hash this out in front of a would-be voyeur.

I try to rise, but my legs don't hold me. I stagger. Luckily, Jaeger and Kaiser are on either side of me to prop me up, and I allow them so we get out of here faster.

Inara spins in a slow circle in the middle of the darkroom. There's a sink in the corner and photographs papering the wall. "Exactly as I envisioned," she murmurs. "He took pictures of his victims as trophies." She heads to the freezer chest beside the sink and opens it. "And here are the dead birds."

I don't want her to linger too long in such macabre surroundings. "Inara," I call. The twins pause so I can turn to her.

She's still studying the room, a slight frown on her face. She's in detective mode.

But I don't want to leave her. I want her with me. I need her, I realize. Leaving her behind feels like ripping my heart in half.

I stretch out my hand and let vulnerability bleed into my voice. "Please."

It's all I can bear to say, but she understands. Her eyes light up, and her expression softens. She joins me, taking my hand, and I'm able to breathe again.

INARA

For the first time ever, I'm giddy. It must be the after-effects of adrenaline and a combination of relief and excitement at finding Rex and solving the case. Bubbles fill my chest like I've been sipping champagne. I can't stop touching Rex, which is good because he's kept hold of me since we left Ted's dark room. It's almost as if he's afraid I'll run away.

When we get a moment alone, I'll have to tell him there's nothing to fear. From now on, I only run toward him.

"What I don't understand is how Ted incapacitated you," I ask Rex. We're back at Roy Manor, doing a post-op debrief with Mina and Hamish.

Rex's face is stony. He hates this conversation. He hates any weakness. "It was a gas. Laughing gas, actually. He flooded the morgue room with it, then was able to inject me with a paralysis agent," Rex says.

"We think Ted used gas on the Walker family, too. He might have even gotten the idea from you." I would poke Rex, but he's already holding my hand in both of his. He frowns down at it now.

"We spoke to the morgue attendant—" Hamish says.

"He was in on it," Mina interrupts. "The morgue attendant was working with Ted. He helped Ted steal the victim's remains from the morgue to lure you out. And once you were incapacitated, they loaded you onto a gurney and into an ambulance. Ted used that to get you to his place."

I shake my head.

"We've also found evidence that Ted was blackmailing a number of people, threatening to release incriminating photos," Hamish reports. "One of his targets gave him access to the helicopter."

"This was his endgame," Rex says. "He called in every favor and exhausted all his resources. He must have been planning it for some time."

He and Mina start comparing notes on all of Ted's movements. My body starts to droop as the last of the adrenaline leaves my system.

I don't want to know every detail of Ted or BK's final days. For once, I don't care about building a body of evidence so the DA can prosecute the perp. The case is over. The two men who haunted my dreams are dead.

"You okay?" Rex murmurs to me. He's looking a lot better than he did a few hours ago, and I'm probably looking worse.

"Yeah." I let myself lean into him. "I'm glad it's over."

He pulls me into his lap and into a hug. I melt into him, letting his scent ground me.

I don't remember closing my eyes, but the next thing I know, I'm waking up, still in Rex's arms. I sit up slowly, blinking, and check the corners of my mouth for drool. "I must have dozed off."

"You did." Rex looks amused.

Hamish and Mina are gone. Rex must have sat here and let me nap on him.

I never thought I'd say this, but I hope he lets me nap on him again. Often.

But first, business. "What did I miss?"

"Fraternitas found the ambulance down the block from Ted's apartment building, with the remains of Emily Rodriguez inside. Her body's been returned to the morgue. Her family is making arrangements for a memorial service on Sunday."

"I'd like to go."

Rex nods as if he expected me to say that. "She was a nurse. I've instructed the Roy Foundation to set up a scholarship fund in her name."

"She would've liked that."

"The Green Street neighborhood has planted trees in honor of the family who died. We can do the same for your family in Elyria, if you'd like."

"That would be nice."

"I'll make it happen." He presses his lips to my forehead.

It feels like another ending, but one I chose. Closure. I don't have to carry the burden of loss any longer. Rex and I can bury the dead and honor them, letting the memory of their love enrich our lives. As long as we feel their love, they will always be with me, and I can let the grief go.

Rex has more to say. I can feel the tension in his body.

"What is it?" I reach up to caress his face to put him more at ease.

"We need to deal with Ted's body. How would you like us to handle it?"

"I don't care."

"We can stage a scene and make sure his body is found. Or we can just make him disappear forever."

He's waiting for me to put up a fuss and insist we bring in the police.

"You decide," I shrug. "But whatever you do, let's do it quietly. The news loves a serial killer and he doesn't deserve to be famous. Let him be forgotten."

Rex smiles like I knew he would. "Your wish is my command." He looks absolutely villainous.

I roll my eyes, then sober. "There is one thing I'd like done. There's a retired detective who told me about the Blackbird murders. I want him to know we closed the case."

"Consider it done." He hesitates, then says, "There are still questions about your involvement in BK's death. Detective Bonds has some theories he'd like to confirm."

"I'll talk to him. Soon." I feel no urgency to rush into work and wrap up the case. The only thing I want is to remain in bed or bed-adjacent with Rex for a solid month.

Another first for me. I've never thought I could get close to someone long enough to nap on them or want to be with them for longer than a scene. I might have longed for it, but

I couldn't have it. I was afraid that death would come to anyone I loved.

Now I want every moment. I want mornings and evenings and workday lunches, as well as nights in the dungeon. Naps and holding hands and deciding what's for dinner. The quiet hours together when we're relaxing or dressing for work or brushing our teeth before bed. The mundane details of the day. All the things Rex was ready for the minute we met. All the things I resisted while he wound his web around me, drawing me slowly in.

As for the fear, I don't feel it anymore. Most of that lifted from my shoulders the second Rex saved me. The little that remained disappeared today when I took out the threat to Rex.

Our fate wasn't fixed, and I did what was required. For once, I used my visions to rewrite the future. I've finally used my gift the way it should be used: saving people. Not seeking justice for the dead but stopping evil in its tracks. I fulfilled my purpose, my calling, and my reward is this new life.

So I did die on the roof. The old Inara is gone, and I am reborn. And I'm no longer afraid.

I can tell Rex all of this. More importantly, I'm going to show him. I'm going to be with him, all in. As all in as he's been with me.

That's why I'm not rushing back to work. My long days working on cases were an endless penance, a never-ending punishment for allowing my family to die. I don't need to do that any longer.

No wonder I feel so free.

I wonder if Rex will ever feel the same freedom. If he will allow himself to heal deeply from the trauma of his childhood. I want that for him. Maybe I can help him.

I look up at his solemn face, his stony mask. He thought losing me was his worst nightmare, but what just happened was actually what he feared most: being out of control. He might need more help than I can give, but that's okay. He can afford therapy.

I cup the hard planes of his cheeks and brush a kiss on his surly mouth. His expression doesn't soften, doesn't change.

"It's over, Rex. It's done. You know what that means?"

"What?" He's watching me carefully. He's still hiding behind his armor, but I understand that. I lived most of my life in mine. If it takes longer for him to shed his, that's okay. At first, it'll feel like being a turtle without a shell. It's so uncomfortable, but he'll learn it's safe to let down his guard around me.

I lean in and whisper. "It means we can be together."

He blinks, and there it is. His eyes soften as tense muscles relax.

"I love you," I say, and suddenly I'm holding back tears. "I love you." I thought it would be scary to say it, but it's not. It's a relief. It's wonderful. "I'm sorry I was afraid to tell you before now—"

"You mean when you're not leaping off a roof to your death?"

He's still trying to forgive me for that.

"Yes. That." I never expected to have this life. But now that I have it, I'm going to live.

"I love you," I say again, and I'm crying and laughing at the same time. I mess up his hair and that does it; he grasps my wrists and chuckles at my enthusiasm. "And I'm so happy we get to be together right now.'

"Finally," he deadpans, and I laugh.

It's such a pleasure to be with him right now, without

any danger hanging over our heads. And maybe we'll never be a normal couple. We're probably too fucked up for that, but we're fucked up in the ways that make us fit each other.

Alfie's voice echoes through the cave, breaking the moment. "Message from Kaiser: Mission Wifey complete, over."

"Message to Kaiser, Affirmative. Over," Rex dictates.

"Wifey?" I wrinkle my nose at him.

"Your codename."

"Ugh. Wifey? Really?" I want to be with Rex, not be that cringy couple from the suburbs.

It's worth it, though, because Rex is now wearing a small smile. "I knew you'd hate it."

"Just for that, we're inviting Victor to the wedding." I feel a thrill at the word wedding. Another thing I never thought I'd want, and here I am, adding career criminals to the guest list. The assassin deserves a place of honor after he saved me. "And the twins." Fraternitas may be the scourge of the city, but the twins made themselves useful. And I'm curious to meet their partners. Apparently, Kaiser is going through with an arranged marriage, which I find fascinating and unexpected.

"Fine. But not St. James."

"According to Hamish, he'll show up anyway."

"Yes." Rex glowers. He's jealous. I kinda love it.

"And I'm making your code name 'Hubby.'"

"I can live with that." He smirks, and I roll my eyes. Of course, he loves it. He thinks marriage is a form of owner-ship, and he loves that he's getting his way. He's lucky I'm still not insisting on a divorce. "Shall I tell Nadia to plan for a spring wedding?"

"I don't know. I still haven't gotten a proposal." I go to

playfully punch his arm and squeak when his fingers snap around my wrist.

"Careful, little bird." His voice drops to the lowest register, and my stomach does a slow somersault. Holding my gaze, he carefully presses a kiss to my wrist. I inhale sharply as my entire core clenches like he hooked his finger behind my belly button and tugged. "You know I'd get on my knees for you." He nuzzles my sensitive skin. "But I believe you prefer it the other way around."

"Yes." My voice grows breathy as lust rolls over me. I'm already wet for him, just from his voice and attention. "Take me to bed."

"Not the dungeon?" He's using his dom voice, and my body goes heavy as I lean into him.

"You decide—"

"That's right."

"My king," I add softly and have the pleasure of watching his eyes darken.

"Yes. But first. . ." He lifts me in his arms, rising and turning to place me back on his seat.

What? I don't understand what he's doing until he takes one knee. He clasps my hand—the one that already bears his ring.

"Inara Ramos, will you marry me?"

I'm surprised by a sudden rush of tears pricking my eyes. "Yes, I will. Again."

"Will you wear my collar and be my submissive? Will you kneel for me and let me watch over you. . . and tell me when I go too far?"

It's more than I've ever hoped for. It's everything I want. "Yes."

"Will you let me have you? All of you?"

"Yes." I start to speak, and he rests a finger over my lips. He's serious, giving me his vows.

"Will you let me worship you?"

"Yes."

"Will you let me keep you?"

"Yes."

"Will you let me love you?"

"Yes, yes, yes." I'm too excited. I slide off the chair and onto my knees to be with him. "Yes, sir."

He laughs and lifts me again. We're off to the bedroom, or the dungeon, or wherever he decides. It doesn't matter, as long as I'm with him.

25

R^{ex}

I'VE NEVER ENJOYED WEDDINGS. After years of delving into the dark secrets of New Rome citizens, I know too much. Everywhere I look in society, I see sinister motives bubbling under the superficial smiles. It's hard to make small talk with the mayor's wife when you know he's cheating on her.

On the other hand, if someone was good and pure-hearted, they held no interest for me.

I didn't trust any show of happiness. Most of it was fake, and when it was real, it was bland.

This wedding is different. This one is mine. I stand at the altar, vibrating with readiness. The guests murmur to each other in their seats, but I can't hear or see anything. I'm waiting for Inara.

The string symphony starts up and the guests quiet. Inara appears, and my heart stops.

She's breathtaking in a white sheath and gold jewelry. Her right hand now bears a ring with the Roy crest, the roaring lion. It's obvious to everyone she belongs to me.

What the guests don't know is that my wife's ass has cane marks all over it. Remnants of our revelries last night. They don't know that even now, she also wears a harness of soft white leather crisscrossing over her entire torso because she is rarely out of bondage anymore. They don't know that the golden circlet at her neck is really a collar. Or maybe they do. St. James is smirking in the corner. The bastard invited himself like we thought, and I don't even care.

Inara walks toward me. I want to run to her. I want to banish all the guests and make her crawl to me.

Maybe later.

She meets my gaze, and the rest of the world ceases to exist. There's only the two of us and our promise to each other.

Will you let me hold you?

Yes.

Will you let me collar you?

Yes.

Will you let me keep you?

Yes.

Every step she takes is another affirmation of her commitment to us. *Yes, yes, yes.* She draws near and I take her wrist, pulling her closer. The officiant starts officiating, but I can't hear a word. I can only hear my little bird saying *I love you* over and over again.

~

I NARA

. . .

BEFORE REX, I'd never been to a wedding, much less imagined one for myself. This one is more beautiful than I could've dreamed.

Nadia and her team outdid themselves again, transforming the lawns of Roy Manor into a jasmine-scented paradise. Giant urns are overflowing with flowering vines, and peacocks stroll past the guests. They installed seven new fountains and extended the labyrinth.

I feel like I'm floating. As soon as Rex took my wrist, my feet left the ground. I'm flying and never coming down.

When it's time for our first dance as a properly married couple, I take Rex's hand, noting how his eyes crinkle when he pulls me in. His back straightens, and his chest swells, and I know he's feeling triumphant. Just like he did the first time we danced.

"No gloves," he murmurs.

"No." I never want anything between us again.

He spins me around, and I glide easily in the direction he guides me. My back twinges a little, reminding me my muscles are sore from our scene last night. But the leather harness I'm wearing holds me together. It's a reminder of both Rex's care and control. I'll never be without it again.

We dance and drink and laugh under the stars, surrounded by our friends. When it's time for the guests to dance, I see Victor's white-blond head across the way. He's dancing with a dark-haired diva who's wearing red lipstick and a form-fitting navy dress.

Mina and Lacy are sitting in places of honor. They're my first stop when I make the rounds.

"Damn, girl." Mina waves her drink around, making champagne slosh everywhere. "Is this your house?"

"It is now." I grin at her, then turn to Lacy and give her a hug.

"I'm so proud of you," she whispers.

"Thank you," I whisper back.

I notice Hamish has seated himself between both of them. I drift away, confident that Hamish will take care of drunk Mina. Although he seems to be more interested in keeping Lacy's glass filled.

Silva waves at me when I pass. He's got not one, but two dates, both masc-presenting and gorgeous. Bonds is seated at their table, watching the throuple with an amused look on his face.

Our Fraternitas guests have their own table, as far away from my cop friends as possible.

"Look." I nudge Rex. "St. James came."

Rex grunts. St. James raises his glass in a toast to us. I wave while Rex seethes.

"At least he's behaving," I say.

"Unlike those two." Rex points out Victor, who is leading his lady toward the labyrinth. "Shall I send security to break up their fun?"

I remember the times Victor had my back in a dangerous place and how he became a silent shadow. "He'd probably find a way to elude them."

"Too right. But maybe I will send security after them, just to make things interesting."

I wait until Rex gets cornered by the mayor and slip away to find St. James. He's lingering on the edge of the dance floor, studying the dancers. For a moment, the torchlight plays on his face, and he looks lost. Then the shadows flicker, and the vulnerable expression is gone as if it never was.

He turns to me. "Congratulations, Mrs. Ramos."

"Roy-Ramos. We're going to hyphenate."

"Ah. In any case, well done. You've tamed the lion."

"I don't know if he's very tame. And it might be fair to say he tamed me."

St. James dips his head to show his agreement, and I sense a beam of light glowing deep in the foggy depths of his aura. I have a premonition that he'll soon find the submissive he will want to cage forever. Then it will be his turn to have someone drive him out of his mind and break all his iron-clad control.

"What is it?" he asks. His gray eyes miss nothing.

I shake my head. "I just wanted to thank you. For everything." On impulse, I push up to tiptoe and kiss his cheek.

His breath huffs out of him, and he goes still, as if the touch of my lips turned him to stone. Then his lips curl up slightly. "You're playing with fire."

I look past him to where Rex is glowering at both of us. "I know. He's not going to be happy with me."

"Ah, the bratty games of a masochistic sub," St. James chuckles. "You better return to him before he tries to kill me in front of the mayor."

"I won't let him do that. He has to get permission from me before he murders anyone else. We agreed." But I move on, returning to Rex's side.

"Do you want to spend another night in the dungeon?" he growls in my ear after he extricates us from another boring conversation with a senator.

"You know I do." His fingers tighten on my arm and I get a thrill.

"Don't test me, little bird. I will put you in a cage."

"I know." That's what I'm hoping for.

He thinks he's clipping my wings, but I know the truth. Before Rex, I was in a cage, and now I fly free.

And tonight, when the guests have gone and we're in the dungeon together, he undresses me himself. My gown falls away, leaving only the body harness framing my breasts and my sex. I feel perfect like this, bound and on display and owned.

Rex starts with gloves, stroking his leather-clad fingers down my skin until I'm mindless. Then he removes them and pinches my nipples until the pain washes me clean. We repeat our vows.

"Will you let me cage you?"

"Yes."

"Will you let me keep you?"

"Yes."

"Will you let me love you?"

"Yes, yes, yes."

He grazes his teeth along my shoulder, biting into my skin until I cry out. I hope that he leaves not just a mark but a scar. I want this moment written on my skin. This blissful feeling, this all-encompassing love.

I can't imagine feeling any more happy than I do right now.

But there's more. Another revelation for us to share. Another frontier to conquer together.

It starts with a dream.

I'M LYING in bed clutching my plush toy rabbit, pillow soft under my cheek. There's a noise outside my door. A rush of air, a crackling sound, then I'm drenched in smoke and heat and flickering flame—

I JERK upright out of the dream. Rex is awake almost before I am. His hand slides over my back. The gentle touch brings me to the present moment.

"What is it?" Rex asks. "A dream?"

"A vision."

"Past or present?" He's not using his dom voice, but the commands help me focus.

"Future." I squeeze his arm and nod to let him know I want him to keep prompting me.

"What did you see?"

"Smoke. Fire." I describe the scene as best I can. It's not a memory, although it felt like one. At first, I thought I was in my childhood bedroom, but it wasn't mine. I explain this to Rex. "It was an apartment building. There was a window looking out onto the city."

"Where? Can you give me any details?"

Please, I beg the gods, or my own mind, or whatever the supernatural source of the visions is. *Please give me what I need.*

The picture comes clearly. "There are four bell towers. A church. . ." I describe the view. "It's a family. Mom, dad, four children. Twin toddlers and an older brother. And a little girl." I saw everything through her eyes.

"All right." Rex rises. I know he's headed to his lair and surveillance system. He's going to search the city, using the details of vision to try and help. If anyone can do it, it's him.

I both want and don't want him to go. I'm still half asleep, my heart sick with adrenaline. I'm too afraid to hope.

He pauses beside the bed, turning like he's attuned to me. "It's okay, Inara." He kisses my forehead. "You rest. Call me if you get a vision of anything else."

"Be careful," I whisper, but he's disappearing out the door.

~

THE LITTLE GIRL sleeps curled with Binky, her plush rabbit. The much-beloved toy has one eye missing and matted fur, but to her, it's the most perfect thing in the world. She dreams of sunshine and playtime in the park. But her nose wrinkles when a gust of air coats her face with smoky heat.

She comes awake with a start. Something is wrong. There's no shouting, only a soft, strange noise, but it alerts her all the same. She calls for her mom and then her dad.

She's too afraid to stand up and leave her bed. Her instincts scream at her to run, but she can't move.

And then the door opens, and a huge figure stands between her and the scary heat in the hall.

She's too frozen to cry out, but maybe if she doesn't move, he won't see her.

But the monster does see her. "It's okay," he says, moving toward her. His steps are silent, as if he's made of shadow. She should be afraid of him, but something tells her he's a nice monster.

He says, "Your mom and dad are waiting. I'm going to get you out."

And then she's in his arms. She's still wrapped in her favorite yellow blanket and clutching Binky to her chest. Safe.

"Close your eyes," the shadow monster says, and she does. The heat flares, making her flinch. There's a roaring sound that swallows up the tinkling of glass breaking before night air is cool on her face. She feels like she's flying.

And then it's over. She's set down on the ground. It's cold, but she has her blanket.

"Oh my gods," someone screams. "She's here. She's okay." It's her mother, crying, "Baby, you okay?"

Her father pulls her into his arms.

She opens her eyes, but there's no sign of the monster.

She turns her head, searching. There he is, slipping into the shadows. Becoming one with the darkness. But she knows he'll be back if she ever needs help.

"What happened?" Her mother cups her face, drawing her attention back to her parents. Their eyes are wide and frightened, but she doesn't feel scared.

"It was the monster, Mama. He saved me."

⁓

*I*NARA

I SIT HUDDLED in Rex's office chair. Hamish was here earlier and brought me a mug of tea, but I haven't touched it.

My eyes are glued to the TV screen where a news reporter is standing outside a burning apartment building. "The building was home to over seven hundred tenants. Preliminary evidence points to an electrical issue that started the fire—"

I mute the sound. I can't take it anymore. The camera pans away from the reporter, showing the fire trucks lining the streets. Next to one ambulance, a little girl stands clutching a worn yellow blanket and stuffed animal. My breath catches. *It's her.* The girl in my dream. *She's alive.*

The door opens and Rex walks in, the silky hair at his temples still sweaty like he just stripped off his protective helmet. He smells like smoke.

I burst into tears.

"Hey," he says and crouches down, letting me pour myself into his arms. Then we're seated together, and he's nuzzling me. "It's okay. The fire's almost out. No one was hurt."

I can't speak. There's a pain in my chest, but it's purging. Rex seems to understand. He strokes my back and lets me cry it out.

"You did it," I say. "You saved them."

"No." He cups my face and thumbs away my tears. "You did."

I sob harder because it's true. It's true, and it feels so right. My emotions bleed out of me, one tear at a time. It's cathartic, a baptism.

"You did it." He kisses my wet cheek. "No more hiding. You told me about your visions. You let me help you."

Now I know why I held so much back, why I kept myself behind thick, impenetrable walls. I needed someone who would conquer me. Someone strong enough to stand in the breach between me and my nightmares.

I needed him. And now that I have him, I can let go. From now on, I can live fully as myself. No fear.

"I'm so glad you found me," I tell him, and he sighs against my mouth.

"I am too."

We hold tight, gazing into each other's eyes. It's almost too much, overwhelming our ability to speak. It's enough to be together, breathing together, feeling the moment between us swell into something sweeter. A sense of belonging, a quiet joy that will last the rest of our lives.

The next morning, I wake from the most delicious dream. Rex is slumbering next to me, so I move carefully to keep from waking him. I roll toward the side table where I keep my sketchbook.

As I draw, I relive it.

The garden is filled with topiaries and jasmine-covered arches. Rex and I are strolling hand in hand.

Shrieks of laughter in the distance. A hide-and-seek game. I tug Rex's hand, wanting to walk quicker to get a glimpse of the children playing in the labyrinth.

And I see her. A small child, only tall enough that her head comes up to my hip. Two dark braids down her back. She turns, and I catch the curve of her chubby cheek. She looks like me but has Rex's dark eyes.

"I'm hiding from my brudders," she tells me in her little girl voice. I lean down, and her eyes sparkle. My skin tingles with the magic. "I lub you, Mama," she says sweetly and smiles.

When Rex rouses, I'm wiping away tears.

"What is it?" He orders a light on. When he sees the tear tracks shining on my face, he grows sober. "Did you have another bad dream? Another vision?"

"No," I choke out. I don't want him to worry, so I give him a watery smile. "I saw something beautiful."

"What did you see?"

"Us." I turn the sketchbook toward him. "I saw all of us."

His brow furrows as he takes in the page. The face of a child with dark eyes. Rex's eyes. "Our daughter," I say and watch hope light his face. I turn the page and show him the rest. "Our sons. Our family."

His head drops, and his body shudders as if he's overcome. I know how he's feeling. It's strange to be so happy. Strange, but I'm getting used to it. It's my new way of life.

I cup his cheek with one hand. "I love you."

He turns his face and kisses my palm. His tears leave my fingers wet. "I was born to love you."

In the end, we get to have it all.

I'M NOT CRYING. You're crying! I hope you loved the story of Inara and Rex.

I have plans to return to New Rome and our crime-fighting couple in Joker's story. But first, Kaiser and Poison Ivy get their story in His Perfect Poison.

Before you ask, yes, St. James is getting a book. I've been plotting it since 2020 when I wrote St. James into the end of Beauty and the Rose, but he's such a dark character I needed a bit more time to ease into his level of sadism.

Victor already has his book! Read Vengeance is Mine here. It is dark and intense.

Happy reading!

<3 Lee

Enter Lee Savino's dark world (The VinoVerse)

Start with:

- Innocence - Hades & Persephone retelling
- Beauty's Beast - Beauty and the Beast retelling

Then. . . the Mafia Brides series

- Revenge is Sweet - as close to a rom-com as a mafia story can be
- Vengeance is Mine - the exact opposite of a rom-com. Dark with BDSM torture. Victor's story

And then. . . the Fraternitas series

- His Perfect Prey - Jaeger's story. Little Red Riding Hood retelling

- His Perfect Poison - Kaiser and Poison Ivy

Coming soon...

- Sebastian St. James and Wellesley's story
- Damien (the Devil) and Eve's story
- More Mafia Brides and Fraternitas

FREEBIE - THE DARKNESS IN HIM

Get Roy Roy's point of view in The Darkness In Him, a freebie available here: https://geni.us/thedarknessinhim

JOIN LEE'S INFLUENCER TEAM

If you're a Booktok or Instagram influencer, you can sign up here to join my street team:
https://forms.gle/JHgXFD8ebwxfJC2P8

Influencer team members are eligible for ARCs, special edition books and other book mail, peeks behind the scenes, live launch parties and more!
Come join the fun!
<3 Lee

ALSO BY LEE SAVINO

For film and TV rights inquiries: <u>lee.savino@</u>
<u>leesavino.com</u>

Want more dark romance? Check out His Perfect Prey, book
one in the *Fraternitas* series.

Dark and Mafia Romance

Mafia Brides
Revenge is Sweet
Vengeance is Mine

Fraternitas
His Perfect Prey
His Perfect Poison

His Perfect Darkness
His Perfect Darkness
Darkest Before Dawn

A Dark Mafia Romance trilogy with Stasia Black
Innocence
Awakening
Queen of the Underworld

Beauty and the Rose trilogy with Stasia Black

Beauty's Beast
Beauty & the Thorns
Beauty & the Rose

~

Contemporary Romance

Royally Wrong
Royally Bad
Royally Fake Fiancé

Bad Boy Heroes
Her Marine Daddy
Her Dueling Daddies
Beauty & The Lumberjacks
Snowed in with the Lumberjack
Rescuing Regina

~

Paranormal romance

Berserker Saga
Sold to the Berserkers
Mated to the Berserkers
Bred by the Berserkers (FREE novella only available at
www.leesavino.com)
Taken by the Berserkers
Given to the Berserkers
Claimed by the Berserkers
Rescued by the Berserker
Captured by the Berserkers

Kidnapped by the Berserkers
Bonded to the Berserkers
Berserker Babies
Night of the Berserkers
Owned by the Berserkers
Tamed by the Berserkers
Mastered by the Berserkers
Surrendered to the Berserkers

Berserker Warriors
Aegir
Siebold with Ines Johnson

Bad Boy Alphas with Renee Rose
Alpha's Temptation
Alpha's Danger
Alpha's Prize
Alpha's Challenge
Alpha's Obsession
Alpha's Desire
Alpha's War
Alpha's Mission
Alpha's Bane
Alpha's Secret
Alpha's Prey
Alpha's Blood
Alpha's Sun

Shifter Ops with Renee Rose
Alpha's Moon
Alpha's Vow
Alpha's Revenge
Alpha's Fire

Alpha's Rescue
Alpha's Command

A Very Merry Alpha's Solstice

Bad Boy Bears with Renee Rose
Alpha's Claim

Midnight Doms with Renee Rose
Alpha's Blood
His Captive Mortal
The Virgin and the Vampire
(All Souls' Night anthology exclusive)

Werewolves of Wallstreet with Renee Rose
Big Bad Boss: Midnight
Big Bad Boss: Moon Mad
Big Bad Boss: Marked
Big Bad Boss: Mated
Big Bad Bully

Sci fi romance

Planet of Kings with Tabitha Black
Brutal Mate
Brutal Claim
Brutal Capture
Brutal Beast
Brutal Demon

Tsenturion Warriors with Golden Angel

Alien Captive
Alien Tribute
Alien Abduction

Dragons in Exile with Lili Zander
Draekon Mate
Draekon Fire
Draekon Heart
Draekon Abduction
Draekon Destiny
Daughter of Draekons
Draekon Fever
Draekon Rogue
Draekon Holiday

Draekon Rebel Force with Lili Zander
Draekon Warrior
Draekon Conqueror
Draekon Pirate
Draekon Warlord
Draekon Guardian

Cowboy Romance

Rocky Mountain Mail Order Brides
Rocky Mountain Dawn
Rocky Mountain Bride
Rocky Mountain Rose
Rocky Mountain Romp
Rocky Mountain Rogue
Rocky Mountain Daddy

Rocky Mountain Ride
Possessing Pearl

Wild Whip Ranch with Tristan River
Cowboy's Babygirl
Taming His Wild Girl

ABOUT THE AUTHOR

USA today bestselling author Lee Savino has written over 69 steamy romance novels. Bad boys, mafia men, wolf shifters, and dragon shifters in space—her dominant, alpha-hole heroes will stop at nothing to possess their one true love. Happily-ever-after and book hangover guaranteed!

Download a free book at leesavino.com.

Connect with Lee Savino in her fabulous Goddess Group: https://www.facebook.com/groups/LeeSavino

Goodreads: http://bit.ly/2tqaH28
Bookbub: http://bit.ly/2h8N6le
TikTok: https://www.tiktok.com/@authorleesavino
Instagram: https://www.instagram.com/authorleesavino

Text copyright © 2025 Lee Savino
All Rights Reserved

No part of this book may be reproduced in any form or by any electronic or mechanical means including information storage and retrieval systems, without permission in writing from the author. The only exception is by a reviewer, who may quote short excerpts in a review.

This book is a work of fiction. Names, characters, places, and incidents either are products of the author's imagination or are used fictitiously. Any resemblance to actual persons, living or dead, events, or locales is entirely coincidental.

www.ingramcontent.com/pod-product-compliance
Lightning Source LLC
Chambersburg PA
CBHW031611100726
47898CB00006B/1748